Witch Is Where The Lights Went Out

Published by Implode Publishing Ltd

Printed in Great Britain
by Amazon

11640013R00174

Web site: AdeleAbbott.com
Facebook: facebook.com/AdeleAbbottAuthor

Witch Is How... (Season #3)
Witch is How Things Had Changed
Witch is How Berries Tasted Good
Witch is How The Mirror Lied
Witch is How The Tables Turned
Witch is How The Drought Ended
Witch is How The Dice Fell
Witch is How The Biscuits Disappeared
Witch is How Dreams Became Reality
Witch is How Bells Were Saved
Witch is How To Fool Cats
Witch is How To Lose Big
Witch is How Life Changed Forever

Witch Is Where... (Season #4)
Witch is Where Magic Lives Now
Witch Is Where Clowns Go To Die
Witch Is Where Squirrels Go Nuts
Witch Is Where Rainbows End
Witch Is Where Unicorns Cry
Witch Is Where The Lights Went Out
Witch Is Where Fairies Wing It

Susan Hall Investigates
(A Candlefield/Washbridge Series)
Whoops! Our New Flatmate Is A Human.
Whoops! All The Money Went Missing.
Whoops! Someone Is On Our Case.
Whoops! We're In Big Trouble Now.

Murder On Account (A Kay Royle Novel)

ALSO BY ADELE ABBOTT

The Witch P.I. Mysteries (A Candlefield/Washbridge Series)

Witch Is When... (Season #1)
Witch Is When It All Began
Witch Is When Life Got Complicated
Witch Is When Everything Went Crazy
Witch Is When Things Fell Apart
Witch Is When The Bubble Burst
Witch Is When The Penny Dropped
Witch Is When The Floodgates Opened
Witch Is When The Hammer Fell
Witch Is When My Heart Broke
Witch Is When I Said Goodbye
Witch Is When Stuff Got Serious
Witch Is When All Was Revealed

Witch Is Why... (Season #2)
Witch Is Why Time Stood Still
Witch is Why The Laughter Stopped
Witch is Why Another Door Opened
Witch is Why Two Became One
Witch is Why The Moon Disappeared
Witch is Why The Wolf Howled
Witch is Why The Music Stopped
Witch is Why A Pin Dropped
Witch is Why The Owl Returned
Witch is Why The Search Began
Witch is Why Promises Were Broken
Witch is Why It Was Over

"So, where's our money?"

"I'll write you a cheque."

And so it was, for the second time in as many weeks, I found myself handing over a cheque to refund fees.

After the three leprechauns had stormed out of my office, I could feel Winky's gaze burning into me.

"Say one word. Just one word. And you'll be an ex-cat."

within a matter of days. I've no doubt they're here to show their gratitude—probably flowers or chocolates. I hope it's chocolates."

Barry, Harry and Gordon were dressed immaculately once again, but they didn't come bearing chocolates or flowers. And there was something about their demeanour that suggested they weren't here to sing my praises.

"We want our money back!" Barry said.

"Gentlemen, please. Why don't you take a seat?"

"We'd prefer to stand," Gordon said. "Now hand over the money that you took under false pretences."

"There must be some kind of misunderstanding. You asked me to stop the man from DOPA stalking you, and I did that."

"So you say, and yet that green-suited pest is still on our trail. He's making our lives a misery."

It was only at the mention of the green suit that the penny finally dropped.

"Just a minute. Are you three gentlemen—err—"

"Are we what?"

"Leprechauns?"

"Of course we are. What did you think we were?"

"But you aren't dressed in green?"

"Why would we be? What sort of stereotyping have you bought into? I'll tell you who is dressed in green, though. The man who will not give us a moment's peace. The man we paid you to stop."

"Ivers."

"What did you just say? Do you know the man?"

"Know him? No, of course not."

"You just said his name. You called him Ivers."

"No, I didn't. I said *I-ver* no idea who he is."

scam, which spanned the human, paranormal and ghost worlds. Thanks to me, two of the masterminds behind it are behind bars, and the other one—well, let's just say he won't be committing any more crimes for the foreseeable future."

"Are you actually getting paid for that case?"

"Yes, I am. In fact, the authorities in Ghost Town have already paid my bill. More importantly, thanks to yours truly, the people responsible for the murder of Detective Susan Shay are now in custody."

"Did you make any money for doing that?"

"No, but I got something more important than money."

"Salmon?"

"I got to clear my name. I no longer have to worry about spending the rest of my days in prison. So, you see, Winky, I have a lot to feel pleased with myself about."

"Cough—*Todfoster*—cough."

"I might have known you'd throw that in my face. What you fail to understand is that the sign of a true professional is someone who is able to own their mistakes, learn from them, and come back even stronger. And, as I'm sure you'll agree, by solving these two major cases, I have put that sorry, but minor, episode behind me."

Mrs V came through the door.

"Jill, I have those three short gentlemen to see you again. I told them you might be busy, but they're quite adamant."

"That's okay. Just give me one minute and then show them in, would you?"

"Of course."

"See, Winky, this is what I mean. These three gentlemen came to me with a problem that I was able to resolve clearly been devastated by the loss of their father."

"How did you know Christine was involved?"

"Why else would she have chosen to stand next to the waitress, as they both had a cigarette? Christine had worked out which was the one spot that would be covered by the hotel's CCTV. That gave them both an alibi while the other twin attacked Susan Shay."

"Very impressive work."

"Thanks. What are you going to do about the sisters?"

"They're being picked up as we speak."

"Right. If there's nothing else, I'll be on my way."

"Sure."

I started for the door.

"Jill, I'm sorry for what we put you through. It was nothing personal, you understand."

***

"What's up with you, Winky? Are you still grinning about that photo?"

"No, I'm just amused by how smug you look."

"Rubbish."

"You're like Smugitty McSmug. If you looked up smug in the dictionary, I bet there'd be a photo of you there."

"It's true. I am feeling rather pleased with myself at the moment."

"Smug."

"Not at all. Just a sense of professional pride at what I've managed to accomplish recently."

"Have you been tidying your paperclips again?"

"I've managed to wrap up two major cases in the course of only a few days. First, I foiled a multi-million pound

"I don't want them coming to the house."

"Okay. Shall we?"

Dawn Brakes was rather surprised to see me, and even more surprised to hear the recording of Christine confessing to the murder.

"One thing I don't understand, Jill," Brakes said. "Is how you got her to admit she'd done it."

"I just got lucky. I think the guilt must have caught up with her."

"I've just had a quick word with Christine, and she seems to be under the impression that Melodie and Coral gave her up."

"She's probably in a state of shock. She's not thinking clearly."

"How did you work out what had happened that night?"

"I'd always believed there was someone in the locked cubicle. When I discovered the loo had actually never been faulty, I figured whoever had reported it must be involved. I discovered that it was the waitress who had made the report, but she'd been alibied by still image from the hotel's CCTV. It was later that I realised she seemed to change her dominant hand. In the restaurant, when she was taking the orders, she used her right hand, but earlier when she signed in, she'd used her left hand."

"Don't identical twins have the same dominant hand?"

"I thought so too, but apparently not. Once I'd worked out that twins were involved, I went back and checked some of my earlier research. When I reread the article about the man jailed for Feltham's murder, I discovered that Melodie and Coral were identical twins. They'd father was convicted of murdering, isn't it?"

"Yeah. Bridget Feltham. She was Melodie and Coral's next-door neighbour. Their father, Len, discovered her body, and reported it to the police. During the course of the investigation, I got to know him and his daughters. He was a good man. An honest man. He wasn't a murderer."

"I take it Shay thought otherwise."

"The only thing she was interested in was getting a conviction, and she didn't seem too bothered who it was. I tried to reason with her. Tried to get her to widen the scope of the investigation, but she wasn't interested. Len's DNA was all over Feltham's body, but only because he'd been trying to revive her."

"You're saying that Shay knowingly sent an innocent man to jail?"

"Yes."

"I take it you got to know his daughters during that time?"

"I tried not to let it show, but they knew I didn't support the way the investigation went."

"And then, their father died in prison."

"I was devastated when I heard about it. I went to the funeral. That's when I saw the twins again."

"Whose idea was it to kill Shay?"

"That was never the plan; they just wanted revenge. They were only meant to hurt her."

"And they asked you to help."

"I should have said no. I got carried away with the emotion of it all."

"How do you want to play this, Christine? I can take you down the station, or I can make a call and ask someone to come here."

"It's going to be okay. Trust me."

"I still don't like it."

"It'll be alright unless you do stupid stuff like this. We can't be seen together. Understood, Melodie?"

"Okay."

"Coral?"

"Yeah, understood."

"I'm going to drop you here, and then I'm headed home. I need a drink."

Moments later, there was the sound of the car pulling over, the doors opening and then banging closed.

I had to hand it to the twins, they had done a masterful job.

Hoyle was back on the sofa, looking dazed. I didn't think she was likely to do a runner, so I went through to the kitchen and got her a glass of water.

"Drink this."

"Those girls have screwed me over."

"They didn't really have much choice. I told them things would go better for them if they could get you to confess."

I switched on the second recorder that was in my pocket.

She took a sip of water. "I didn't mean for them to kill her, you know. They were just supposed to give her a beating. That idiot Coral didn't know when to stop."

"I know you believe Shay cost you a promotion, but surely she didn't deserve to die?"

"You think I did this because of a *promotion*?" She laughed. "You don't understand at all."

"Explain it to me, then."

"We worked on the Feltham case together."

"*Feltham*? That's the woman who Melodie and Coral's

"This will go much more smoothly if you just tell me the truth. I know that you felt Shay cheated you out of a promotion, but surely that didn't warrant killing her."

"I did not kill her!" She jumped to her feet. "That's an outrageous thing to say. You're the one under investigation for the murder."

"I know you didn't actually strike the fatal blow. That was Melodie. Or was it Coral?"

"Get out! Now!"

"I think you should hear this." I took out the recorder and pressed the play button.

The first voice on the tape was Hoyle's.

"What are you two doing here? Have you lost your minds?"

"We needed to see you."

"And you thought you'd come here? Quick, get in my car."

The next sound was of the car's engine starting. The rest of the conversation took place as Hoyle drove around the area.

"A private investigator came to see us."

"What? When?"

"Yesterday. She knows everything."

"Don't be stupid. No one knows anything."

"She knew why we'd stood where we did to have a cigarette."

"And she knew I was in the cubicle in the loo."

"And she knew I wasn't the real Angela Fredricks."

"You both keep saying 'she'. Who's she?"

"She said her name is Maxwell."

"I should have known. She's married to an ex-cop, and she was at the restaurant that night. She's the one who's in the frame for the murder. You two just need to keep your heads. No one is going to listen to her wild accusations."

"That's easy for you to say. You're not the one who'll go down for murder."

Chapter 28

"Yes?" Unsurprisingly, Christine Hoyle looked a little flustered when she opened the door and saw me standing there.

"Hi, Christine."

"Sorry, do I know you?" she said, rather unconvincingly.

"Not really. Although, we were both at Norman Whitelea's retirement dinner at the Red Lion."

"You're Jack's wife."

"That's right. Jill. I'm sorry to trouble you at home, but I wonder if you might spare me a few minutes?"

"Now isn't a good time."

"It is rather urgent."

"Look, if it's about the murder, I really can't help you. I'm not on that case."

"I'm pretty sure that you can, actually."

"How did you find out where I live?"

"I really do think we should go inside and talk."

"I don't have time. I really must ask you to leave."

"That's a shame. Coral and Melodie speak so highly of you."

"What did you just say?" All the colour drained from her face.

"You don't look well, Christine." I took her arm. "Let's go inside."

In something of a daze, she put up no resistance, as I helped her onto the sofa.

"Why did you do it, Christine?"

The question seemed to snap her out of it. "Do what? I don't know what you're talking about."

now." I started for the gates.

"Hang on," Amber called after me. "Haven't you forgotten something?"

"What?"

"You need to help us to reverse these 'doppelganger' spells."

"You're sitting on my bench."

"I don't think you can reserve them. There are plenty more. Look over there."

"TimTim is expecting me."

"Tim?"

"No. TimTim."

"Couldn't you and TimTim sit on a different bench?"

"No, because that's my—"

"Okay, I get it." I decided it would be less painful to relinquish the bench than to continue that conversation, so I stood up and walked to the gate. When I looked back, I saw the man holding out what appeared to be a handful of nuts. Moments later, a squirrel ran down a nearby tree, across the grass, jumped onto the bench beside the man, and began eating from his hand. TimTim, I assumed.

"Jill!" Amber came rushing into the park, followed closely by Pearl.

Not that either of them looked like themselves.

"How did it go?"

"Perfect!" Pearl said. "We were brilliant."

"No problems, then?"

"No. She reacted just like you said she would. I thought she was going to have a coronary when she first saw us. She made us get in the car and then drove around while we talked."

"What about the recorder? Did you remember to switch it on?"

"Oh ye of little faith. Of course we did." Amber reached into her pocket and handed it to me.

It was with bated breath that I pressed the play button and listened.

"Well done, you two, that's perfect. It's over to me

show him the ropes."

"And he picked it up okay?"

"Better than you did."

"Cheers. Okay, then, let's get this show on the road."

It was a painful process, but I eventually managed to get the twins to successfully cast the 'doppelganger' spell, and then I magicked us all to West Chipping.

"Are you sure you know what you have to do?" I asked.

"Yes, Jill," Amber said. "We've got this."

"Okay, and make sure this is switched on." I handed her the recorder. "Good luck. We'll meet in the park when you're done."

"Will do."

***

I couldn't recall the last time I'd felt so nervous. So much depended upon the events of the next hour, and its success or failure was all in the hands of the twins. They'd appeared confident enough when I'd left them, but would they be able to keep their cool under pressure?

I'd already walked three laps of the park, and I'd looked at my watch a thousand times. They'd been gone for almost an hour, and I was beginning to get really worried. What if it had all gone pear-shaped, and they couldn't bring themselves to face me? I daren't ring them in case they were still playing their roles. Eventually, I took a seat on the bench closest to the gate.

"That's my bench."

"I looked up to see a strange little man with a carrier bag in his hand.

"Sorry?"

'doppelganger' spell?"

"*Doppelganger*?" Amber frowned. "I'm not sure I ever learned that one."

"I did," Pearl said.

"Great."

"But I could never get it to work properly."

This was going to be much more difficult than I'd imagined.

"Okay, don't worry about that. I'll go through the spell with you both, to make sure it works okay. We can cast the spell here in Candlefield, and then I'll magic us all over to West Chipping."

"What exactly do you want us to do?"

I explained what I needed from them, and although they were a little nervous, they said they were up for it.

"When do you want us to do it?" Pearl said.

"Ideally, right now."

"Now?" Amber looked horrified. "I thought we'd have time to practise."

"You don't need to rehearse. It'll come across better if it's spontaneous. What do you say? Can you get someone to watch the shop for a while?"

"None of our assistants are in today because we knew it was going to be quiet."

"Drat." I could already see my cunning plan going up in flames.

"I've got an idea." Amber rushed upstairs and returned a minute later, accompanied by Bobby.

"Hi, Jill," he said. "I'm going to look after the shop."

"Err, right?"

"It's okay," Pearl said. "Bobby has been really bored with no visitors to talk to, so yesterday he asked us to

***

I was about to do something that I never dreamed I'd do. I was about to ask the twins to help me with one of my cases.

Yes, I do realise it sounds like a crazy idea, but sometimes in life you have to take a chance.

"Hey, you two. Have you heard from the dragon inspectors yet?"

"Not yet," Pearl said. "But they've promised to get back to us by the end of the week."

"It's been really dead in here," Amber said.

"I bet you get bored when it's so quiet, don't you?"

"Yeah. I much prefer it when we're busy."

"I might be able to help alleviate the boredom. I need a small favour."

"No," they said in unison.

"I haven't even told you what it is yet. I think you'll change your mind when I do."

"I doubt that," Pearl said.

"How would you both like to work undercover for me, just for an hour or so."

"How do you mean, *undercover*?" Amber said. "If you want us to dress up in silly costumes, you can forget it."

"No, nothing like that. I need you to help me crack a murder case in the human world."

That seemed to get their attention.

"Murder?" Pearl said. "Won't it be dangerous?"

"I would never ask you to do something that might put you in danger. Are you interested?"

They exchanged a glance and then nodded.

"Great. Can you both remember how to cast the

"Something clearly is."

"I was just thinking how good you looked in that Morris dancing outfit."

"You've seen the photo, I assume?"

"It's a pity your sister didn't take a video. I would have liked to see you ringing that bell."

"I don't want to discuss it."

Mrs V came hurrying into my office, carrying a box of chocolates in her good hand. "I'm sorry I wasn't in when you arrived, Jill. I nipped out to get these for you."

"For me? Why?"

"For stepping into the breach on Saturday of course."

"Thanks, but I still feel like I let you down."

"Rubbish. It was a great success, and best of all, Armi and I are back on speaking terms."

"How's the hand?"

"Getting better. It's just a pity that it had to be this hand. I do everything with my right hand."

"Say that again, Mrs V."

"I said I do everything with this hand."

"Because you're right-handed?"

"Yes."

"Mrs V, you're a genius."

"I am?"

A little puzzled by my outburst, she returned to the outer office. I fired up the computer and brought up the restaurant CCTV footage to check my hunch, and sure enough, I was right. Next, I brought up the article I'd studied earlier when trying to find people who Sushi had recently put behind bars.

And there it was. Bingo!

who had stepped out in front of him.

"No problem. You don't happen to know where I can find Angela Fredricks, do you? I'm new here."

"That's her over there."

"Near the watercooler?"

"Yeah, with the orange jumper."

"Thanks."

The woman had her back to me, so she didn't see my approach, which was just as well because she might have recognised me from the restaurant.

"Angela?"

She turned around. "Yes?"

I was struck dumb for a moment. "I—err—"

"What do you want?"

"*You're* Angela Fredricks?"

"Yes. Who are you? Was it you in reception, pretending to be my sister?"

"Err—sorry, my mistake."

I turned around and legged it out of the office, and then out of the building. The woman I'd just spoken to clearly was Angela Fredricks, but she certainly wasn't the waitress from the restaurant. She looked nothing like her. So who was the waitress?

***

When I arrived at the office, there was no sign of Mrs V. I'd just taken a seat at my desk when Winky jumped in through the window, sat on the windowsill, and grinned inanely at me.

"What's amusing you?"

"Nothing."

"I'm not sure."

"What's it in connection with?"

"I'm her sister and it's a personal matter. An *urgent* personal matter."

He tapped away on his computer. "There's an Arthur Fredricks in Finance."

"It's Angela."

"Hmm." He tapped away a little more. "Here she is—housing department."

"Great. If you can just direct me to her, I'll—"

"I'll need to let her know you're here first." He picked up the phone and made the call. "Angela Fredricks? It's Richard on the main reception. I have your sister here. She'd like to speak to you on an urgent personal matter. What? You don't? Right, okay. Thank you." He turned to me. "She said she doesn't have a sister."

"What? She's just joking. You know what siblings are like."

"I'm going to have to ask you to leave."

There was no point in arguing with Mr Jobsworth, so I mumbled something under my breath, then made my exit.

When I returned, a few minutes later, I was invisible. There was an abundance of signage in the building, so it wasn't difficult to find my way to the housing department. Once inside the large open-plan office, I stooped down behind a long row of filing cabinets and reversed the 'invisible' spell. Now, to find Angela Fredricks.

As I stepped out from behind the cabinets, I almost bumped into a spotty young man, pushing a trolley full of what appeared to be internal mail.

"Sorry," he apologised, even though I'd been the one

Grandma if she could think of a suitable punishment."

"And she came up with the idea of putting him in a jam jar?"

"Yeah. I shrank him first, obviously."

"Won't he suffocate in there?"

"Just how cruel do you think I am? We put air holes in the top."

"How long does he have to stay in there?"

"Grandma said a month ought to do it, and before you ask, she has promised to give him food and water every day. Hopefully, she won't forget."

"Then what? After his month is up?"

"We'll let him go."

"What if he goes to the police or the papers?"

"And says what? A couple of witches shrank him and put him in a jam jar? Somehow, I doubt that he'll do that."

***

I wanted to speak to the waitress, Angela Fredricks, who I now knew had only taken the job at the restaurant a couple of weeks before the night of Sushi's murder. If I had driven all the way across town to her house, there was a good chance that she would have already left for work, so I stayed at home until just before nine o'clock, then drove to the council offices.

It was years since I'd been inside that particular building, but it hadn't changed at all.

"Yes?" said the man behind the enquiries desk. Clearly, he was a man of few words.

"I'd like to see Angela Fredricks, please."

"What department does she work in?"

Chapter 27

The next morning when I came downstairs, Jack and Florence were at the kitchen table, both of them looking at Jack's phone.

"Look, Mummy, Auntie Kathy has put your photo on Insy Gram."

"I don't want to see it, thank you."

"But you look really good in the Morris dancing costume." Jack grinned.

"Don't you two know it's rude to look at a phone at the table?"

"But you always look at yours, Mummy."

"That's different. That's for work. Have you fed Buddy yet?"

I already knew the answer to that question because the dog was jumping up my leg to get attention.

"I forgot," Florence said.

"Would you do it now, please?"

"Okay." She gave a huge sigh for such a little girl.

"I didn't get the chance to ask you last night," Jack said. "How did you get on with that Frankenstein case?"

"It turned out to be nothing of the sort. It was just a straightforward scam involving a human, a sup and a ghost."

"Oh yeah. That sounds really straightforward." He grinned. "What happened?"

"Long story short, the sup is behind bars in Candlefield, the ghost is behind bars in Ghost Town, and the human is in a jam jar in Grandma's office."

"He's *where*?"

"I couldn't hand him over to the police, so I asked

"Let me go!" the wizard shouted.

"Sorry, no can do." I made a call to Daze. "Hi, it's Jill. There's someone here I'd like you to meet."

Twenty-minutes later, Daze and Blaze had collected the wizard and taken him to Candlefield.

"You might as well let me go," Greenlight said. "It's not like you can hand me over to the police, is it?"

"Be quiet. I'll be back in a minute."

"Jill?" Grandma was clearly surprised to see me appear in her office. "You could have given me a heart attack."

"Sorry, but I need some advice."

"It had better be quick. I'm a busy woman."

I quickly told her how I'd foiled the Restore scam.

"That's all very interesting, but what does it have to do with me?"

"The rogue retrievers have arrested the wizard. Mad is going to apprehend the ghost, but I don't know what I can do about the human. It doesn't seem right that he should get off scot-free. I was just wondering if you had any suggestions?"

"Oh yes. I know just the thing."

like I can hand him over to the police here in the human world. They already think I'm a murderer. If I tell them that I've just broken up a criminal ring based in the human, paranormal and ghost worlds, they'll think I'm a nutter too."

"You can't just let him go, though."

"Don't worry. That's not going to happen. Anyway, I'd better get back before they smell a rat." I returned to the dining room. "I'm so sorry to keep you waiting, Mr Greenlight."

"No problem, your ladyship. If you could just let me have the agreed payment, I'll leave you and your brother to catch up."

"The thing is, I don't actually have your money."

"What? Why not?"

"Because I'm not in the habit of handing over money to scamsters such as you and your colleague here."

"I don't know what you're talking about. Your brother is right here, as promised."

"I have no idea who this gentleman is, but he is no more the colonel than I'm Lady Tweaking." I reversed the 'doppelganger' spell.

I'm not sure which one of them looked the more shocked, and for the longest moment, neither of them moved or spoke. Eventually, the phoney colonel reversed his spell, and revealed his real self.

"She's a witch!" he shouted at Greenlight. "What were you thinking?"

"How was I supposed to know?"

"Be quiet, both of you." I used magic to bind their hands and legs together, causing them both to fall to the floor.

apartment at first, and I was just about to force an entry when Cilla came to the door. The two of them had clearly been drugged."

"Are you sure they're alright?"

"Positive. At least, they will be once the effects of the drugs have completely worn off. What's happening at your end?"

"Greenlight, that's the guy from Restore, has just introduced me to my 'brother', the colonel."

"How did he manage to do that?"

"The guy who is supposedly the colonel is actually a wizard, using the same spell that I used to make myself look like Lady Tweaking."

"How do they hope to get away with it?"

"Why *wouldn't* they get away with it? Just think about it for a minute. Their typical victim is desperate to believe that the person standing in front of them is their loved one, restored from the dead, and so they hand over the cash. As soon as they do, Greenlight is on his way."

"And the wizard?"

"I imagine that he mysteriously disappears shortly after. Leaving the victim a half-million pounds worse off."

"What's your plan, Jill?"

"I'm going to give these two gentlemen the surprise of their life, then I'll call Daze. I'm sure she'll be happy to put the wizard behind bars in Candlefield. Can you sort out the GT end?"

"Sure. The colonel has given me details of the person he dealt with at this end. As soon as I'm done with this call, I'll go and introduce myself to him. What about the human, though? Greenlight or whatever his name is."

"I'm not sure what I'm going to do about him. It's not

wrong-footed.

"It's lovely to be back, Caroline," said the man standing in front of me, who looked just like the colonel. He even sounded like the colonel. But there was one thing I was absolutely sure about: He was *not* the colonel; this man wasn't even a human. He was a wizard who had no doubt used the same 'doppelganger' spell as I had. These days, I routinely used the 'block' spell, so other sups wouldn't realise I was a witch. That gave me the upper hand because although I knew that he wasn't the colonel, he had no idea that I wasn't the real Lady Tweaking.

It was now obvious that I'd been barking up totally the wrong tree. I'd been working on the assumption that Restore were digging up bodies to breathe new life into them. In fact, the truth was much more straightforward: It was a simple scam devised between a human, a ghost (or ghosts) and a sup.

"There's just the small matter of the payment," Greenlight said.

"Of course. Why don't we go through to the dining room? My safe is in there."

"Lead the way, your ladyship."

We'd just entered the hall when my phone rang.

"I'm sorry, but I have to take this. Please take a seat and I'll be back in a couple of minutes."

Greenlight wasn't happy at the delay but he did as I asked. He was clearly keen to be on his way with his ill-gotten gains. The 'colonel' took a seat next to him.

"Mad? Did you find the colonel?"

"I did."

"Is he okay?"

"More or less. I didn't think anyone was in their

"I'll go and see what I can find out."
"Thanks, Mad. Keep me posted."
"Will do."

I was intrigued to find out what Greenlight had in store for me. I'd been completely wrong about my new neighbours down the corridor, but it was still possible that The Count could have set-up in business with the people at Restore. I still found it hard to believe that they actually had the capability to bring someone back from the dead, but if I was wrong, how would I react when I came face to face with the resurrected colonel?

I would find out soon enough.

Although I'd previously gone head-to-head with zombies, I was uncharacteristically nervous about what was about to happen. As promised, Caroline had vacated the manor house for my use. I deliberately arrived early, and only when I was inside, did I use the 'doppelganger' spell to transform into Lady Tweaking.

At ten o'clock on the dot, there was a knock on the door. Greenlight greeted me with much enthusiasm, but I was too busy looking at the man standing next to him to respond.

"Aren't you going to give your brother a hug, your ladyship?"

It was at that precise moment that I realised I had no idea what the colonel's first name was. I was supposed to be his sister, so I could hardly address him as Colonel.

"It's so good to see you again, *bro*." I gave him a big hug.

And yes, I do realise that Lady Tweaking was unlikely to call anyone 'bro', but I'd been caught completely

"The vicar must have done it. It's a good job you saw it and took it down."

"This isn't the only one. He's put them up all over the village."

Oh bum!

***

I'd called Mrs V to tell her that I wouldn't be in until later because I was headed to Tweaking Manor. I had a meeting with Alex Greenlight who claimed he would be accompanied by the newly *restored-to-life* colonel.

Speaking of whom, I'd been trying to get in touch with the colonel ever since I'd taken the phone call from Greenlight, but all my calls had gone straight to voicemail, and he hadn't responded to any of the messages I'd left.

I decided to give Mad a call; she would hopefully be back from her holiday.

"Hey, Jill."

"I wasn't sure if you'd still be away?"

"We got back yesterday."

"I need a favour."

"Sure. Name it."

"I'm a little worried about the colonel."

"Why? What's happened?"

I quickly brought her up to-date on the Restore situation.

"And you think something might have happened to him?"

"I hope not, but it's too much of a coincidence that ever since Greenlight spoke to me I've been unable to get hold of him."

"Those goldfish are blowing bubbles again," Jack said when we came downstairs.

"You give Florence her breakfast, and I'll go and see what's wrong this time."

I stormed into the lounge. "What's up with you two? I really am not in the mood for this."

"Why did you get rid of the cats?" Wanda said.

"Because they were making such a racket they were keeping us awake. I thought you'd be pleased."

"It was entertaining, teasing them, wasn't it, Mabel?"

"Hilarious. Those felines are so stupid."

"I'm dreadfully sorry if I've spoiled your fun, but it was either that or never sleeping again. The two of you will just have to suck it up."

"Charming," Wanda huffed.

"Some people are so inconsiderate," Mabel said.

"What's up with them?" Jack asked when I returned to the kitchen.

"They're annoyed because I got rid of the cats."

"That doesn't make any sense."

"I'm beginning to think nothing in my life does."

We were almost out of bread, so Jack popped to the village store. When he returned, he had a loaf in one hand, and a sheet of paper in the other. "Look at this."

"Are the Stock sisters running a promotion?"

"It isn't from the store. I found it attached to the lamppost." He handed it to me.

Beware!

There is a huge, stray dog roaming the village (last seen at the old watermill).

Be extra vigilant - it may be vicious.

"Are you sure it wasn't Buddy you saw?" I said.
"No. The beast I saw was enormous." The vicar had his nose pressed against the glass door.
"Do you see him?" I said.
"No, but maybe he's hiding in the bushes."
"I'll go and check."
"No, Jill, wait!"
But I was already through the door. "Doggy? Are you there? Doggy? Come out."
"What's going on?" Jack appeared in the kitchen, still dressed in his pyjamas.
"The vicar thought he saw a dog jump over our fence."
"It was enormous." He held out his arms to illustrate the point.
"There doesn't appear to be anything out there now." I shrugged.
"I'd better go and check the rest of the village." The vicar left in a hurry.
"Care to explain all of that?" Jack said.
"Brute was just chasing the cats away."
"*Brute*?"
"I turned myself into a Doberman."
"And you didn't think to check that the coast was clear first?"
"It's a quarter to six in the morning. Who goes for a walk at this time of day?"
"The vicar does, apparently."

***

There had seemed little point in going back to bed, so Jack and I had breakfast, and then I got Florence up.

to vacate this property and never return."

"Or you'll do what?" the ginger tom sneered. "It looks to me like you're stuck behind that fence."

"I'll count to five and by then, you'd better all have left. One, two, three—"

The cats, led by the ginger tom, all chorused, "Four." They clearly thought I was bluffing.

"Five!" I took a few steps back, then took a run at the fence. The five cats had scattered before I landed. "And don't you dare come back."

Mission accomplished, I leapt over the fence again, went back into the kitchen, and resumed human form. I was just deciding whether it was worth trying to grab another half hour in bed, or to have breakfast, when there was a frantic knocking on the door.

Who on earth was that at this time of the morning?

"Vicar?"

"Jill, are you okay?"

"Err, yeah. Fine."

"Are all of your doors locked?"

"What's wrong, Vicar?"

"He must be in your garden."

"Who must?"

"A monster of a dog. I was just taking my early morning constitutional when I saw him leap over your fence, chase off a pack of cats, and then jump back over the fence again."

"Deary me. I'd better go and check."

"I can't allow you to do it alone. It might be dangerous." And before I could stop him, he'd squeezed past me, and was headed towards the kitchen.

As soon as Buddy saw him, he began to yap.

Chapter 26

"That's it!" I jumped out of bed. "I've had enough."

"Where are you going?" Jack just about managed to open one eye. "What time is it?"

"Can't you hear them?"

"Oh yeah. How long have they been at it?"

"The best part of an hour."

"What are you going to do?"

"Make sure they never come back to our garden."

"You're not going to kill them, are you?"

"Of course I'm not going to *kill them*, but I am going to give them the biggest scare of their nine lives."

"I'm hungry," Buddy said.

"It's not six o'clock yet. You'll have to wait."

"But I'm starving."

"Tough. If you were doing your job and keeping the neighbourhood cats away, I wouldn't have to do this."

"I don't like cats. They scare me."

Of course they did. How did I end up with a cat that was scared of mice and a dog that was scared of cats?

"Watch and learn then." I opened the door into the garden, then turned myself into a Doberman.

"Yikes!" Buddy scurried away.

The caterwauling was even louder outside. I put my two front paws onto the fence, so that I could see into the front garden where there were five cats, all staring at the window.

"Err, guys. Excuse me."

The cats all turned their gaze towards me.

"Who are you?" The biggest of the clowder sneered.

"I'm Brute, and I live here. I'm going to ask you politely

Unfortunately, it wasn't good enough to win the competition. Armi's group were awarded the win, but only on a split decision. Everyone in Mrs V's troupe was gracious in defeat, but I couldn't help but feel I'd let the side down.

"Thanks for stepping in, Jill," Mrs V said.

"I feel like I let you down."

"Don't be silly. If it hadn't been for you, we wouldn't have even been able to take part."

Armi put his arm around her shoulder. "Can we call a truce now, Annabel?"

"Of course we can. Until the next competition, anyway."

actually started to enjoy it.

"Jill? What are you doing?"

As soon as I heard the voice, my heart sank. I spun around to see Kathy, Peter, and both kids standing there.

"Oh, hi."

"You didn't tell me you'd taken up Morris dancing." Kathy grinned.

"I haven't. I'm just ringing this bell." Oh bum! I'd been so distracted by Kathy's arrival that I'd taken my eyes off Mrs V, who was now looking daggers at me. How many prompts had I missed?

Ignoring Kathy and the family, I focussed on Mrs V for the rest of the routine, but I knew I'd already blown it.

When the music stopped, Mrs V came hurrying over. "What happened, Jill?"

"Sorry."

"Hi, Mrs V," Kathy said. "You were very good."

"Thank you, dear."

"Why don't you stand next to Jill, so I can get a photo of you both?"

Mrs V did as Kathy said and the two of us somehow managed a smile, even if it was through gritted teeth.

"I'd better leave you to it," Kathy said. "The photo will be on Facebook and Instagram if you want to check it out later."

"I really am sorry, Mrs V," I said.

"Don't worry about it. We have two more routines. You need to concentrate from now on."

"I will. I promise."

For the next two dances, I never took my eyes off her for a moment, and although I say so myself, my timing was perfect.

dance commenced.

"How will I know when to ring it?"

"Just watch me," Mrs V said. "Every time I raise my right arm, you ring the bell. Got it?"

"I guess so."

The two groups were to take turns dancing, and it was Armi's group who went first. Now, I'm no expert in matters Morris dancing, but their routine looked to be tightly choreographed, and very well executed.

Mrs V did not agree.

"Did you see that, Jill?" She tutted. "Sloppy if you ask me."

"I thought they did okay."

"To the untrained eye, maybe, but I doubt the judges will agree."

Once Armi's group had finished, they moved to the edge of the square, and our troupe took centre-stage.

"Good luck, Mrs V," I said.

"Luck doesn't come into it, dear. Now, don't forget, whenever I raise my right arm, ring the bell."

"Okay."

Although I felt a little foolish wearing the oversize costume, at least I wasn't expected to dance. All I had to do was stand behind the dancers, and ring the bell when prompted. Jack and Florence were watching from the other side of the square. Before leaving them, I'd threatened Jack that he mustn't take any photographs. I didn't want a permanent record of today's events.

As soon as the music started, the dancers began their well-rehearsed routine. I was watching Mrs V like a hawk, and every time she raised her right arm, I rang the bell. It was much easier than I'd expected, and after a while, I

coo over his model, which made me feel a little better about the money I'd just handed over. A *little* better, but not very much.

"What's wrong with Mrs V?" Jack said.

She was wearing full Morris dancing costume and had a bandage around her hand.

"Hello, you lot." She still managed to greet us with a smile.

"Are you okay?" I gestured to her hand.

"It swelled up overnight."

"Did you ought to be dancing?"

"I'll be fine with the dance, but I do have a tiny favour to ask you, Jill."

***

"Mummy looks funny, doesn't she, Daddy?" Florence giggled.

"Laugh if you dare," I threatened Jack.

"I wouldn't dream of it. That outfit really suits you." He broke into hysterics.

The tiny favour Mrs V had asked of me was to ring the bell, which she was unable to do because of her swollen hand. Like an idiot, I'd agreed to do it before she'd explained that I would have to dress in full Morris dancer costume. That was bad enough, but the only spare costume they had was two sizes too big. By the time I'd realised what was required of me, it was too late to back out because Mrs V was so excited at the prospect of winning the competition and getting one over on Armi.

I'd had to dash to the nearby public toilets to get changed, and I only just got back in time before the first

Jack shot me a puzzled look, and before I could speak, the man said to him, "I assume it's for you?"

"What is?"

"Oh dear, I hope I haven't spoiled the surprise, but I can't hold onto it any longer without payment."

"Jill?" Jack said.

"I—err—"

"I'm sure you'll be delighted with the Bristol Blenheim."

"The Blenheim?" Jack's face lit up. "Did you buy me the Blenheim?"

"I—err—"

He threw his arms around me and gave me a kiss. "What a brilliant surprise! I had no idea. Thanks, Jill."

"No problem."

"What is a Blenbum, Daddy?"

"The Blenheim is an aeroplane. Mummy has bought me a model of it to build."

"Can I help you do it?"

"We'll see. Let's go and get it."

We followed the man into the shop where he produced the model kit from under the counter. "There you are."

Jack's eyes lit up again.

"Would you like a bag for it?"

"No, it's fine as it is. Thanks." Jack and Florence left the shop, and I was just about to follow.

"Excuse me, madam, I think you've forgotten something."

"The glue?"

"No. The glue is in the box. You haven't paid yet."

"Of course, yes. Silly me."

As we made our way to Wash Square, Jack continued to

with it?"

"No, just this." I grabbed the sauce and headed back to the table.

"I thought you'd got lost," Jack said.

"You wouldn't believe the hoops I had to jump through to get these."

"I've finished, Mummy." Florence was still playing with her puzzle. "Can we go and watch the Morris dancing now?"

"Mummy hasn't finished her meal yet, pumpkin," Jack said. "We have to wait for her."

"Your chips have gone cold, Mummy."

"I prefer my chips cold." I dipped a couple of them into the sauce. "Mmm, yummy." I was going to eat them if it killed me.

We still had half-an-hour before the start of the Morris dancing competition, which was to be held in Wash Square. To pass the time, we took a walk down the high street.

"Hey there!" The voice came from somewhere behind us.

Jack turned around. "I think that guy is calling us."

I glanced around and, to my horror, I realised it was the man from the model shop.

"I don't think so. I think he's calling to someone across the road. Come on, let's go."

"No, he's definitely calling us."

Oh bum!

"Thank goodness I spotted you." The man was still trying to catch his breath. "I was beginning to think you'd forgotten."

two need any?"

They didn't, so I went in search of more supplies. I thought there might be some on the stations where the napkins and bins were kept, but there was no sign of them. The queues at the counter were ten-deep, so I went to one side, and caught the eye of one of the servers.

"Excuse me, can I get some tomato sauce, please?"

"Sure, but you'll need to use the screens." He gestured towards the touchpad screens that Jack had used to order the meals. "Or the app."

"I don't want a meal. Just some tomato sauce. Couldn't you pass me some?"

"That's not possible, I'm afraid. You'll need to use the screen."

"Are you telling me that I have to pay for extra sauce?"

"No, of course not. It's free, but you do need to—"

"Use the screen. Yeah, I get it."

Still fuming about the ridiculous system, I went over to the touchscreen. Whereabouts on the stupid Fun Menu would I find the tomato ketchup? After two dead-ends, I eventually located it under 'Miscellaneous'. Quantity? After all that messing around, I deserved at least three pots. Once I'd finished, the screen informed me I was order number seventy-six.

As I only wanted tomato sauce, I'd assumed that my order would go straight to the top of the queue, but no, it was firmly at the bottom. I was getting madder and madder as I watched my number slowly but surely rising up the list.

"Number seventy-six," a young woman shouted.

"That's me."

"Tomato sauce? Is this all you wanted? Nothing to go

"This is really yummy, isn't it, Mummy?" Florence took a bite of her cheeseburger.

"Yeah, it's great." The burgers were surprisingly tasty, but that didn't make up for everything that went with the experience.

A few weeks ago, Fun Burgers had opened a restaurant and drive-thru on the outskirts of Washbridge. Since then, every time I'd driven into the city with Florence in the car, I'd taken a different route. I knew if she saw the brightly coloured building with the signs advertising kids' Fun Burger Bags, she'd be all over it like a rash. My plan had worked fine for a while, but I hadn't accounted for the playground grapevine. Last week, she'd come home from school full of tales of the toys in the Fun Burger Bags.

I had hoped that the excitement of going to see the Morris dancing competition might have made her forget about Fun Burgers, and that we would be able to pick up lunch in the city centre.

No chance.

As soon as we got into the car, she began to sing the Fun Burger song; goodness knows where she'd learned that. I'd suggested we could go through the drive-thru, to avoid the pandemonium inside, but she would have none of it.

So, there we were, seated in a *Fun* Booth, eating *Fun* Burgers, while Florence played with a puzzle from the *Fun* Burger Bag.

Was I having *fun*? What do you think?

"This burger actually isn't bad," Jack said.

"They didn't give us enough tomato sauce." I sighed.

"You had three pots of it. How much do you need?"

"More than that. I'm going to get some more. Do you

As soon as I'd finished talking to Greenlight, I called Caroline.

"It's Jill. I know this is really short notice, but is there any chance that I could have the use of Tweaking Manor again tomorrow morning? If everything goes to plan, I expect to apprehend the slimeballs behind the art scam."

"Of course. I'll give Trudy Majors a call and arrange brunch and a morning's shopping. Do you want me to give Sears the morning off too?"

"Yes, please. I really am grateful for all your help."

"Don't mention it. It's my pleasure."

Next, I called the colonel. I'd promised to keep him updated on events, and he would no doubt find it amusing to hear that he had been brought back to life. Unfortunately, I didn't get the chance to give him the news because the call went straight to voicemail. After leaving him a message, I tried to go back to sleep, but it was no good because I was wide awake, so I showered, got dressed and ate breakfast.

Afterwards, I took out my laptop and brought up the articles I'd found when looking for details of anyone who Sushi had recently put behind bars. The two I'd investigated: Dave 'The Sword' Fisher and Harper had both proven to be a bust. There had been one other article, which initially I'd dismissed because the crime had taken place two years ago, and the perpetrator had died behind bars. However, I was now convinced that I'd been wrong to dismiss it, and if my hunch was right, it could lead me to Sushi's murderer.

***

Chapter 25

It was Saturday morning and Jack had volunteered to take Florence to dance class while I enjoyed a well-deserved lie-in. I planned to stay in bed until just before they were due back, then we'd all grab lunch, ahead of going to watch Mrs V and Armi fight it out in the battle of the Morris dancers.

At least, that had been the plan, but no sooner had Jack and Florence left than my burner phone rang. The only person who had that number was Mr Greenlight from Restore.

"Lady Caroline Tweaking speaking," I said in my poshest voice.

"It's Alexander Greenlight, Lady Tweaking."

"Do you have good news for me?"

"I do indeed. Your brother, the colonel, is back amongst the living, and he's very keen to see you."

"That's excellent news. Did everything go okay? What I mean to say is, is he in good shape?"

"Absolutely. I have to ask if you have the agreed fee?"

"I do indeed. Although, I'm a little nervous about holding so much cash in the house."

"The sooner I take it off your hands the better, then." He laughed. "Would it be convenient for me to come around tomorrow morning?"

"Of course, but I insist on seeing my brother before handing over the cash."

"We wouldn't have it any other way. I can assure you that he'll be there with me. Does ten o'clock work for you?"

"Yes, I'll be waiting for you then."

paranormal world, had come as a huge disappointment.

If they weren't behind Restore, then who was? And how did they intend to bring the colonel back to life? I'd find out soon enough because I'd given Greenlight my phone number and they had promised to call as soon as the colonel was ready to be reunited with his 'sister'.

"He was to be our first guinea pig."

"You're using a rabbit as a guinea pig? You do realise how ridiculous that sounds."

"We did try using a guinea pig, but it wouldn't sit still long enough."

"I don't mind giving it a go," the rabbit chipped in. "It sounds like fun."

"Are you crazy?" I said. "You might get fried."

"It's a risk I'm willing to take in the name of science."

"May we continue?" Black said.

"I suppose so."

He placed the rabbit on the machine and threw the lever.

Ten minutes later, after much noise, lots of flashes, but thankfully, no power cut, the rabbit said, "I'm still here, guys."

"Back to the drawing board." Black sighed.

Tired and hugely disappointed, I set off for home. The roads were quiet at that time of day, and as I drove, my mind played back the night's events. I'd been totally convinced that my neighbours were behind the Restore operation. It had all fitted together so neatly. I'd seen them in the graveyard in Candlefield, and I'd seen them carrying a coffin-shaped box up the stairs (which tonight they had explained contained parts of the machine I'd just seen). Even the way they dressed all fitted. And when Daze had told me that The Count had been released from prison, I was convinced that he and Black were one and the same person. To discover that Black wasn't The Count, and that the two brothers were actually involved in some cockamamie attempt to transport humans to the

bunny up and held him out to me. "You can take him. He hasn't been harmed."

"I don't want the rabbit. I want the colonel. Where is he?"

They looked at one another, and then Black's brother said, "We don't know who the colonel is."

"What are you doing here?" I demanded. "What is this machine?"

"We can't tell you that," Black said.

"You can and you will. Otherwise, you'll have to explain it to the rogue retrievers."

"Don't call them. Please."

"Then you'd better start talking."

"We call it the Tporter."

"And what does it do?"

"Nothing yet. It's still in the development stage."

"What will it do when it's finished?"

They both hesitated. "Would you be prepared to sign an NDA before we tell you?"

"No, I won't sign an *NDA*. Tell me what it is now, or I call Daze."

"Okay, okay. If everything goes to plan, it will allow us to transport humans to the paranormal world."

"You're crazy. That's impossible."

"That may be true now, but the Tporter will change that. We just have to iron out a few bugs."

"These *bugs* that you mentioned. Would they include causing power surges that took down the power grid for miles around?"

"I'm afraid so. We hadn't anticipated that the process would use so much energy."

"What's with the rabbit?"

moment I thought they might go out altogether.

"Right, you stay here."

"Like I had any intention of following you." Winky jumped off the sofa and crawled underneath it. "Tell me when it's all over."

There was no need to tiptoe down the corridor because they would never hear me over the racket coming from their unit. The thought of seeing the colonel's rotting body filled me with dread, but it had to be done. After a couple of deep breaths, I magicked myself inside the unit.

The machine was enormous and looked very much like I'd imagined. It was shaking and making the most awful noise. Standing beside it, with their backs to me, was Black, AKA The Count, and the man I assumed was his brother.

"Stop what you're doing!" I shouted at the top of my voice.

They spun around, clearly stunned to see me standing there.

"Stop immediately! And return the colonel's body to its resting place."

Black reached up and pulled on a large lever, which turned off the machine. Even though it was now silent in the room, my ears were still ringing.

"Step aside and let me see the colonel."

"Who's the *colonel*?" Black said.

"Don't come the innocent with me. Step aside now."

They did as I said, and for the first time I saw who was on the machine. Or perhaps I should say *what* was on it.

"What have you done with the colonel? Where is he?"

"Is that what he's called?" Black pointed to the rabbit. "We didn't think he belonged to anyone." He lifted the had to wake you up to stop that horrible snoring."

"I was *not* snoring. I was just catnapping."

"I could hear you from the bottom of the stairs."

"Why do you always feel the need to exaggerate?"

I took out the ham sandwiches that I'd made at home and put them on my desk.

Winky eyed them, and said, "What did you bring for me?"

"Nothing."

"You can be so selfish sometimes."

"Shush, I need to listen for any movement next door."

"If they start up that machine of theirs, you'll hear it, trust me."

By one o'clock in the morning, I'd heard nothing from next door, and I was beginning to think this was another bust. Winky kept dozing off, but every time he started to snore, I gave him a gentle poke. If I wasn't going to get any sleep, neither was he.

"That crazy bring-back-the-dead hunch of yours isn't looking very promising," he said while trying to stifle a yawn.

"It has to happen tonight. They promised the colonel would be restored to life within forty-eight hours."

"You do realise how barmy that sounds, don't you?"

Before I could reply, an almighty banging sound started up next door. It was so loud that the whole building seemed to be shaking.

"See!" Winky was up on his paws. "What did I tell you?"

"I didn't realise it would be this loud."

The lights in the office began to flicker, and for a

the house."

"I won't."

"What's with her sudden interest in worms?" I asked Jack once Florence had gone outside.

"I think they were talking about them today at school. Are you sure you're going to be okay going out again tonight?"

"I don't have any choice. Tonight's the night they're going to do the deed."

"Do you want to go and put your head down for a couple of hours after we've done here? I can take Florence to bed."

"Thanks, but I reckon if I have a sleep, I'll feel like death warmed up when you wake me. I'll be fine, and besides I've got a lie-in in the morning to look forward to."

***

As soon as I walked into the office building, I heard an unearthly noise, but it wasn't coming from my neighbours' unit. It was Winky snoring.

I unlocked the outer office, made my way on tiptoe past Mrs V's desk, and then let myself into my office as quietly as I could. Winky, the cat who insists he doesn't snore, was flat out on his back on the sofa, doing a fantastic impression of a pneumatic drill.

"Boo!"

He jumped so much, that he toppled off the sofa onto the floor.

"Are you insane!" he screamed. "I could have broken my neck."

"Don't be ridiculous. Cats always land on their feet. I

"Are you okay? Do you want me to run you to the hospital?"

"No, it isn't that bad, but I'm not sure how I'm going to ring my bell now."

"What bell?"

"In the competition tomorrow."

"I thought you were dancing."

"We are, but I also have to ring a bell."

"Can't you use your other hand to do that?"

"I doubt it. I normally do everything with my right hand."

***

"Who's Morris, Mummy?" Florence asked while the three of us were enjoying the roast dinner Jack had made.

"I don't think I know anyone called Morris, darling."

"But Daddy said we're going to watch Morris dancing on Saturday afternoon."

"Morris isn't a person. It's the name of a kind of dancing."

"Can I Morris dance?"

"No, we'll just be there to watch. Mrs V from the office will be dancing, though. We can cheer her team on."

"Is it a competition?"

"Yes, it is."

"What does the winner get?"

"I don't know."

"I've finished now. Can I go and play in the garden?"

"Yes, why don't you throw the ball for Buddy?"

"He never runs after it. I'm going to look for worms."

"Don't pick them up, and definitely don't bring them in

Clearly horrified, Sushi stood up and began to remonstrate with the waitress who became visibly upset. The manager, Terry Surefoot, quickly intervened, sending the waitress out of the room while he tried to calm Sushi down. It was at this point that the waitress had joined Hoyle outside for a cigarette. Unimpressed by the manager's apologies, Sushi stormed out of the room and headed for the toilet where we were to have our brief encounter. Shortly after, Sushi's husband stood up and left too. I knew now that he had gone to the men's toilet where he had been seen by a member of the restaurant staff. Over the next few minutes, everyone returned to the room and retook their seats. Everyone except for Sushi.

"Any minute now, and it'll all be over for me," Winky said, as he glanced down at the road below. "Then you'll be sorry."

"Okay, okay, I'll give you some food. It's not like I'm doing anything important." I stomped across the room and took a tin of salmon out of the cupboard. "Just trying to save myself from a murder conviction."

The bowl was no sooner on the floor than he began to tuck in, seemingly unconcerned about my dire predicament. I was just about to return to my desk when I heard a scream from the outer office.

Mrs V, who was clearly in some pain, was shaking her hand around.

"What happened?"

"I trapped my fingers in the drawer."

"Why did you do that?"

She shot me a look. "I didn't plan to do it. I was distracted by a cute little bird that landed on the windowsill."

"Much more important. Now, get down and let me concentrate."

"Charming." He huffed, and then jumped onto the windowsill. "I might as well throw myself out of this window. No one would care."

"Just be careful you don't land on someone's head. I don't want to be sued."

As I'd done on my first viewing of the CCTV footage, I skipped forward to the point where all the guests had just taken their seats. Hoyle was looking daggers at Sushi, who was returning the look with interest. A few moments later, Sushi's husband said something to her, which resulted in them having heated words. A waiter and the waitress, who would later spill the soup on Sushi, began to go around the table, taking everyone's orders. While we waited for the first course to arrive, there was much banter, most of it between Norman Whitelea, the guest of honour, and the others. From what I could recall, they were all recounting their favourite 'Norm' moment.

It was at this point in proceedings that Christine Hoyle stood up and left the room. I knew now that she was on her way outside for a quick smoke before the starters arrived. Not long after, I too stood up and made my way out of the room, en route to the toilet.

A few minutes later, the waiter and waitress reappeared, carrying trays full of starters. A couple of the guests had requested prawn cocktail, but the majority had asked for soup. The waitress placed the first bowl in front of Whitelea, the next in front of Sushi's husband, and then came the flashpoint: As she was leaning forward to place the bowl in front of Sushi, she appeared to lose her grip for a moment, and some of the soup spilled.

"Sure." She tapped away on her computer for a couple of minutes. "Would you like me to print it for you?"

"Yes, please." I studied the printout. "Angela Fredricks. I see she only joined your staff a couple of weeks before the incident."

"That's right."

"Okay, thanks for that."

After leaving the restaurant, I made my way to the address on the printout, a small townhouse five miles away. I knocked, but there was no response. I was looking through the front window when the next-door neighbour came home.

"Are you looking for Angela?"

"Yeah."

"She'll be at work."

"I've just come from the Red Lion. She wasn't there."

"She works in the council offices."

"Oh? Are you sure?"

"Positive."

That was kind of weird, but then maybe the waitressing was just a side gig. "What time does she get home?"

"About six, usually."

***

Back at the office, I decided to take another look at the CCTV footage from inside the dining room.

"Is there any chance of getting fed today?" Winky jumped onto my desk.

"You'll have to wait. This is important."

"More important than your darling cat?"

Chapter 24

Back in my car, I mulled over everything I knew about the Sushi murder. It was now clear to me that the toilet in the locked cubicle had never actually been faulty. But reporting it as such had resulted in it being locked, awaiting repair. As I'd suspected all along, there must have been someone in the locked cubicle, and whoever it was had been waiting for Sushi. My turning up in the loo could have potentially scuppered their plans, but once I'd left, they had struck with deadly effect.

That theory was fine as far as it went, but there were a couple of gaping holes, which I would need to fill in if I were to take it to the police. The obvious candidate was the waitress who had reported the toilet faulty—the same waitress who had spilled the soup on Sushi. But she had an alibi. At the time Sushi was murdered, she'd been caught on the hotel's CCTV, standing next to Christine Hoyle; the two of them enjoying a cigarette.

My *something smells off* radar was sounding a warning. If there were separate, designated smoking areas for staff and customers, how come Hoyle and the waitress had decided to smoke in a different location altogether? It was almost as though they knew that was the one place they would be captured on the CCTV of the hotel next door. I needed to speak to the waitress who had spilled the soup over Sushi.

I hurried back into the restaurant.

"Did you forget something?" the receptionist said.

"Can you give me the address of the waitress who was on duty on the night of the murder? The one who spilt the soup."

"Is that for staff?" I said.

"Yes, I'm afraid we still have a few members who indulge."

"What about customers? Do they use that same area?"

"No, there's another smokers' area near to the main entrance. You may not have noticed it because it's located behind the bushes. Sorry, I have to dash."

"Thanks for all your help."

I took a look at the invoice for the repair of the toilet. The only item on there was a callout charge. Beneath that was a hand-written note that said the toilet was found to be working, so there would be no additional charges for parts or labour.

"Yes, please."

He returned a couple of minutes later, flicking through the pages of a green, A4, hardback notepad. "This looks like it. According to this entry, the toilet wouldn't flush."

"What time was the report made?"

"It doesn't give a time, just the date."

"And it was the date of the murder?"

"That's right."

"Why bother entering something as minor as that into the log? Why not just get your maintenance man to sort it out?"

"We don't actually have a maintenance man on staff. There isn't enough work to warrant it. We use a few local tradesmen who we call in as and when required."

"And is that what happened here?"

"Yes, but they weren't able to carry out the repairs until after your people released the crime scene."

"Is there a note to say what the nature of the repair was?"

"No, but there will be an invoice if you'd like to see that."

"Yes, please."

He disappeared out of the office again, and returned clutching the invoice, which he handed to me. "I don't mean to be rude, Constable, but I have a dental appointment in a few minutes. Are we likely to be much longer?"

"I'm done here. Is it okay if I hang onto this invoice?"

"Yes, of course. I'll walk you out."

He led the way outside through a side exit. A few metres from the exit was a small covered area with a sign indicating it was for the use of smokers.

The assistant manager walked into reception, and the first thing he did was drop the pile of folders he'd been carrying. "Sorry about that. I'm Gerry Safehands, I believe you were asking for Terry?"

"That's right, but I'm sure you'll be able to help."

"Do you mind if I pick these up first?"

"Of course. Let me give you a hand."

The man was a liability. Every time he picked up one folder, he managed to drop another one. "Sorry about this."

"Why don't you let me carry some for you?"

"That would be a great help." He led the way to a small office where we deposited the folders onto the desk. "Thanks. I really appreciate that. Now, how can I help you, Constable?"

"I'm part of the team working on the murder case. I understand that on the night in question, one of the cubicles in the ladies' toilets was locked because it was faulty."

"You're telling me something I wasn't aware of. Terry has been the liaison with the police. I haven't really had anything to do with it."

"Okay, well you can take it from me that we were informed that the cubicle was locked because it was faulty. I'd like some more details about that, specifically what the fault was, who reported it and when."

"Right. I should be able to help because we keep a general log of all maintenance carried out in the building."

"Can you take a look, please." I gestured to the computer on his desk.

"It won't be on there. It's entered into a book which is kept in Terry's office. I can go and get it if you like?"

And even if they had been up to their shenanigans, I probably wouldn't have heard them over your snoring."

"What did you just say? That's an outrageous accusation. I do *not* snore."

"Really, so how come ten minutes after I got here, you were going at it like a road drill?"

"Rubbish. So, what's the plan now?"

"If they're going to meet the deadline to bring the colonel back to life, they'll have to do the deadly deed tonight."

"Does that mean I'll have the pleasure of your company again?"

"It does, and this time, try to stay awake, will you? I'm not sure I can handle another night of your snoring."

***

I couldn't shake the feeling that the locked toilet cubicle held the answer to who had murdered Sushi. According to the police's report, which I'd read at the station, that cubicle wasn't occupied, and had only been locked because it was faulty. Maybe that was true, but when Sushi had been letting rip at me, I'd been sure I'd heard someone else in the room with us. So, to double-check, I once again adopted the disguise of a police constable and paid another visit to the restaurant.

"Hi, can I see Mr Surefoot, please?"

"I'm afraid the manager isn't in today. It's his day off."

"Does he have an assistant?"

"Yes, Mr Safehands. Would you like me to call him for you?"

"Yes, please."

some. My money is as good as anyone else's."

"Trust me, Mr Keller, if we brewed beer, I would gladly sell you some, but as I'm sure you can see, this is not a micro-brewery."

"You could be brewing it off the premises. This is probably just your sales office."

"We have absolutely nothing to do with the brewing or selling of beer. Whoever gave you my name was mistaken. I'm a private detective, and I'm extremely busy, so I'm going to ask you politely to leave."

"What's behind that door?" He pointed to my office.

"If I let you look in there, do you promise to leave?"

"Yeah, okay."

I opened the door, stepped aside, and allowed him inside. "See, no beer in here."

"Why's that cat only got one eye?"

"He got tired of the other one. Now, if you don't mind."

"Okay." He took out a pen and notepad, scribbled something, tore out a sheet and handed it to me. "But if you change your mind, give me a call. I'm prepared to pay top dollar."

"Who was that guy?" Winky asked after Keller had left.

"He thinks we're running a micro-brewery."

"There's an idea. You'd make more money than you do playing at being a P.I."

"I do not *play* at being a P.I. I am a consummate professional."

"I probably shouldn't mention the Todfoster case at this juncture."

"You'd better not."

"Did you catch the body snatchers at it last night?"

"No, there weren't any sounds from next door at all.

all about?"

"It's a protest at being moved out of the window," Wanda said. "Isn't it, Mabel?"

"It is, dear. You had no right to move us out of there."

"You were drawing the attention of half the cats in the neighbourhood."

"That's not our fault and it's certainly no reason to deprive us of our view."

"Okay. If I put you back in the window, do you promise to stop this nonsense?"

"Of course. We're both reasonable people, aren't we, Wanda?"

"We are, Mabel, dear."

And so, back into the window they went.

"What about the cats?" Jack asked when we were back in the kitchen.

"I'll just have to think of something, but it'll be worth it because at least it's got those two prima donnas to be civil to one another."

***

When I arrived at work, there was a man in the outer office, looking behind the filing cabinet.

Mrs V rolled her eyes. "This is Mr Keller, Jill."

He looked up. "Are you the boss around here?"

"Yes, I'm Jill Maxwell."

"I know it's here somewhere. My wife's auntie's husband's best friend's neighbour gave me a bottle. It was superb."

"I assume you're talking about beer?"

"Yes, I can't understand why you won't let me purchase

weren't any sounds from down the corridor. I'll have to try again tonight."

"You're going to kill yourself at this rate. Can't you give yourself a night off?"

"I can't. If they're going to bring the colonel back to life in time to meet their promised deadline, they'll have to do it tonight."

"Fair enough. At least you'll be able to have a lie-in on Saturday."

"How will I? I have to get up to take Florence to dance class."

"I'll do that. You can stay in bed."

"Have I ever told you that you're my favourite husband?"

"You might not say that when you go into the lounge."

"Why? What did you do?"

"I did what you asked me to; I took charge of the goldfish situation. You'd better come and see."

I followed him into the lounge, to find Wanda and Mabel's bowls back on the sideboard. On the carpet, next to the sideboard was a sheet of plastic, and on that were two buckets.

"What's going on? Why are there two—?"

Before I could finish the sentence, the water in both bowls began to froth so violently that it splashed over the side, onto the sideboard, and then dripped into the buckets. The two fish, in what was clearly part of a coordinated plan, were swimming around at breakneck speed.

"Hey, you two, stop that right now!" No response. "Stop or I'll take you both back to the pet shop." This time they did as I said. "Would you like to tell me what this is mean."

"Maybe if I said the name *Christine*, it would jog your memory."

Oh bum!

"Err, I—err—"

"Before you come up with one of your fanciful tales, I should tell you that I had a text just now from Christine Hoyle, saying that it was nice to chat to me the other day."

"I needed to eliminate her from my enquiry."

"So, you thought you'd pretend to be me?"

"She was hardly going to open up to me otherwise, was she?"

"You can't go around impersonating me, Jill. It isn't on."

"I'm sorry. It's not like I do it often."

"*Often*?"

"What I meant to say is it's not like I've done it before."

"And did you manage to eliminate her from *your* enquiry?"

"Yes, I think so. And, please don't try to tell me that I should allow the police to do their thing because *their thing*, as far as I can tell, is going to result in me spending the rest of my life behind bars."

"Fair enough, but you should at least have told me what you were up to."

"You're right, and I'm sorry."

"Okay, let's forget it. What time did you get back last night?"

"Just before two."

"Did you catch your neighbours, trying to bring the colonel's body back to life?"

"No. I hung around there until one-thirty, but there

Chapter 23

Once again, I was still fast asleep when it was time to get up. The only reason I stirred then was because Florence had come running into our bedroom and leapt on top of me.

"Get up, Mummy. Daddy says it's time for your breakfast."

"I'll be down in a minute."

"Daddy said you would say that. He says you have to come right now."

"Okay. I'm coming."

Florence clearly didn't trust me because she waited beside the bed until I was up, and then she took my hand and led me down the stairs.

"I'm making scrambled eggs on toast for Florence and me," Jack said. "Do you want the same?"

"Yes, please."

Thankfully, Tigkey and Monger had decided to give breakfast a miss, so I wasn't forced to look at those monstrosities while I was eating. Florence finished her breakfast in record time before announcing she was going to make some new beanies, and disappearing back upstairs.

Jack had barely said two words since he'd asked me if I wanted scrambled eggs; I assumed that was because he knew I was only half awake.

I was wrong.

"Is there anything you'd like to tell me, Jill?"

"What?"

"I asked if there is anything—"

"I heard what you said. I just don't know what you

messed up big time."

He jumped from the windowsill onto my desk. "There's no point in beating yourself up. We all make mistakes, even me."

"Okay, what's the punchline?"

"I'm being serious. You screwed up, but the trick is to forgive yourself and move on. That's what I always do. Take the Feline Fortunes stuff for example."

"What about it?"

"You were right all along."

"I was?"

"Yeah. It's cheap, nasty and way overpriced."

"When did you realise that?"

"As soon as I unpacked the boxes."

"What are you going to do about it?"

"I've already done it. I've offloaded my entire stock."

"You must have lost a pretty penny getting shut of that lot. Still, at least you saw sense in the end."

"*Lost money*? Do you think I'm crazy? I didn't lose any money. In fact, I made a profit. Only a tiny one, but better than nothing."

"How did you manage to sell it at a profit?"

"Easy, I just told my friend, Graham the Gully, about the money to be made, and he snatched my paw off."

"How could you con one of your friends? I assume he's called Gully because he's gullible?"

"Actually, he's called Gully because he's so useless at ten-pin bowling. His bowls always end up in the gully. And, I'll have you know that he was delighted with his purchase."

with you running away to Spain with your boyfriend."

"I honestly didn't plan any of this."

"Really? Why do I find that hard to believe?"

"I mean I didn't intend to fall in love with someone else, but the heart wants what the heart wants, doesn't it?"

"I'm not sure it's your heart that's the problem here. What about all that rubbish you fed me about wanting to visit your family in Candlefield?"

"That was a lie, I'm afraid. I don't get on with any of them, so I rarely go back there."

"And all the photos you sent me?"

"Ronnie took them."

"Did he? Well, that's just great. If word of this gets out, it could ruin my professional reputation. I've already had to give your husband a full refund."

"That sucks. Sorry, Jill, I have to go because they're calling our flight."

"Hang on. Wait a—"

She'd already hung up.

I couldn't believe what had just happened. It wasn't only that I'd missed the signs, I'd actually provided cover for her by forwarding the photographs to Richard. I'd even congratulated myself on the easy money that I was being paid on the case. This was a wake-up call. Never again could I allow myself to be so complacent. Never again would I take anything on trust.

Thirty minutes later, Winky reappeared at the window.

"Is it safe to come in? I promise I won't mention the Todfoster case again."

"It's okay. I deserve everything you throw at me. I

professional misconduct." And with that, he stormed out of the door, slamming it behind him.

"Whoops!" Winky was on the sofa, grinning from ear to ear.

"Don't you dare say a word."

"I wouldn't dream of it. I'm not one to rub salt in the wound."

"Good."

"I was just wondering—"

"What?"

"It doesn't matter."

"Go on. Spit it out."

"How come you didn't remind him to leave you a review on TrustA-PI?"

"I'm going to kill you."

He was out of the window before I could put my hands on something heavy enough to do the deed.

Ten minutes after Todfoster had left, I was still in a bit of a daze. Ava had promised me that she wasn't seeing anyone else and that she needed alone time, so she could magic herself back to Candlefield to see her family. What a liar!

I took out my phone, found her number and made the call, but with no expectation that she would answer.

"Jill, hi. How are you?"

"How do you think I am? I've just had a visit from your husband."

"Oh dear. How is Richard?"

"Not very happy."

"I honestly didn't want to hurt him."

"Really? You have a funny way of showing it. What

tailing her, she's always alone."

"Really?"

His reaction surprised me a little. I'd assumed he would be delighted by my report, but if anything, he seemed to be getting even redder in the face.

"Are you okay, Richard? Why don't you take a seat? Would you like a drink? Tea? Coffee?"

"I'd prefer to stand, and I don't want a drink. What I do want, though, is my retainer refunded immediately."

"I'm sorry. I don't understand."

He took out a screwed-up sheet of paper and threw it onto my desk. "Read that!"

I unfolded it, and quickly read the scribbled note, which had been signed by Ava.

Oh bum!

"Care to comment?" He glared at me.

"I—err—don't understand."

"Which bit exactly don't you understand? The part where she says she has been seeing *Ronnie,* her personal trainer? Or the part where she says she has left me and is going to live with him in Spain? How did you manage to follow her for over a week, and yet never once spot her with her lover?"

"I—err—"

"Yes? I'm waiting."

"It seems I may have missed the signs."

"Call yourself a private investigator? You're a disgrace. Now, about that refund?"

"Okay." I took my cheque book from the desk drawer, wrote him a cheque to cover his retainer, and handed it to him. "I'm really sorry."

"Think yourself lucky I'm not suing you for

they're based on reality. All the evidence pointed to the fact that the epicentre of the Restore operation was right next door. If I were right about this, it meant they would be bringing the colonel's body up those stairs within the next couple of days. Maybe even tonight. And when they did, I'd be waiting for them.

***

Mrs V came through to my office and closed the door behind her, which was never a good sign.

"Jill, Mr Todfoster is out there."

I'd been hoping that I might be able to drag that particular case out for a few more days. Sending a photo to him once a day was some of the easiest money I'd ever made.

"I don't remember him making an appointment for today."

"He didn't. He just turned up and he doesn't look very happy about something."

"Don't worry. He'll be a whole lot happier when I give him the good news. Send him in, would you?"

Mrs V hadn't been exaggerating. Todfoster was red in the face with rage and looked like he might explode at any moment, so I decided to get in first with my report, which was bound to calm him down.

"Richard, I was going to call you later today. You'll be pleased to know that your fears are unfounded. Ava certainly does have a very busy social life, but she isn't cheating on you."

"Is that so?"

"Yes. As you'll see from all the photos I've taken while

"I have my sources. Meanwhile, I've been awake half the night because of those 'considerate' neighbours of ours."

"I take it they were doing more alteration work last night?"

"I've no idea what they were doing, but the noises coming out of there were enough to wake the dead."

"What did you just say?"

"I said, I don't know what they—"

"No, not that part. The last bit."

"The noises coming out of there were enough to wake the dead."

"That's it! You're a genius!"

"I've been telling you that for years."

"Come here. Let me give you a kiss."

"Yuk, stay away from me." He shot under the sofa. "What on earth has got into you?"

"I think you may have just solved one of my cases."

"Do I get a cut of the fees?"

"No, just my eternal thanks."

It was all slowly starting to make sense. My new neighbours, who claimed to be funeral directors, must be the human side of the Restore operation. I'd seen them carrying a large box up the stairs; a body-shaped box to be more precise. Black, as he insisted on calling himself, was probably The Count, and his companion was most likely his brother. The horrific noises, which Winky had described, must have been the machinery used to reanimate the corpse. I'd seen them in Frankenstein movies.

Yes, I do realise that movies aren't real, but sometimes

right?"

"I'm not sure. I told him he was wrong and that if he didn't believe me, he was welcome to pay us a visit. Hopefully, that will have convinced him he's barking up the wrong tree. Jill, you and the family are still coming to watch the Morris dancing competition on Saturday, aren't you?"

"Florence goes dancing in the morning."

"The competition isn't until two in the afternoon. I'm sure she'll enjoy it."

"Okay, sure. Why not."

My phone rang; it was Daze.

"Jill, I'll have to make this quick, but I've just had an answer back about The Count. It appears he was released from the asylum about a month ago. According to the authorities over there, he's a cured man. I'll believe that when I see it."

"Any idea where he might be?"

"Someone said he might be staying with his brother, but no one seems to know for sure."

"Okay, Daze, thanks very much for that."

That certainly gave me food for thought. Restore were claiming to be able to breathe new life into dead bodies, and the start of their operation seemed to coincide with the release of The Count. Could that be a coincidence? Somehow, I doubted it.

"It must be nice to only work half days," Winky said.

"I'll have you know I was working all morning."

"If you count spending half the morning in a tea room, eating a full English as working."

"How do you know what I had for breakfast?"

"Yeah. A complete nutter."

"You said you thought he was in an asylum, I believe?"

"That's right, somewhere near the Dark Forest."

"Would you do me a favour? Would you check to see if he's still there?"

"Is this connected to those scam artists who claim to be able to bring back the dead?"

"Yeah."

"Okay. I'll make some calls and get back to you later."

"Thanks, Daze."

***

Mrs V was eating another bacon cob at her desk.

"You're becoming addicted to those."

"I know. It's only because I have to walk past that new takeaway every morning, although I did manage to resist this morning."

"So, what's that in your hand?"

"When I popped there to pick up a salad for lunch, they were still serving the bacon cobs. Apparently, they serve them all day."

"So you had that instead of a salad?"

"Yes, but I've made a firm promise to myself that tomorrow will definitely be salad day."

"Until tomorrow comes." I grinned. "Any more calls?"

"That Mr Keller rang again."

"The man who was after the beer?"

"Yeah. He's convinced that we are a micro-brewery. He seems to think we're denying it because we only want to deal with a certain select clientele."

"The man is bonkers. Did you manage to put him

Chapter 22

Although Mr Greenlight had refused to give any details about how Restore were able to bring someone back from the dead, he appeared to have suggested they were somehow able to breathe life back into a dead body. Why else would he have said that their service was only available to those who had been buried, not cremated?

I was still ninety-nine percent sure the whole thing was a scam. No one could bring back the dead, unless you counted zombies. The only reason I wasn't a hundred percent sure was because of the recent discussion I'd had with Daze and Blaze. They had mentioned that someone, called The Count, had claimed to be able to restore the dead.

To put my mind at ease, I gave her a call.

"Daze, are you busy? Can you talk?"

"Is it a quick one? We're just on our way to a meeting with our boss."

"You're not in trouble, are you?"

"No, in fact quite the opposite. He's going to give us a commendation."

"Well done."

"Not really. The whole thing is a farce. All we did was find that stupid cousin of his."

"The Yeti guy?"

"Big Foot, yeah. It turned out he'd been on a bender all weekend, and was sleeping it off at one of his buddy's apartments. Not the sort of thing they should be handing out commendations for."

"When I was talking to you and Blaze, he mentioned someone called The Count."

reached into the inside pocket of his coat and took out a single sheet of paper. "Our contract is deliberately short and straightforward. Essentially, it says that upon the safe return of your brother, you will pay us the fee of five-hundred thousand pounds. Please, take a moment to read it, and if you're happy, add your signature at the bottom."

There wasn't very much to read because he'd pretty much summed up the contents, so I scribbled something which I hoped resembled Caroline's signature and handed it back to him.

"Excellent."

"How quickly can I expect to get my brother back?"

"He should be standing by your side within forty-eight hours."

After Mr Greenlight had left, the colonel said, "Do you think they can really do this?"

"Before he came, I would have said there was no chance, but the fact that they are confident enough not to ask for payment until the deed is done—" I grinned. "Doesn't change my mind. I'm convinced the whole thing is one big scam."

"What next?"

"I'm going to find out what these people are really up to."

"Yes, he's over there by the fireplace."

"Excellent. I'm pleased to meet you, Colonel."

"My brother says likewise. Why don't we sit down?"

At my beckoning, the colonel took a seat at the head of the table, I sat beside him, and Mr Greenlight sat on my other side.

"If it's alright with you, Lady Tweaking, I'll get straight into it."

"Yes, I'd prefer that."

"We at Restore have developed a method to *restore* the dead to life."

"That's a very bold claim, Mr Greenlight."

"But it's one we can back up."

"And how exactly do you back up your claim?"

"We will ask for no money until your brother is standing before you. Alive once again."

"I see. That certainly does demonstrate your confidence. And how much does this *service* of yours cost?"

"Five hundred thousand pounds."

"Half a million? That's a lot of money."

"Yes. And worth every penny, I'm sure you'll agree."

"If it brings my darling brother back to me, then yes, I suppose so. But how on earth are you able to bring someone back to life?"

"I'm afraid I'm unable to divulge that information."

"Surely, you must be able to tell me something?"

"I can tell you that we're only able to offer this service for those loved ones who were buried. It won't work for those who were cremated."

"Are you saying that you retrieve their bodies and some how bring them back to life?"

"I'm very sorry, but I've already said too much." He

'doppelganger' spell and transformed into Lady Tweaking.

"That's incredible, Jill. If I hadn't seen it with my own eyes, I would never have believed it possible. Now, how do you want me to play this?"

"I think it would be best if you allow me to do all the talking, unless he asks you a question directly. Is that okay?"

"Absolutely. I'll remain shtum."

"Let's go through to the dining room. We'll hold our meeting in there."

The guy from Restore was clearly keen because he arrived dead on time. I told the colonel to stay in the dining room while I went to let him in. I hadn't been sure whether to expect a human or a sup, but the diminutive man was one-hundred percent human. Even though it was quite a balmy day, he was wrapped up as though we were in the throes of a wintry blast. His scarf was so high on his face that I had to ask him to pull it down so I could hear what he was saying.

"I'm Alexander Greenlight, and you must be Lady Tweaking."

"That's right. Please follow me. We're in the dining room. Wouldn't you like to take off your coat? Scarf? Gloves?"

"I'd prefer to keep them on if you don't mind. I feel the cold more than most."

"As you wish."

As we stepped inside the dining room, the man hesitated and looked around. "Is your brother with us?"

It was only then that I realised he couldn't see the colonel.

"I asked him that very question, and he said his uncle's wife's auntie's best friend's neighbour had recommended us. Or was it his auntie's husband's neighbour's best friend? I don't remember."

"Not to worry. I'll see you later."

Maybe I should move into the brewing business. It would probably pay better and certainly be a lot less hassle.

The day before, when I'd spoken to Caroline, I'd asked if she would give her butler the day off, so that I would have the house to myself. She'd been a little hesitant at first, but she'd eventually agreed to my request. As promised, she'd left a key for me under the urn by the front door. She had also given me the alarm code, so I was able to disable that once I was inside.

I'd only been there a matter of minutes when the colonel appeared.

"Good morning, Colonel."

"Morning, Jill. You'll have to excuse me if I'm not looking my best. I've grown a little lazy in my retirement, and I'm not used to these early mornings."

"You look as dapper as always to me."

"It's kind of you to say so. Cilla was still wrapped up in bed when I left her." He looked around the large entrance hall. "I have to say, this place is even bigger than I expected."

"What time did the guy from Restore say he'd be here?"

"It won't be the same person that I've been dealing with in GT. He told me that his representative in the human world will arrive at—" The colonel took out his pocket-watch. "Any minute now, in fact."

"Okay, in that case, I'd better do my thing." I cast the

Who do they think you murdered?"

"A police detective called Susan Shay."

"The woman who was murdered at the restaurant the night I babysat for you?"

"Yeah."

"Why do they think you did it?"

"Because we had a history of butting heads, and I was the last person with her in the loo before she was found murdered."

"You didn't—err—?"

"No, Kathy, I didn't, and I'm hurt that you should even have to ask."

The full English went down a treat and tasted even better because Kathy was picking up the bill. She spent most of the time talking about her shops and her plans for further expansion. But that was okay. It helped to take my mind off my problems for a few minutes at least.

As we headed out, I managed to grab a quick look through to the garden where Henry, Henrietta and the two gnomes appeared to be very much at home.

***

Because breakfast had taken longer than I'd expected, I called Mrs V to let her know that I wouldn't get into the office until much later that morning.

"Have there been any calls?"

"Just one from a Mr Keller. He wanted to know if we were still brewing speciality beers."

"Where did he get the idea that we were in that line of business?"

that made my heart sink. "They've opened the garden. Why don't we have our breakfast outside?"

"No!"

"Why not? It's a lovely morning. Come on, the fresh air will do us both good."

"I can't."

"Why not?"

"I had a coffee out there a couple of days ago, and I ended up with a terrible streaming nose."

"How come? You don't have hay fever. You've never had it."

"That's what I thought too, but they do have some unusual plants out there. One of them must have kicked it off. I can't afford to risk it just before I go to work."

"Okay. We'll stay in here and you can tell me all of your news."

"I don't really have any. Just the same old same old. Oh, apart from the fact that my daughter has started making those horrible monstrosities."

"You should be encouraging her artistic streak. Surely, there must be something else going on in your life? What about work? Have you got any juicy cases?"

"You know I can't discuss those."

"Go on. I won't tell anyone."

"I'm keeping surveillance on a woman because her husband thinks she's cheating on him."

"Is she?"

"No. He's just being paranoid."

"Anything else?"

"Not really. Oh yes, the police think I murdered someone, so I'm trying to find the real killer."

"I assumed you were joking about that the other day.

gave me for my birthday. The one I had to take in to be resized."

"Oh yeah, that one." He couldn't have sounded less convincing if he'd tried.

"I should get it back this weekend. Come on, let's go get breakfast." I hustled Kathy out of the door before she could ask Jack any more awkward questions. I knew from experience that he would soon buckle under interrogation.

"It's taking them a long time to sort out your ring," Kathy said as we walked through the village. "If it was me, I'd be in there every day, giving them hell."

"I'm sure it'll be ready by the weekend."

"Peep Inside?" Kathy pointed to the sign. "That's a strange name to choose for a tea room."

"Their name is Peep. Joe and Flo."

"They don't have a small daughter called Bo, do they?"

"Hey, I'm the one who cracks jokes about names in this family."

"Good morning, Jill." Flo greeted us at the door. "You're our first customer of the day.

"The bacon smells nice."

"Seeing as how Jill isn't going to introduce me, I'd better do it myself." Kathy stepped forward. "I'm her sister, Kathy."

"It's very nice to meet you. Grab a table anywhere and take a *peep* at the menu." She laughed. "Sorry, our little joke. I'll be over in a few minutes to take your order."

"I think I'll have the full English," Kathy said. "It'll set me up for the day."

"I'll have the same."

"Hey, look, Jill." Kathy pointed to a notice on the wall

"Auntie Kathy is here!" Florence came running down the stairs with Tigkey in one hand and Monger in the other. As soon as I opened the door, and before I'd even managed to greet Kathy, Florence was straight in there. "Look, Auntie Kathy. Look what I've made."

"Those are brilliant. Let me have a closer look." She took them from Florence.

"That's Tigkey and that one is Monger."

"Wow! Good job, Florence. Isn't she clever, Jill?"

"Yeah." I forced a smile.

"You must be so proud of her."

"Very."

Jack came through from the lounge. "Hi, Kathy, would you like tea or coffee?"

"Actually, on my way over here, I remembered reading in The Bugle that the tea room in your village has recently changed hands. I thought maybe we could go there this morning. It'll be my treat."

"I'm not sure I've got time for that," I said. "I have to get Florence ready for school."

"I can see to Florence." Jack put his arm around my shoulder. "You and Kathy go and get breakfast at the Peeps."

"Err, okay, then. Florence, give Mummy a kiss." I bent down and she gave me a hug and a big smacker. "Have a lovely day at school."

"I will. I'm going to show Monger to Wendy."

"Haven't you got your ring back yet, Jill?" Kathy was staring at my hand.

"Err, I—err—"

"What ring?" Jack looked puzzled.

I quickly turned to face him. "You know. The one you

Chapter 21

"Can I show Auntie Kathy my new beanies when she gets here?" Florence said, in between spoonfuls of muesli.

"If there's time, but you have to get ready for school first."

"Okay, Mummy."

"You should take some time out, Jill," Jack said. "Have a relaxing cup of tea with Kathy before you go to work."

"I can't. I've got loads to do."

"I'm sure an hour won't make any difference. Come on, you've got to start being kinder to yourself."

"Okay, I'll try."

"By the way." Jack picked up Florence's empty bowl. "Did you hear those cats going at it during the night? I reckon there must have been three or four of them out there. It took me ages to get back to sleep."

"I didn't, but then I was dead to the world. You can blame Wanda and Mabel for that."

"What do you mean?"

"Didn't you notice they're both in the windowsill now?"

"Yeah. I meant to ask why you'd put them there."

"Because they said they were fed up with the view. Now, half the cats in the neighbourhood are hanging around outside, staring at what they hope will be their next meal."

"What are you going to do about it?" Jack said.

"*Me*? I thought I was supposed to be relaxing. Being kind to myself. You could help me to do that by taking over the goldfish duties."

"Sure, I can do that."

"What time?"

"About seven-thirty, eight, something like that. Will you be around?"

"Err, yeah, sure. I'll see you in the morning."

"Are you okay? You sound exhausted."

"I'm fine. I've just been doing some digging."

disappeared into thin air.

I wouldn't have believed it was possible to hate anyone as much as I hated that woman. Had this all been an elaborate ruse? There was only one way I was going to find out.

Another hour later, and I was on the point of giving up when the trowel hit something solid. With renewed energy, I dug even faster. A couple of minutes later, I pulled the small box from the soil. I hesitated a moment before opening it, terrified by what I might (or might not) find inside.

It was the stone. I was so happy I could have cried. I now had the first three compass stones. Only one more to go.

"Look at the state of you." Jack stared at me in disbelief when he walked into the lounge.

"I've got it!" I held up the stone, then rushed across the room and gave him a big hug.

"That's great. Well done, you."

I stepped back and realised that I'd covered him in mud too.

"I'd better go and get a shower."

"Good idea. I'll join you."

After our shower, which took a little longer than usual—not that I'm complaining—I had a phone call from Kathy.

"Jill, I have to visit one of my shops first thing tomorrow morning, which will take me right by Middle Tweaking. I thought I might drop by for a coffee and a chat if that's okay."

old watermill, but I didn't want to risk waking Florence as I rummaged through the shed. Instead, I brought up my trusty spell book app on my phone and began to search for a suitable spell.

I'd felt sure there would be a spell that would magic up a spade for me, and I was right. Almost. The only spell I could find was for a trowel. You would have thought that someone would have come up with a spell for a full-size spade, but no. It was a trowel or nothing. I even tried to customise the 'trowel' spell, but ended up with a garden fork, which was even less use.

And so it was that I was on hands and knees, digging up the grave with a trowel, which let me tell you isn't the easiest thing I've ever done. Progress was extremely slow, not helped by the fact that we hadn't had any rain for days, so the ground was rock hard.

"Need a hand?" the familiar voice came from the bushes behind me.

"Come out! Show yourself."

"Long time, no see." Ma Chivers grinned. "Have you missed me?"

"Is the compass stone down here?"

"*Compass stone*? What's that?"

"You know very well what it is. Is it under here?"

"That would be telling, wouldn't it?"

"Why would you pretend to be dead? Your own son believes you are."

"That waste of space? He'd believe the sky was green if I told him it was."

"Is the compass stone here?"

"Maybe it is. Maybe it isn't. There's only one way for you to find out. Be seeing you, Jill." And with that, she supper in the window?" the moggy sitting in the middle of the three said without once looking at me.

"Those goldfish are not your supper," I snapped. "Those are valued members of our family."

Okay, a bit of an exaggeration, I admit, but the occasion called for it.

"Surely, you could spare one of them?" the white Persian said. "You'd never miss it."

"No, I can't, now shoo!" I walked towards them with some purpose, waving my arms around. For a moment, I thought they were going to stand their ground, but when I was within a couple of feet of them, they finally relented and scooted off.

I might have to rethink the goldfish placement question, but that would have to wait until tomorrow. I had a grave to dig up.

***

Question: hypothetically speaking, if you were on a mission to dig up a grave, what would be the one thing you would be sure to take with you?

Yes, I realise you would never dig up a grave. And, yes, I do realise it's a terrible thing to do, but remember, it wasn't really a grave. I was working under the assumption that Ma Chivers wasn't actually down there, and that she was most probably still alive. So, back to my original question, what would be the one thing that you'd be sure to take with you?

No, not a small flask of whisky. The answer is obviously a spade. I say, *obviously*, and yet I was standing graveside sans said spade. I could have magicked myself back to the

Jack had made a fabulous roast dinner, spoiled only slightly by Florence's insistence on having Tigkey and Monger on the table beside her.

"Which one do you like best, Daddy?"

"They're both nice, but I think I like Tigkey best."

"What about you, Mummy? Which one do you like best?"

"I liked them better when they were tiger and monkey."

"Yes, but which one do you like the best now?"

"Tigkey, I suppose."

"I'm going to make lots more of them today."

"That's great."

When it was Florence's bedtime, I gave her a goodnight kiss before Jack took her upstairs to read her a story. I was in the lounge, psyching myself up, and waiting for darkness to fall before I magicked myself over to Candlefield cemetery.

I just happened to glance out of the window to see not one, but three cats, sitting on our front lawn, all staring into the house. It took me a minute to realise what they found so fascinating, but then the penny dropped. I hurried outside, expecting my sudden appearance to spook them, but they never budged. They didn't even bother to look my way; instead, they just continued to stare at the window.

"Excuse me!" I shouted.

"You must be one of those two-leggeds that can talk to us," the ginger tom said.

"Yes, and I'd appreciate it if the three of you would vacate my front garden."

"If you didn't want us here, why have you placed

"There's nothing wrong with the sideboard. I picked it out myself."

"There's no accounting for taste. Anyway, the point is, that I need a better view. Something more interesting."

"I could move you to the kitchen, I suppose."

"So that I can stare at a kitchen sink all day? No thank you."

"I'm not moving you into our bedroom."

"You're right about that. I have no desire to watch the night-time antics of you humans. I've heard the stories. Disgusting. What I had in mind is that you could put me on the windowsill, so I can see outside."

"It might get too hot in the window."

"No, it won't. That window never gets the sun on it."

"Okay, anything for a peaceful life." I cleared the ornaments out of the windowsill, and put her bowl on there. "How's that?"

"Much better."

I'd just got back onto the sofa when Mabel started. "That's not fair! How come she gets to see out of the window when I'm stuck down here looking at your ugly feet?"

"My feet are *not* ugly."

"I want to look out of the window too."

"Fine." I jumped up, grabbed her bowl, and put it in the windowsill next to Wanda's. "And the first one of you to complain that you don't like to be near to one another is getting fed to the neighbours' cat."

What? Of course I didn't mean it. Sheesh! There isn't even a cat next door. But if they did dare to complain, they'd be going straight into the brook.

"A *what* bird?"

"Decipher. They only live in the paranormal world. They look a bit like parrots but they have a special skill which allows them to solve cryptic clues."

"Did you buy one? Where is it now?"

"I got it on a sale or return basis. I've taken it back to the shop. Anyway, the point is that the bird reckons the clue meant the compass stone was buried in Ma Chivers' fake grave, and that she's still alive. I couldn't dig it up in broad daylight because it might have caused a bit of a stir, so I'm going back there tonight."

"Are you sure that's a good idea? Digging up a grave in the dead of night, I mean?"

"Do you have a better one?"

"No."

"Right, so will you make the dinner while I try and catch my breath?"

"Of course. Go and put your feet up."

I had just sat on the sofa when it started.

"Hey, you!" Wanda was staring at me through the glass.

"Not now, Wanda, I'm having a really bad day."

"Poor little you. I've been having a bad couple of weeks. Not that you care."

"Can't it wait until tomorrow morning?"

"No, it can't. I told you I had a complaint last week, but you haven't even asked me what the problem is."

"Okay, I'm all ears. What's the problem?"

"The view from here."

"What about it?"

"It's boring. I'm fed up of looking at that sofa, that armchair and that awful sideboard."

"Nothing concrete."

"Is there anything I can do?"

"It's supposed to be my turn to make dinner. If you could do it, that would be great because I have to go out tonight."

"Working on this case?"

"No, actually I'm going to dig up a grave."

"I wish you'd take this seriously."

"I am being serious, but it isn't anything to do with the Sushi murder."

"Why on earth do you need to dig up a grave?"

I checked the stairs to make sure Florence wasn't in earshot. "It's the third compass stone."

"Do you know where it is?"

"I think so. It's in Ma Chivers' grave."

"Are you saying it's in there with her?"

"No."

"I'm confused. You just said you were going to dig up her grave."

"I am, but there's a very good chance Ma Chivers isn't down there."

"You mean someone may have moved the body?"

"I don't think her body was ever there. In fact, I don't think she's dead."

"Wow. This just gets weirder and weirder. How do you know all this?"

"A little bird told me."

"Jill!"

"I'm deadly serious. I was struggling to solve the cryptic clue engraved on Ma Chivers' headstone, so Grandma suggested I get a decipher bird to solve it for me."

your old stomping ground earlier this afternoon."

"You were in the police station? Which one?"

"Washbridge. By invitation of Dawn Brakes and some other detective called Swinton."

"Sid Swinton?"

"You know him?"

"Only by reputation. He's a bit of a hard-ass."

"He was playing bad cop to Brakes' good cop."

"What did they want?"

"To talk to me about a parking ticket. What do you think?"

"I know you're upset, but there's no need to get shirty with me."

"Sorry, it's just so infuriating. If they'd put their resources into finding out who actually did murder Sushi, instead of harassing me, they might actually make some progress."

"What did they say?"

"They just asked me the same questions over and over again. Swinton said that if I admitted I'd pushed her, but hadn't intended to kill her, it would go better for me."

"What did you say?"

"I signed a confession there and then, obviously. What do you think I said? I told him he could stuff it where the sun doesn't shine."

"Please tell me you didn't?"

"No, I didn't, but I wanted to."

"What now?"

"Same thing as always. I'll have to find the real killer because it's obvious that those incompetents are never going to do it."

"Do you have any leads?"

away with digging up a grave in broad daylight. I would just have to go there that night as soon as it was dark.

***

"Mummy, Mummy, look!" Florence held up a Frankensteinesque beanie, but not one I'd seen before.

"I—err—where did that come from?"

"I made it. Lizzie told me how to do it. This is a Tigkey. Do you like it?"

"I—err—"

"It's half tiger and half monkey. I'm going back upstairs to make a Monger out of the other bits." She hurried away.

Jack was seated at the kitchen table, grinning to himself.

"Did you know she was going to make those?"

"Yes, she mentioned it this morning."

"And you didn't think to tell me?"

"You had to rush out, remember? And besides, I knew it would only set you off."

"What do you mean, *set me off*?"

"I know you don't like seeing those beanies being cannibalised."

"*My* beanies, you mean?"

"They stopped being *your* beanies a long time ago. They were Lizzie's beanies and now they're Florence's beanies."

"Yes, but—"

"And she can do with them as she pleases, can't she?"

"I suppose so. I just wish she wouldn't show the results to me."

"You seem a bit tetchy. Are you alright?"

"Not really. I spent a very unpleasant couple of hours in

Chapter 20

"You again?" Wilhelmina (Will to her friends, which clearly did not include me) was obviously not very thrilled to see me.

"Hi. I'm sorry, but I'm going to have to return Dorothy."

"I'm surprised you had time to find out her name; you've only been gone for just over an hour."

"I'm afraid it didn't work out with Rhymes."

"Your tortoise?"

"That's right. Unfortunately, he's rather intimidated by her."

"By this tiny, gentle creature?"

"Crazy, isn't it? But like I said, Rhymes is very highly strung."

"Hmm." She took the cage from me and examined the bird. "She doesn't look any the worse for her excursion. Okay, I'll take her back. Bye, then."

"Hang on. We agreed a fifty percent refund if I had to return her."

"Oh yes." She put the bird back with the others, then went over to the till and gave me my refund. "I hope the prize is worth it."

"What prize?"

"The prize for the crossword, scavenger hunt or whatever it was you needed the bird to help you solve."

"I have no idea what you're talking about. Bye, and thanks."

After leaving Everything Feathers, I considered going straight to Candlefield cemetery, but I didn't think I'd get

"As I said, it's only a guess. It may not be referring to your mission."

"No, I'm sure you're correct and that it does refer to my mission. But I will *not* fail. I *will* save my daughter. I can promise you that."

"Tell me what you do understand, please."

"When she says she *chose a different compass,* I believe she is referring to the life she led. She had a different moral compass to you. To most people."

"What else?"

"She says you *shouldn't weep for her.*"

"Because she was happy with the choices she made?"

"Possibly, but I don't think so."

"What then?"

"I may be wrong about this."

"Tell me, anyway."

"She says *still it waits.*"

"What does?"

"The thing you're searching for. The compass stone."

"Where?"

"*Where you stand.*"

"That doesn't make any sense."

"It would have done at the time you first read the text."

"When I was at the graveside?"

"Correct. It was below your feet at that moment."

"You're saying the compass stone is buried with Ma Chivers?"

"Possibly, but I don't think so. The reason it says you shouldn't weep for her is that she isn't dead. It's not her body that is buried there, but the compass stone."

"Are you sure?"

"Not one hundred percent, no."

"What does the last line mean? *Where you fail?*"

"I'm guessing she means you will fail in your mission."

"To save my daughter?"

"I think so."

"That's wrong."

something called a compass stone."

"Is it some kind of scavenger hunt?"

"No, this is much more serious. It's a matter of life and death. My daughter's life to be precise."

"Surely even you wouldn't stoop so low as to lie about that."

"No, I wouldn't. I have to find four of these stones if I'm to have a chance of protecting my daughter. I already have two of them. This is the clue to the third one."

"Let me see it again."

The bird studied the text for several minutes, and then said at last, "Sorry, but I have no idea what this means."

"What do you mean, *you have no idea*? I thought decipher birds could solve any cryptic clue."

"Whoever told you that was lying. It's true we can solve most of them, but by no means every one. I'm very sorry."

"Please, take another look. You're my only hope."

"It still doesn't make any sense. Maybe if you gave me more background; put the clue in context."

"Like what?"

"Like, where did you find the clue? What do you know about the person who left it for you? That kind of thing."

"Okay. The woman who left the clue was called Martha Chivers, but everyone knew her as Ma Chivers. Like me, she was a witch, but a very evil one. She did many bad things and she had very few friends."

"You said *was* and *did*. Is she dead?"

"Yes. This text is from the headstone of her grave."

"Why didn't you tell me that before? That makes much more sense."

"It does? What does it mean?"

"I don't understand all of it."

fell silent. At last, I would be able to get the cryptic clue deciphered.

"Jill? What on earth is going on in here? I heard the most awful noise." Mrs V came into the room and caught sight of the bird. "Where did that come from?"

"I—err, sorry, Mrs V." I cast the 'forget' spell, and then led her back to her desk.

"Okay, bird, it's just you and me now."

"*Bird*? How would you feel if I referred to you as *witch*?"

"Sorry, I'm forgetting my manners. My name is Jill."

"I'm Dorothy."

"It's very nice to meet you, Dorothy. I'm sorry about the issue earlier."

"The *cat*, you mean?"

"Yes, I'm sorry about the cat."

I took out my phone and brought up the photo of the cryptic text. "Now, if you could just solve this little puzzle for me, we can—"

"She was right about you, wasn't she?"

"What do you mean? *Who* was right about me?"

"Will."

"*Will*? Oh, you mean Wilhelmina Birdman."

"It's Will to her friends."

"Right."

"She had you sussed straight away. You just want someone to solve your crossword puzzle."

"Look, I'll come clean with you."

"Like you did with Will, you mean?"

"No, honestly, this is the truth. This isn't a clue from a crossword puzzle. It's a clue to the whereabouts of

"But—"

"But?"

"But I would only be able to refund you fifty percent of the purchase price."

"Half? What if I only had the bird for like a day?"

"Fifty per cent would be the best I could do."

"Okay. I'll take it."

"Which one?"

"That one."

"I thought you said you like this one?"

"Err, yeah, that's what I meant. That one."

And of course, I had to buy a cage too; on the same fifty percent sale or return basis. Still, it would all be worth it if it helped me to solve the cryptic clue. With cage in hand, I magicked myself back to the office.

Big mistake! What was I thinking? The woman had only just told me that decipher birds were terrified of cats.

As soon as it spotted Winky, it let out an ear-piercing screech.

"Make it shut up!" Winky clamped his paws over his ears.

"You'll have to go outside!"

"What?" He shook his head because he couldn't hear what I was saying, so I had to walk over and prise one of his paws away from his ear.

"I said you'll have to go outside!"

"Why can't you take that bird out of here?"

"Just do it! It'll only be for a few minutes."

"Okay, anything to get away from that row." He sprinted out of the window.

Thankfully, as soon as Winky had disappeared, the bird

"So, can I take a closer look at them, please?"

"Yes, but you'll need to leave your bag here on the counter."

"Why?"

"Some people are very crafty. They pretend they're going to buy a bird, and then they whip out a crossword, get their answer, and do a runner."

"How disgraceful."

She stayed close by my side as I walked up and down the line of cages. "Have you seen one that you like yet?" She was clearly eager to get back to her budgie count.

"That one looks friendly."

"They're all friendly. Decipher birds are known for their pleasant disposition."

"Before I choose, I do have one question."

"Yes?"

"Do you offer the birds on a sale or return basis?"

"*Sale or return*? This is a living creature you're purchasing, not a new cardigan."

"Quite, but I'm a little worried about how my tortoise will adapt to having a bird in the house. He has quite a nervous disposition."

"In that case, it might be better if you didn't buy a bird at all."

"No, I'd really like to give it a try. But if the worst happens, and Rhymes can't get—"

"Rhymes?"

"That's my tortoise's name. If he can't get on with the bird, would I be able to return it?"

"I suppose so. I wouldn't want your tortoise to be distressed."

"That's great."

"Ah, right. I've never actually seen one before, so I didn't know what I was looking for. They're quite similar to parrots, aren't they?"

"Not if you know what to look for."

"Right. Why is there a barrier in front of the cages?"

"That's to stop all the timewasters."

"I don't understand."

"You wouldn't believe the number of people we get in here who are only interested in solving a cryptic clue for their crossword. Before we installed the barrier, we used to have crowds of them over there."

"That's terrible. The cheek of some people."

"Do I take it you're interested in purchasing a decipher?"

"You don't hire them out by any chance, do you?"

"Hire them out?"

"By the hour, preferably."

"No, we do not *hire them out*. Have you never heard of the saying, a pet is for life?"

"Of course, and I couldn't agree more. I have several pets of my own already."

"No cats, I hope. I couldn't possibly allow one of my darling birds to go to a home with a cat. These delicate birds are terrified of them."

"*Cats*? No. Just a tortoise."

"That's alright, then."

I had no intention of buying one of her birds, but I figured if I could get to the other side of the barrier, I'd be able to distract her long enough to show the bird the text from Ma Chivers' headstone. Once they had provided me with a solution to the cryptic clue, I would be out of there in a flash.

In an attempt to take my mind off the fact that I was clearly in the frame for Sushi's murder, I magicked myself over to Candlefield. I had previously visited Everything Rodent, and Everything Aquatic, but this was to be my first visit to Everything Feathers who, according to the Candlefield Pages, were the premier supplier of pet birds.

The woman behind the counter had her back to me, and she appeared to be counting something.

"One hundred and eighty-one, one hundred and eighty-two, one hundred and eighty—"

"Excuse me."

She spun around and glared at me. "Yes?"

"I hope I didn't interrupt anything."

"I was counting the budgerigars. I've been at it for the last three quarters of an hour, but it's fine. I'll just start again when you've gone."

"Sorry about that."

"It's perfectly alright. I'm Wilhelmina Birdman, owner of this establishment."

"Is that really your name?"

"Why would I lie?"

"It's just that—err, well I guess you must have heard of Everything Rodent and Everything Aquatic?"

"No, I don't think so."

"What about Bill Ratman or Bill Fishman? You must be familiar with them?"

"I haven't heard of either of them. Now, is there something I can help you with or not?"

"I'm looking for a decipher bird. Do you happen to have any?"

"You mean apart from the fifty of them in cages over there?"

"I didn't think I'd be seeing you again until the trial," Winky said.

"Very funny."

"I hope you've made provision for me in case they bang you up for the rest of your natural."

"Of course I have. If anything happens to me, Mrs V will adopt you."

"The old bag lady? I'd walk the streets first."

I'd just finished my coffee when the temperature dropped, and the colonel appeared in front of my desk. Fortunately, Winky was dozing under the sofa—no doubt catching up on his lost sleep.

"Hi, Colonel."

"I have great news, Jill. Those Restore scoundrels have taken the bait."

"Really? I wasn't expecting you to hear anything so soon."

"Me neither, but it seems that the mention of Lady Tweaking and Tweaking Manor has made them more than a little eager. They called a few minutes ago and asked if we could meet there tomorrow morning. I told them that would be alright. I hope that's okay."

"Let me check with Lady Tweaking." I gave her a call. "Caroline, it's Jill. About that thing we discussed, is there any chance we could do it tomorrow? I realise it's short notice. You can? Excellent. I'll be over first thing in the morning." I gave the colonel the thumbs up. "All systems go."

***

"Yes?"

"I spoke to Susan Shay." Another short delay to build the tension.

"Yes?"

"Then, I left the loo and returned to the dining room."

"After you'd pushed Shay?"

"No. I never laid a hand on her. When I left her, she was alive and well. We can sit here all day, and you can ask me the same question a thousand times, in a thousand different ways, but my answer is always going to be the same. If you had any evidence whatsoever, you would have charged me by now, so I suggest we stop wasting each other's time, and call an end to this farce."

Did they do that? Of course not. The interview lasted almost another hour, during which time we covered the same ground over and over again. It was only when they eventually realised that I wasn't going to change my story, that they brought proceedings to an end.

"Thank you for coming in today, Mrs Maxwell." Brakes stood up.

"The pleasure was all yours."

"We may need to speak to you again," Swinton said.

"I'll look forward to it."

"Is everything alright, Jill?" Mrs V said.

"Everything is just dandy."

"They don't still think you had anything to do with that poor woman's murder, do they?"

"They're absolutely sure I killed her. Unfortunately for them, they don't have a shred of proof. Could you get me a coffee, please, Mrs V?"

"Coming right up."

So that was their game: the old, good cop, bad cop routine. Such amateurs.

"I understand you and Susan Shay had a somewhat rocky relationship?" Brakes said.

"We had a few disagreements, that's true."

"From what I hear, you seem to have a problem with the police, generally." Swinton put on his best 'bad cop' face.

"I married one, so that can't be true."

"What were you and Shay arguing about in the toilet on the night she was murdered?"

"Who says we were arguing?"

"Were you?"

"No, I had better things to do than waste my time arguing with her."

"But you did have words?"

"She told me that I'd ruined my husband's career, and then she expressed surprise that we were still together."

"That must have made you angry."

"Not really. Her opinions were of no interest to me."

"What happened, Maxwell?" Swinton said. "Did you get angry and push her?"

"No."

"You didn't mean to hurt her, but she hit her head. Is that what happened?"

"That would be another *no*."

"It will go better for you if you tell us the truth now."

"Okay." I stared down at the table for a minute. "I'll tell you the truth."

"Good. Now we're getting somewhere. You'll feel better when you get it off your chest."

"I went to the loo." Pause for effect.

"Why?"

"Detective Brakes would like to question you about the death of—"

"I know what it's in connection with, but why couldn't she come here and ask me her questions? Why can't *you* ask me them?"

"If you wouldn't mind, madam. The sooner we get down there, the sooner you'll be able to get on with your life."

"And if I refuse?"

"I hope it won't come to that."

I was so very tempted to tell him to get stuffed, but I could hear Jack's voice in my head, telling me not to antagonise the police unnecessarily.

"I assume we're going to West Chipping police station?"

"Actually, no. Detective Brakes is working out of Washbridge station today."

"Good. Let's get this over with, then."

I was shown straight to one of the interview rooms where, as expected, I was left to stew for almost thirty minutes, all the time getting more and more angry.

"Sorry to keep you waiting," Brakes lied when she eventually showed up.

She was accompanied by a man who introduced himself as Detective Swinton.

"How long is this going to take? I've already been here for half an hour."

"It'll take as long as it takes," Swinton snapped.

"Now, Sid, let's cut Mrs Maxwell some slack," Brakes said. "I'm sure she's a very busy woman."

Chapter 19

"Did you sort them out?" Winky said.

"I've had a word with them."

"Yes, but did you read them the Riot Act?"

"No, but only because it turns out they were actually trying to be considerate."

"By scaring me witless and keeping me awake all night?"

"They're making some alterations to their internal walls, and they thought that by working during the night, they wouldn't disturb their neighbours."

"I *am* their neighbour and they disturbed me."

"Yes, but to be fair, they couldn't have anticipated that they'd have a cat living next door."

"It sounds to me like you're making excuses for them."

"Not at all. They said they'd be done in a few more days."

"What am I supposed to do in the meantime?"

"Invest in some earplugs?"

The door opened and Mrs V popped her head inside. "I thought I heard you talking to someone, Jill?"

"No, just to myself."

"I have a Detective Greybotham to see you. I did tell him you're very busy, but he's insistent."

"You'd better send him in, then."

Greybotham didn't look old enough to be a school prefect, let alone a detective. His drab suit and coat matched his name.

"What can I do for you, Detective? Do take a seat."

"I won't, thanks. I'm here to ask you to accompany me to the police station."

"That was considerate of them."

"Oh, and I found out what kind of business it is; they're funeral directors."

"Oh dear."

"I saw you in Candlefield cemetery."

"That's not really surprising. Our line of business takes us there regularly."

"And you're planning to open a similar business here in the human world? Isn't that going to be a bit weird?"

"Not at all. The nature of the business is exactly the same in both worlds."

"Okay, but what's with all the noise?"

"I don't hear anything."

"I don't mean now. I'm talking about in the middle of the night. It's happened twice now."

"Oh that."

"Yes, *that*. What's going on?"

"We're having some of the internal walls removed. We didn't want to disturb you during office hours, so we've had the work done at night. We had no idea that you'd be working at that time."

"I don't usually. Has the work been finished yet?"

"Not quite, but a few more days should see it done."

"Fair enough. And when do you expect to open for business?"

"Next week or the week after."

"My name is Jill, by the way."

"Black."

"Is that your name? Mr Black?"

"No, just Black. Is it alright if I get back to what I was doing now?"

"Err, yeah. Sure."

"Did you find out what they're up to?" Mrs V said.

"They're knocking down some of the internal walls."

"In the middle of the night?"

"They didn't want to disturb us during office hours."

"What for?"

"I left some paperwork here by mistake." I hurried out of the door before Mrs V could fire any more awkward questions at me.

The front of the unit was still boarded up, but I could hear movement inside, so I began to hammer on the temporary door. As expected, there was no response, but I had all the patience in the world, and I was quite prepared to stay there all morning if necessary.

After ten minutes, I'd clearly worn them down because the door opened a couple of inches and one of the weird men poked his head out.

"Yes?"

"I'd like a quick word."

"We're busy."

"Look, friend, we can do this the easy way or the hard way. It's up to you."

"I've just told you we're very busy."

"Either you step outside and talk to me or I call my good friend, Daze—you may have heard of her; she's a rogue retriever—and tell her that there are two wizards in my building who I believe are up to no good."

From the speed at which he stepped out into the corridor, it was clear that he knew who Daze was, and had no desire for her to pay them a visit.

"What do you want?"

"You can start by telling me exactly what you're up to in there."

"We're just getting everything ready."

"What's *everything*? What kind of business do you run, exactly?"

"We're funeral directors."

"What does it have to do with me? I'm not the one making the noise."

"No, but as my guardian, my welfare is your responsibility."

"Since when was I your *guardian*? You're always telling me that ours is an equal partnership."

"And so it is, but it's not like I can go around there and complain, is it?"

"I suppose not. Was it the same kind of noise as before?"

"Yes. A vibrating sound that grew louder and louder. The only difference is that this time the power didn't go off to stop it."

"How long did it go on for?"

"At least an hour."

"And this would have been about what time?"

"Around midnight."

"Okay. That's obviously not acceptable."

"So, you'll have a word with them?"

"Yes, I'll do it now."

As soon as I walked back into the outer office, Mrs V said, "Have you remembered?"

"Remembered *what*?"

"How you got rid of the mole? I thought you'd come out to tell me."

"No, sorry. I'm going down the corridor to have a word with our new neighbours. They've been making all manner of noises in the middle of the night."

"How do you know?"

Oh bum! That was a good question. How did I know? I could hardly tell her that Winky had told me.

"I—err—had to come back to the office late last night."

Yes, I know. I'm a terrible person. There's no need for you to rub it in. But I would remind you that this only came about because I was trying to help the gnomes and elves. Once again, it seems that where I'm concerned, no good deed goes unpunished.

As I walked towards the office building, I received another photo from Ava Todfoster who was at a coffee morning. That woman seemed to live the life of Riley. I quickly fired off an email to her husband and then hurried up the stairs to the office.

"Morning, Mrs V."

"Good morning. Do you by any chance know anything about moles?"

"A little. Why?"

"One of the little blighters has decided to dig up our lawn. How did you manage to get rid of yours?"

"I—err—don't remember. It's quite a long time ago now."

In fact, I remembered the affair like it was only yesterday: I'd shrunk myself to mole size and gone looking for the pesky creature. Mortimer, that was his name, had turned out to be a very reasonable sort. After I'd explained that he was ruining my lawn, he'd moved to the next-door neighbour's garden. Poor Megan. Snigger.

"If you do remember, will you let me know, Jill? Armi was talking about laying a trap for it, but I don't want to harm the little creature."

"Of course I will." As soon as I walked into my office, Winky handed me a small sheet of paper. "What's this?"

"Read it."

"A formal complaint? About what?"

"The noise coming from next door."

the guy has no clue what the problem is."

"Look, I think Peter's waving to you," I lied.

When she turned back to the house, I reversed the 'power cut' spell.

"I don't see him."

"Sorry. It must be the light playing tricks."

Just then, Peter came rushing out of the door. "It's fixed! The power is back on."

"It is?" Kathy said. "How? What did he do?"

"I don't know. I don't think he does either. It just came back on."

"But if he doesn't know what caused it, who's to say it won't happen again?"

"It'll be fine," I said. "Come on, let's go inside."

The electrician left, refusing to take a payment because he hadn't been able to pinpoint the problem. He said he'd never encountered anything like it in his fifteen years in the trade.

A few minutes later, Peter left for work, leaving Kathy and me to enjoy a cup of tea.

"Is there anything I can do before I shoot off, Kathy?"

"I don't think so. I'll nip down the supermarket in a few minutes to replace the stuff we lost in the freezer."

"What about the garden ornaments?"

"Pete says it's a waste of time reporting it because the police won't be interested in the theft of a few gnomes."

"He's probably right. Will you replace them?"

"I don't think so. We're ready for a change. We might put some decking in."

***

"No, they're elves."

"How much do we owe you, Jill?"

"Nothing."

"Don't be silly. You have to let us pay you for them," Flo said.

"No, honestly. My friend was just glad to get rid of them."

"I can't think why." Joe picked up Henry. "These little guys are fantastic."

"At the very least, the next time you and your family pay us a visit, it will be on the house," Flo insisted.

"Okay, that's very kind. Do you think we could take them through to the garden now because I really have to get going."

"Of course. I'll take the two elves, and you two can bring the gnomes."

Between the three of us, we carried them through the shop and put them in the garden.

"They look at home already," Joe said.

"I'm sure they'll be very happy living here with you. Now, I must shoot off."

***

I drove over to Kathy's as fast as the speed limits would allow. I'd really messed up this time, and I would have to find some way of putting it right.

She must have spotted me through the window because she came hurrying down the drive to meet me at the car.

"Are you okay?" I said.

"Not really. Pete is staying off work until we get this mess sorted out. He's inside with the electrician now, but between the seats.

"It's the tea room. They have a lovely garden at the rear."

"Ooh, a tea room." Henrietta beamed. "That sounds nice."

"The four of you will need to keep very still and absolutely quiet now. Okay?"

"Okay, Jill."

I drove the car into the village and pulled up outside the tea room. As expected, it was locked, and I couldn't see any sign of life inside, so I knocked on the door. I wasn't sure the Peeps would be in because they'd told me they would continue to live in Wash Edge.

For once, I got lucky because Joe opened one of the windows above the shop and popped his head out.

"Jill?"

"Good morning, Joe."

"Morning. I'm afraid we aren't open for half-an-hour yet."

"I know. I've got the garden ornaments I promised Flo. I realise it's early, but I wanted to offload them before I went into the office."

"Okay, I'll be down in a tick."

A couple of minutes later, the door opened and out stepped Joe and Flo.

"Joe tells me you have our garden ornaments, Jill."

"They're in the back seat." I opened the door so they could see them.

"They're lovely." She cooed.

"What are those small guys?" Joe said. "Goblins?"

Henry flinched at what he perceived as a slight, but fortunately neither of the Peeps noticed.

"What did you do?"

"I had to disable the CCTV cameras so that I could sneak the gnomes and elves out of the garden." I hesitated.

"*And?*"

"And to do that, I had to take out the power for a few minutes."

"*A few minutes*? So how come Kathy said it's still out?"

"I was so busy making our getaway that I forgot to reverse the spell when we left. That's why I need to go over there to sort it out."

"What about your breakfast?"

"I'll grab something later."

"You can't keep missing breakfast. You'll make yourself ill."

"I didn't skip it yesterday. Mrs V got me a bacon cob from a new place just around the corner from the office. I'll probably do the same again today. Where's Florence?"

"In her bedroom, playing with the beanies."

I hurried back upstairs, gave her a kiss, and then rushed out to the car. I was just about to set off for Kathy's when a voice behind me made me jump.

"It wasn't very comfortable back here last night," Henrietta said. "I hope you're going to take us to our new home soon."

Oh bum! With all the kerfuffle with Kathy's power cut, I'd totally forgotten that I had to take the gnomes and elves to the tea room. I had intended waiting until it opened, but I didn't want to keep Kathy waiting any longer than necessary.

"I'm going to take you there now."

"Where is our new home?" Henry poked his head

would do something like that?"

"Did he tell you about the freezer too?"

"No. What about it?"

"We had another power cut, and all the food has defrosted. The power is still off. I can't understand it because none of our neighbours had one."

Oh bum and double bum! I'd totally forgotten to reverse the 'power cut' spell.

"That's terrible," I said.

"Pete called the power company first thing, but they maintain the problem isn't at their end. We've got an electrician here now, but he can't understand what's happened either."

"I'll come over."

"Why? There's nothing you can do."

"You're my sister. I should be with you at times like this."

"I—err—okay. Sure."

"I'll see you in a few minutes." I ended the call and looked across at Jack who was shaking his head. "What?"

"It's not a coincidence, is it?"

"What isn't?"

"You know what. The missing gnomes and the power cut."

"There have been lots of power cuts recently. You know there have."

"General ones, yes, but Kathy said theirs was the only house that was affected last night."

"That is a bit strange."

"Jill! What happened?"

"Okay, okay. It's possible I may have had something to do with it."

Chapter 18

"Jill, wake up. You're going to miss breakfast again." Jack was shaking me gently.

I managed to open one eye. "Why are you getting me up in the middle of the night?"

"It's seven-thirty."

"It can't be." I somehow found the strength to pull myself up into a sitting position. "I've only just closed my eyes."

"What time did you get in last night?"

"I'm not sure. Half-past one, I guess."

"Do you want me to leave you to have a few more hours in bed?"

"No, there's stuff I need to do."

"How did the rescue mission go?"

"Fine. No hitches whatsoever. I just need to take the gnomes and elves to their new home. I'll do that after I've had breakfast. I'll grab a shower and be down in ten."

Showered, and feeling a little more alive, I made my way downstairs to find Jack talking on my phone.

"That's terrible, Kathy. You really are having some bad luck. Jill is here now. Do you want to speak to her? Okay. I'll pass you over." He put his hand over the mic and whispered, "She's found out the gnomes have gone."

"Okay, I'll handle it." I took the phone from him.

"That's not all."

"Huh?"

Before he could respond, Kathy said, "Jill, are you there?"

"Yes. Jack has just told me about your gnomes. Who

around the back into the garden. It was pitch black, so I had to use the torchlight app on my phone to see what I was doing. The two gnomes were next to the tree; Henry and Henrietta were standing by the summerhouse.

"Guys! Come on."

None of them moved.

"Hurry up. I've come to get you out of here."

Again, no one moved, but this time Henry said in a whisper, "The cameras."

"It's okay, I've disabled them. Hurry up."

The four of them followed me out of the garden and around the side of the house.

"Stay here while I go and get the car. As soon as I pull up onto the drive, get into the back seat. Okay?"

They all gave me a nod or a thumbs up.

A couple of minutes later, I reversed the car onto the bottom of the drive, opened the back door, and the four of them jumped inside. Mission accomplished.

"Thanks, Jill," Henry said.

"Where are you taking us?" Henrietta asked.

"To a nice new home in the village where I live."

"Your house?"

"No, somewhere much better, but I can't take you there until the morning, so you'll have to lie low in the car until then."

"No problem. It's just such a relief to escape those cameras."

"What's that?"
"The CCTV will catch you doing it."
"Ah, but there's something you haven't taken into account."
"What's that?"
"I have a cunning plan."

***

Jack went up to bed just after eleven. I planned to wait until midnight before making a move because I wanted to make sure that Kathy and family would all be fast asleep in their beds.

I used the time until then to consult the app version of the spell book. My cunning plan was to disable the CCTV—I just hadn't worked out how to do it yet. I could have used the 'lightning bolt' spell, but that would have destroyed the equipment altogether. I checked the index to see if there were any spells listed under the heading of CCTV, but there was nothing. I'd already reached letter 'N' and, so far, I'd drawn a blank. It was almost midnight when I struck lucky under the listings for letter 'P'. The 'power cut' spell could take out the power for an individual building. That would be ideal because Kathy would assume there had been another general power cut affecting the whole area.

After parking a few streets away, I made my way to the house. As expected, it was in darkness. I went as close as I dared without coming into range of their cameras. After a quick check to make sure there was no one else around, I cast the 'power cut' spell, and the red lights on the CCTV went out. That was my cue to rush up the drive and

reappearance in the kitchen, and he let us know of his disapproval by yapping at the top of his voice.

"Buddy, be quiet. It's only us."

"Why do you have to disappear and pop up again like that? It scares me."

"Sorry. I'll try to make sure you're not around before we do it in future."

"Did you two have a nice time?" Jack said.

"It was brill!" Florence beamed. "Eliza is really nice. She says she wants some beanies just like mine. And her mummy looks just like my mummy. Can I go and play outside?"

"Of course you can, pumpkin. Dinner will be in about thirty minutes." He turned to me. "What about you? Did you have a nice time with your doppelganger?"

"I did. Linda is really nice. She offered to stand in as my double if I ever need one."

"Like a stunt double?"

"No. I'd never ask her to do anything dangerous, but it might come in handy one day. What's for dinner?"

"Pie and chips."

"Steak and kidney?"

"No. Chicken and mushroom."

"That'll do. I'm starving. Oh, and while I remember, I have to nip out tonight."

"On a case?"

"No. On a rescue mission."

"Who are you rescuing?"

"The gnomes and elves in Kathy's back garden. They have no life since Kathy installed the CCTV."

"Right. Gotcha. But I see one tiny flaw with your rescue bid."

her," Linda said. "I guess they must be animals that only live in the human world?"

"Actually, they're not. Take the one that Florence is holding for example. It started life as two beanies: A camel and a moose. Then my wicked sister cut them apart and joined the front of one to the rear of the other, to produce a camoose."

"Why would she do that?"

"Because she thinks it's funny."

"I think it's a bit weird."

"You and me both. Still, I shouldn't be too hard on Kathy because it's her holiday home that we're going to stay in, and she isn't going to charge us anything."

"I was thinking, Jill, I'd really like to give something back to you. I mean, if it wasn't for you, I wouldn't have a business."

"We've discussed this before. I don't want any of the money you earn."

"I know you won't take that, but there might be another way I can pay you back."

"What do you mean?"

"I was thinking that if you ever needed the services of a lookalike when you're working on a case, you could always give me a call."

"If I need to be in two places at once, you mean?"

"Yeah, that kind of thing."

"Actually, that's not a bad idea. I might take you up on it sometime."

***

Buddy was clearly freaked out by our sudden

off immediately, and were soon upstairs in Eliza's bedroom, leaving Linda and me to enjoy a quiet cup of tea.

"This still feels a little weird," I said.

"What does?"

"You and me. It's like I'm watching myself drinking a cup of tea."

"Does it bother you, Jill?"

"Of course not. It's just a little strange. How's the lookalike business?"

"As busy as ever. In fact, I've had to turn down a few gigs recently or I'd never get to see Eliza. What about you? How's the detective business?"

"I've been quite busy too, but we're hoping to get away in the next few weeks, so that's good."

"Anywhere nice?"

"Filey."

"Is that in the human world?"

"Yeah, we can't holiday in the paranormal world unless we leave Jack behind."

"Of course. I was forgetting your husband is a human. That must be pretty weird."

"I'm used to it now."

"What about Florence? Isn't it difficult to make sure she doesn't say anything to her father?"

"Not really. She just treats it like a game."

Eliza and Florence came downstairs for pop and biscuits. They kept glancing back and forth between Eliza and me, and then giggling. They clearly found the fact that their mothers were identical hilarious.

"Those are very strange toys that Florence brought with

"Those don't count."

"What about birds?" I said. "Didn't you have any budgies, parrots or anything like that?"

"No." Pearl shook her head.

"There was Feathers," Amber said.

"He wasn't our pet," Pearl corrected her. "He was Mum's."

"Was Feathers a budgie?"

"No, he was one of those decipher birds."

"I've never heard of them. It's a strange name."

"They can solve cryptic clues," Pearl said. "Mum used to use him to cheat when she was doing the crossword. Do you remember, Amber?"

"Yeah, but she always denied it, and claimed she'd solved them all by herself."

"I assume they're a rare breed?" I said.

"Not really. All the pet shops have them. Are you thinking of getting one for Florence?"

"Not likely. Two goldfish and a dog are more than enough. I was just curious, that's all."

It wasn't easy, but I eventually managed to persuade Florence to say goodbye to Bobby, so that we could go and see Linda and Eliza.

"Bye, Florence." Bobby had tears in his eyes as he waved her goodbye. "Come back and see me again soon."

"We will," I said, as I guided her towards the stairs.

After we'd said our farewells to the twins, we set off across town.

Linda and Eliza were waiting for us in the garden of their small house. As soon as they spotted us, Eliza came running down the street to greet Florence. The two hit it the counter, picked up Florence, and spun her around.

Pearl, who was busy with a customer, called, "Hey, Florence, I'll be with you in a minute. Would you like a milkshake?"

"Yes, please. Strawberry."

Amber put her down and said, "Would you like to go and see Bobby?"

"Yeah!"

"Come on, then. Your mummy will bring your milkshake."

The two of them disappeared up the stairs, and I waited by the counter. Once Pearl had made the drink, she asked one of the assistants to watch the counter, so that the two of us could go upstairs and join the others.

"Thanks, Auntie Pearl." Florence took the milkshake and then went back to playing with Bobby who was clearly delighted to see her.

Amber and Pearl, being surplus to requirements, came to join me.

"You really must bring her over one weekend so she can play with our girls," Amber said. "They're always asking about her."

"I will. I promise." I glanced over at Bobby, who was lying on his back, so that Florence could bounce up and down on his big tummy. It looked painful, and yet he seemed to be enjoying it as much as she was. Turning back to the twins, I said, "Hey, you two, did you have any pets when you were kids?"

"We had a few," Amber said.

"Yeah." Pearl began to count them off on her fingers. "Hamsters, goldfish, a rabbit and a cat."

"You forgot the stick insects," Amber said.

"It looks like hair."

"Why do you have a wig?" Jack said.

"I had to nip into Grandma's shop. She made me model two wigs for one of her customers."

"And you thought you'd steal one?"

"I didn't *steal* it. Grandma let me have it for a highly discounted price."

"Put it on your head again, Mummy."

"Yes, put it on, Jill." Jack grinned.

"Okay." I turned to the mirror, put on the wig, and spent a few minutes adjusting it. "Do you like it? I think I suit curly hair."

"You look funny, Mummy!" Florence giggled.

"Jack? What do you think?"

"Did she let you have it on a sale or return basis?"

***

"Are you sure you want to take those two with you, darling?"

Florence was clutching two beanies of the Frankensteinesque variety.

"Yes, I'm going to show them to Bobby and Eliza."

"They might scare them."

"That's silly, Mummy." She giggled. "They're only toys."

They certainly scared me.

"Okay, but you'll have to tuck them under your arm so you can hold my hand while I magic us there. Ready?"

"Yes, Mummy."

"Okay, here we go."

"Look who's here!" Amber came rushing from behind

Chapter 17

I'd left the office early, so that I'd be home when Florence finished school because I'd promised to take her to Cuppy C to see Bobby. In an attempt to kill two birds with one stone, I'd contacted my doppelganger, Linda, to see if she and her daughter, Eliza, were free. It was ages since she'd first suggested we get together sometime, and this seemed like as good an opportunity as any. As luck would have it, they were free, so I'd arranged to go over to their house after we'd finished at Cuppy C.

I had deliberately timed it so that I would get back to the old watermill before Jack and Florence arrived home from school because I wanted the house to myself for a few minutes.

"Hello? Jack? Florence? Anyone in?"

All clear. Ignoring Buddy's yapping, I hurried upstairs to the bedroom and took it out of the box.

Ten minutes later, I was still checking my reflection in the mirror.

"Jill?" Jack's voice came from behind me.

"Mummy? What's that on your head?"

I hadn't heard the two of them come in because of the racket Buddy was making. I snatched the wig off my head and held it behind my back.

"Nothing." I shrugged.

"Show us your hands," Jack said.

I held out my left hand.

"It's in your other hand." Florence stepped behind me. "Look, it's here. What is it, Mummy?"

"It's—err—called a wig."

"I thought you might be able to decipher the clue."

"*Me*? I wouldn't know where to start. You need a decipher bird."

"A *what*?"

"Don't tell me you've never heard of a decipher bird."

"You've just made it up."

"Why would I make it up? If you don't believe me, ask Lucy. She used to have one when the twins were small."

I still wasn't convinced. This was the woman who had conned me into believing that Death Wings were going to eat Buddy.

"Are we done here?" Grandma said. "I have customers to attend to."

"Hang on."

"What now?"

"Me? Why doesn't she try them on herself?"

"What a brilliant idea," Grandma said. "We hadn't thought of that, had we, Bunty?"

"It's my neck," Bunty said. "I find it very hard to twist around to see all sides through the mirror."

"Try this one on first." Grandma put the blonde one on my head and spent the next five minutes adjusting it. "What do you think, Bunty?"

"Hmm, I'm not sure. Can I see the other one?"

Grandma removed the blonde wig and replaced it with the brunette one.

Bunty walked around me to get a view from all angles. "No, I think the blonde one is best."

Meanwhile, I was looking at my reflection in the mirror and I quite liked what I saw.

"Thanks." Grandma took the wig off my head. "You can go now, Jill."

"I came down here to ask you a question, remember?"

"Will it take long?"

"I wouldn't think so."

"Go through to the back and I'll be with you as soon as I've finished with Bunty."

Ten minutes later, Grandma joined me in the small staff room.

"This will have to be quick. I've still got a shop full of customers out there."

I took out my phone and showed her the photo of the text from Ma Chivers' grave.

"What's this gibberish?"

"This was engraved on Ma Chivers' headstone. I think it might be a clue to the whereabouts of the compass stone."

"It sounds like nonsense to me."

back to the office when Grandma spotted me and beckoned me to go inside.

I popped my head in the door. "It's okay. I can see you're busy. I'll come back later."

"Nonsense. You've come at a very opportune moment."

I didn't like the sound of that. Not one little bit. "I—err—just wanted to ask you something, Grandma."

"Yes, but first, you can help Bunty here." She gestured to a short woman who was standing close by. "Bunty, this is my granddaughter, Jill."

"I'm very pleased to meet you, Jill."

"Likewise."

"Bunty is looking for a wig to wear for her daughter's wedding, aren't you, Bunty?"

"That's right. I can't do much with my own hair these days, so I thought I'd treat myself to a beautiful wig for the occasion."

"Your own hair looks really nice," I said.

"It's kind of you to say so, dear, but this isn't mine." She proceeded to remove her hair, which I now realised was also a wig. Underneath, her own hair was grey and cropped very short. "There's a limit to what I can do with this."

"I see." I turned to Grandma. "I'm still not sure how I can help."

"Bunty is undecided between these two." She pointed to the table where there were two wigs: one blonde, the other brunette.

"You want my opinion? Well, I think—"

"No." Grandma sighed. "She doesn't care what you think. I want you to try them on, so Bunty can see them properly."

Lady Tweaking. "Do you understand now?"

"That's brilliant. I'll get straight back to GT and submit the application."

***

Whenever I'd had a spare moment, I'd taken another look at the photo of Ma Chivers' headstone, in the hope that I might be able to figure out what the wording meant. So far, I'd made no progress. I couldn't even be sure it related to the whereabouts of the compass stone. It was only the fact that the text included the word *compass* that gave me a glimmer of hope.

Grandma was supposedly assisting me in my quest for the compass stones, but so far all she had done was criticise from the side-lines. Maybe she'd have more luck at deciphering the cryptic text than I'd had. I called her phone but got her unhelpful voicemail message.

"*I'm not here. Go away*!"

Undeterred, I called her hotel where, after some cajoling, the receptionist told me that my grandmother was at her wig shop.

"Mrs V, I'm going to my grandmother's wig shop."

"How is that new venture of hers going, Jill? I've been meaning to pop in there to check it out."

"Okay as far as I know. I shouldn't be too long."

"Are you feeling better than you were earlier?"

"Much better, thanks. That bacon cob definitely hit the mark."

I had hoped the shop would be quiet, so that I could grab a quick word with Grandma, but there were several customers in there. I was just about to turn tail and head

"That posh ghost? You know I hate it when you invite those creepy spirits over."

"I don't know what you're so scared of. The colonel wouldn't hurt a fly."

"Call me strange, but I prefer to spend my time in the company of the living." He disappeared under the sofa.

The colonel answered on the first ring. "Jill, I was wondering when I'd hear from you. Have you come up with any bright ideas?"

"I have. Can you pop over?"

"Certainly. I'm on my way." He'd no sooner spoken the words than the temperature dropped, and he appeared in front of my desk. "Okay, Jill, what's the plan?"

"Lady Tweaking of Tweaking Manor is a friend of mine. I've persuaded her to let us use her house for a day."

"How did you manage that? Does she know about—err—?"

"Ghost Town? Restore? No, I think that would have blown her mind. I made up a story about trying to snare an art fraudster. She's going to use the opportunity to go shopping in London."

"You always were a good liar, Jill." He grinned. "So what's the plan?"

"I need you to submit your application to Restore as soon as possible. Tell them that Lady Tweaking is your sister, and that she has made a connection with you."

"Hang on. If I do that, won't they expect to see her ladyship?"

"I'm banking on it."

"Sorry, Jill, I must be a bit slow. I thought you said she'd be in London."

I cast the 'doppelganger' spell and changed myself into

trouble, but yes, I remember."

"You said that you had a super-secret back entrance into that unit."

"So?"

"I need you to use it to find out what's going on in there with the new tenants."

"I assume this is you being nosey again?"

"No. I'm concerned something nefarious might be afoot."

"*Nefarious*? Who says nefarious?"

"Will you do it or not?"

"Double helpings of salmon?"

"Okay."

"Red, not—"

"Pink. Yes, yes, I know the drill. Now hurry up."

The promise of extra salmon was enough to send him on his way with a spring in his step. I was really keen to find out what those two weirdos were up to, so when Winky reappeared minutes later, I didn't even give him the chance to jump down from the windowsill before I demanded, "So, what are they up to next-door?"

"Your guess is as good as mine."

"What do you mean?"

"They've boarded up my super-secret back entrance."

"Drat!"

"Just so you're aware, that doesn't mean that I don't get the double helping of salmon."

The coffee and bacon cob certainly hit the mark, and twenty minutes later, I was feeling much better.

"Winky, just a heads-up, I'm going to ask the colonel to come over."

going on down the corridor."

"What do you mean?"

"Just before the lights went out, there were all kinds of weird noises coming from down there."

"What kind of weird noises?"

"It's hard to describe."

"Voices? Music? Banging sounds? What?"

"It was like something was vibrating really fast. As if something were about to explode. I thought I was a goner."

"How long did it carry on for?"

"About ten minutes. Then the lights went out. Presumably, whatever had been making the noise stopped when the power died. You need to go down there and have a word with those weirdos."

"I've already tried, but they wouldn't let me through the door."

"You should report them to the landlord. We shouldn't have to put up with this, particularly now they've raised the rent."

Mrs V came through the door carrying coffee and a bacon cob.

"There you go, Jill."

"Thanks, Mrs V, you're a lifesaver." I waited until she'd left the office, then said to Winky, "I need you to do me a favour."

"The answer is no. I'm too tired."

"It's only a small one. Itsy-bitsy really."

"I'm listening."

"You remember how when you were trying to cause problems for Bubbles, you sneaked into their place?"

"I resent your insinuation that I was out to cause

"It's getting beyond a joke. I told Armi to call the power company to find out what's going on."

"He'll be lucky to get through. I bet their lines are all red hot."

"Would you like a cup of tea?"

"I'd prefer a coffee. I need something to get me going."

"Did you have any breakfast?"

"Not really."

"That's no good. Why don't I nip to that new takeaway I told you about? Their bacon cobs are delicious."

"That does sound tempting."

"Red or brown sauce?"

"Brown, please."

"Right. Go and have a sit down and I'll be back in a jiffy."

Just the thought of a bacon cob had bucked me up, but it didn't last long.

"I have a complaint," Winky said.

"Not now. I'm not in the mood."

"*You're* not in the mood. How do you think I feel? I barely got a wink of sleep last night."

"So what? You can sleep all day if you want to."

"No, I can't. I have important Feline Fortune business to attend to. Aren't you going to ask why I didn't get any sleep?"

"No."

"I'll tell you why. First, all the lights went out."

"They went out everywhere. There was another power cut."

"It's spooky in here in the dark."

"Don't be such a wuss."

"That's not all. There's something seriously strange

I expected Jack to laugh at that. When he didn't even crack a smile, I knew I was in trouble.

My phone rang, making me jump; it was Kathy.

"Jill, did your power go out again last night?"

"I don't think so."

"Ours went off at eleven for about twenty minutes."

"Jack and I were in bed at ten."

"Really?" She laughed. "It's good to hear that you two are keeping the passion alive."

"Not exactly. We were both dead on our feet. I was fast asleep long before eleven. I'm not sure about Jack. Hang on, I'll ask him." I put my hand over the phone. "It's Kathy. She reckons they had another power cut last night at eleven."

"Yeah, we did too. I was reading when all the lights went out."

"You never mentioned it."

"I'd forgotten all about it."

"Kathy, are you there? Apparently, we had one here too."

"What do you reckon is going on?"

"Beats me."

***

"Are you okay, Jill?" Mrs V said. "You look shocking."

"Thanks."

"Sorry, but I'm worried about you."

"I know, and I'm fine. Just a little tired."

"We had another power cut last night. Did you?"

"Apparently, but I didn't know anything about it because I was already in bed, fast asleep."

"That isn't important. The point is that I took a look around their incident room."

"Jill!" Jack's face was getting redder and redder.

"You promised not to get angry."

"What if someone had seen you?"

"Duh! I've just said I was invisible."

"Right. What did you find out?"

"That I'm their number one suspect."

"You can't know that for certain. Are you sure you aren't just being paranoid?"

"Dawn Brakes said, and I quote, *she had the motive and the opportunity. Right now, she's our prime suspect.*"

"You can't be sure she was talking about you."

"She was pointing to a photo of me at the time."

"Oh. I thought you'd identified a number of other suspects?"

"I had. Lots of them, but one guy is in a coma, another is happily married with a new baby, and according to the whiteboard in the incident room, the other two have both been alibied."

"Didn't you say you thought there was someone else in the toilets with you and Sushi?"

"I did. I had been pinning all my hopes on identifying who was in there."

"What's changed?"

"It turns out that there wasn't anyone in there. The management had locked that cubicle because the toilet was awaiting repair."

"This isn't sounding good."

"You think? I reckon it's only a matter of time before your buddies come knocking on the door, with their handcuffs ready."

Chapter 16

"Mummy, why aren't you having any breakfast?" Florence said, through a mouthful of toast.

"I'm not hungry this morning."

"When *I'm* not hungry, you make me eat *my* breakfast."

"She's got you there." Jack grinned.

"I'll have some breakfast later at work, I promise."

"What will you have?" Florence said.

"Cereal probably."

"What kind of cereal?"

Kids. Don't you just love their enquiring minds?

"Cornflakes."

"Can I go and play with my beanies?"

"Sure."

"Are you okay, Jill?" Jack asked once Florence had gone upstairs.

"Yeah, I'm fine."

"You were very quiet last night too. Something's wrong. What is it?"

"Do you promise not to get mad if I tell you?"

"That depends."

"Forget it, then."

"Okay, I promise. I won't be angry."

"I paid a visit to West Chipping police station yesterday."

"Why would I be angry about that?"

"I was sort of invisible at the time."

"How can you be *sort of* invisible? You either were or you weren't."

"Okay, I was. Except for the onion breath that is."

"What?"

suspect."

The man stepped away from the whiteboard, leaving me to stare at a photograph of myself.

Sushi's murder. Below their names was a still image, which had obviously been taken from the hotel's CCTV. The image quality was poor, but it clearly showed the two of them standing side-by-side, smoking a cigarette.

Sushi's husband's photo was also on the board. The note under his name said he had also been eliminated because he'd been seen in the men's toilet at the time of the murder.

But it was the last snippet of information that delivered the hammer blow. The heading was: **Unknown occupant of toilet stall**. I'd become more and more convinced that whoever was in that stall was the murderer; that they had waited until I'd left, and then struck. But, according to the note on the whiteboard, that stall hadn't been occupied. Its door was locked because the toilet was out of commission and awaiting repair.

I'd visited the police station in the hope of shedding more light on the case, and possibly even finding new leads that I could follow up. Instead, the exact opposite had happened. I now had precisely nothing to go on. Somewhat dispirited, I took a couple of photos of the whiteboard, and one of the CCTV still image, just in case they proved useful later.

I'd just started towards the door when Dawn Brakes and a male detective walked into the room. The man walked over to the whiteboard and pinned another photo to it. I couldn't see what it was because he was blocking my view.

"We'll have to tread carefully, Ma'am," he said. "You know her husband is ex-force, I assume."

"I don't care about that," Brakes said. "She had the motive and the opportunity. Right now, she's our prime

I'd drawn a blank with both of my leads, so I decided I should check if the police had had better luck, which meant another visit to West Chipping police station.

I wasn't as familiar with the layout of that building as I was with the police station in Washbridge, but once invisible, I soon managed to find the incident rooms, which were on the second floor. There were three in total, and the largest one had clearly been assigned to the Sushi murder case because her photograph was pinned to the huge whiteboard at the front of the room.

The only person in the room was a female detective who was studying the computer screen in front of her. When I walked up behind her and peered over her shoulder, she reacted immediately by turning around. For a horrible moment, I thought the 'invisible' spell had worn off, but the fact that she didn't confront me soon dispelled that idea. It was only when she started to sniff the air that the penny dropped. Invisibility might mean I couldn't be seen, but it didn't mask the smell of the cheese and onion sandwiches I'd eaten at Cuppy C.

Note to self: Do not eat onions when you're trying to go unnoticed.

It turned out there was nothing of any interest to see on her computer screen. As far as I could make out, she appeared to be filling in her expenses claim for the month.

The whiteboard, though, provided much more meaningful information. A photo of Christine Hoyle was on there with a note that she'd been eliminated as a suspect by CCTV from the adjoining hotel. A similar note had been added next to the photo of the waitress who had spilled the soup. They had both been captured on camera, having a cigarette outside the restaurant, at the time of

"I've known him ever since we were kids. I moved away from the area after I left school, but then came back about four years ago. When I found out Carl was in prison, I started to write to him. Then, when he came out, we moved in together. Not long afterwards, Leo came along."

"Carl seems happy."

"We both are."

Harper came back into the room and passed me a cup of tea.

"I was just saying to Lacey that you seem a very happy family."

"Leo is the best thing to ever happen to me."

Lacey coughed.

"Sorry, darling. You too."

"Don't you find it hard work living on the top floor? With the little one, I mean?"

"It's not ideal," Harper said. "But we've got our name down on the council list and we're hoping to get a house soon. And, like I told Vera, I started work last week. It's only part-time for now, but they said they might be able to give me more hours in a few months."

"That's great."

Carl and Lacey made a delightful couple, and they spent the next twenty minutes talking about Leo, on whom they both clearly doted.

By the time I left their flat, I was convinced that, despite his past, Harper had turned his life around and was not Sushi's killer.

***

"Just—err—a migraine thing. She should be back next week. You say you saw her yesterday?"

"That's right."

"Sorry. We must have got our wires crossed."

"That's okay. Would you like to come and see Leo?"

"Who?"

"Leo. Come in." He disappeared inside.

According to everything I'd read about Harper, he was an unpredictable and violent man, so I cautiously made my way inside, primed to take evasive action at the first sign of danger.

"Isn't he beautiful?" Harper gushed. "This is Lacey."

Seated on the threadbare sofa was a young woman, nursing a baby who couldn't have been more than a couple of months old.

"Would you like a cup of tea?" Harper offered. "Sorry, I've forgotten your name."

So had I for a moment, but then it came back to me. "Melinda Lawless. Err, yes, tea would be nice."

"Milk and sugar?"

"Just milk, please."

"Lacey?"

"No, thanks, lover."

Harper left the room leaving me somewhat nonplussed.

"Sorry about the mess," Lacey said. "Move those nappies and grab a seat. Carl didn't tell me who you were."

"I'm from the probation service."

"There's nothing wrong, is there? Vera seemed pleased with everything when she came yesterday."

"No, nothing's wrong. Just a mix-up at our end. So, Lacey, have you and Carl been together long?"

***

Next stop, Riverton. In total contrast to Fisher's mansion, Harper was living in a flat on the top floor of an eleven-storey high-rise block. I'd fully expected the lift to be out of order, but as soon as I'd pressed the call button, the lights had sprung into life, and moments later, the doors had opened.

So, why was I walking up the stairs?

I'd taken one step inside the lift, then been driven back out by the awful smell. I'm pretty sure if I'd ridden the lift to the top floor and back down again, I would have been overcome by the fumes.

A decade earlier, Carl Harper had been described in court as a very dangerous individual who cared nothing about anyone but himself. Following a drunken argument, he had killed a man with a single blow. It hadn't been his first offence; he'd had a string of convictions since the age of sixteen, many of them involving violence. After sentencing, as he was being taken out of the court room, he'd threatened to kill Sushi.

He sounded like a seriously nasty piece of work, and I was expecting the worst.

"Hi." The clean-cut man who answered the door greeted me with a smile.

"Hi, I'm looking for Carl Harper."

"That's me."

"Oh, right. My name is Melinda Lawless. I'm from the probation service."

"Oh? What happened to Vera?"

"She's ill. I'm stepping in for her for a few days."

"What's wrong with her? She seemed okay yesterday."

The metal gates were locked, so I pressed the button on the intercom.

"Yes?" a female voice snapped.

"Hi. I'd like to speak to Mr Fisher, please."

"Me too, but I wouldn't hold your breath."

"Sorry?"

"Who are you, anyway?"

"My name is Helen Moneymaker," I said.

"Yeah, but who are you? What do you want?"

"I'm from the Inland Revenue."

"Are you sure your name isn't Money*taker*?" She laughed.

"That's very amusing. I'd like to talk to Mr Fisher about his tax returns."

"You'd better contact his accountant, then."

"I'm afraid I really do need to speak to Mr Fisher in person. It's rather urgent."

"Yeah? Well, you're plain out of luck because Jimmy isn't speaking to anyone."

"Would you at least ask him?"

"You can ask him yourself. Not that it'll do you any good. He's on Shipton Ward at Shawtown hospital."

"Is he ill?"

"He's been in a coma for six months."

"Oh. I'm sorry. I had no idea. What happened?"

"The daft sod got drunk and stepped out in front of a taxi."

It was possible she was spinning me a yarn, but a search on his name confirmed that he had indeed been involved in a road traffic accident, which had left him in a coma.

So much for that lead.

"In a manner of speaking. He told me where I'd find his mother's grave."

"Ma Chivers is dead?"

"Yeah."

"You never did tell us why you were looking for her."

"It was nothing. I'd better be making tracks. Good luck with your application."

***

Dave 'The Sword' Fisher was still serving time for the murder of Ricky Harrow. The two men had been heads of rival drug gangs in Shawtown. Fisher had numerous previous convictions for violence and had been found guilty of murder by a unanimous decision. His nickname was not only a play on the word swordfish, but also reference to the fact that he was known to carry a blade with him most of the time. Harrow had been found stabbed to death in his home, and it was Sushi who had found the evidence, a combination of DNA and CCTV footage from a nearby petrol station, that had ensured Fisher was convicted. After Fisher was jailed, his brother, Jimmy, had taken over leadership of the drug gang. Had he murdered Sushi to avenge his brother?

I intended to find out.

Clearly, the drug trade paid well. The address I'd found for Jimmy Fisher turned out to be a huge, modern house on the outskirts of Shawtown. Set in its own grounds, it was an architectural monstrosity, which just goes to prove that money can't buy taste. The front of the house was ninety percent tinted glass. Very classy.

"Don't go telling her that." Amber had appeared behind me, carrying a coffee, a sandwich and a cupcake. "She's already big-headed enough."

"I am *not* big-headed." I took the coffee and sandwich, and I was about to take the cupcake when she pulled her hand away. "Hands off. This is for Bobby."

"Oh, right. Sorry."

"Jill is going to bring Florence to see me." Bobby popped the cupcake into his mouth.

"That's nice. Maybe we'll get to see her too. Jill never brings her to see us."

"That's not true."

"It's been ages."

"Okay, sorry. I'll bring her over tomorrow if I can, and she can spend time with all of you."

I spent the best part of an hour with Bobby who was now much brighter than when I'd first arrived. Back downstairs, the twins were both poring over the application form.

"Look at this question," Amber said. "What colour are the walls in the room where the dragon will be kept? What possible difference can that make?"

"What about this one?" Pearl stabbed the form with her pen. "Will the dragon have access to food and water? Do they think we're going to let him starve to death? This is bureaucracy gone mad."

"I'd better leave you to it."

"Hey, Jill, was Cyril able to tell you where you could find Ma Chivers?"

"Not exactly, but he put me onto her son."

"I didn't realise she had any children. Poor lad. Was he able to help?"

form that's the problem." She picked up the pile of papers and then dropped them with another thud.

"What does Bobby make of all this?"

"He's upset. He loves having all those visitors. Why don't you go and have a chat with him?"

"Am I allowed to?"

"Yeah. You're not a customer."

"What am I?"

"Let's say you're an honorary co-owner."

"Do honorary co-owners get free coffee?"

"I suppose so."

"And a sandwich?"

"We don't have many left. Just egg and cress or cheese and onion."

"I'll have cheese and onion, please."

"Okay. We'll bring them up to you."

Result!

"Jill!" Bobby was stoked to see me; he came running over to give me a hug. "Have you heard what's happened, Jill?"

"Yeah, the twins just told me."

"I told the man I was happy here and that I didn't need a licence, but he said the twins have to have one. It's lonely up here without my visitors."

"The twins will soon sort it out, and then people will be able to visit you again."

"Could Florence come and see me?"

"Err, I—err—"

"Please, Jill. It would cheer me up no end."

"Okay, I'll see what I can do, but it might not be today."

"Thanks, Jill, you're the best."

"*Amiss*? Who says *amiss*?" Pearl snapped.

"Sheesh, when did you join the dictionary police? It's bad enough that I have to put up with Winky criticising my choice of words. Is something *wrong*? Is that better?"

"They've shut Bobby down," Amber said.

"What do you mean, they've shut him down?"

"The dragon inspectors paid us a visit yesterday, and they said we had to stop customers going upstairs to see him immediately."

"Why? Don't they think the conditions are suitable to keep him here?"

"That's the stupid part," Pearl said. "They actually praised us for the way we were looking after Bobby. And of course, he said he loved it here."

"I don't get it, then. If everything is okay, why have you had to stop customers going to see him?"

"Red tape. Blooming red tape." Amber sighed. "Apparently, we should have applied for a dragon custody licence before we allowed customers to visit him."

"That's not so bad, then," I said.

"Really?" Pearl reached down and brought out a thick wad of papers, which she dropped with a thud onto the counter. "In that case, would you like to fill this lot in for us?"

I picked up the papers and flicked through them. "There are one hundred and eight questions in here."

"Tell us about it. Until we return this together with the fee, we can't allow any of the customers to go up to see Bobby."

"How much is the fee?"

"Not much at all, thankfully. It's this stupid application

babblings of a crazy old witch? I hoped it was some kind of clue because otherwise my mission to find the four compass stones would have failed. I took out my phone and snapped a photo of the headstone. Hopefully, I would be able to make sense of it later.

As I headed towards the cemetery gates, I saw two figures in the distance. Two men, both dressed in black, were standing over a grave. Gravediggers maybe? No, they were too smartly dressed for that. Undertakers more likely. As I drew closer, I caught sight of their faces. It was the two men from down the corridor. Until that moment, I hadn't even realised they were sups.

One of the men caught my eye, said something to the other, and then both of them hurried away in the opposite direction. What was I supposed to make of that? I walked over to the grave, which they had been standing over, expecting it to be a recent burial, but the gravestone showed the person had been buried just under a year ago. Did they work as undertakers here in Candlefield? They were certainly dressed for the part. If so, why open an office in Washbridge? And why all the subterfuge?

***

My visit to the cemetery had been very depressing, so in an attempt to lift my spirits, and because I was starving, I paid a visit to Cuppy C.

The place was much quieter than of late, and judging by the look of thunder on the faces of both Amber and Pearl, something was wrong.

"Is something amiss?" I asked.

him a tenner.

"Whose grave are you looking for?"

"A woman named Martha Chivers."

"Row nineteen. Plot twenty-three."

"Are you sure? I didn't see you consult your database."

"My database is up here." He tapped the side of his head. "Go and see for yourself."

"Don't disappear because if you're wrong, I'll want a refund."

"I'm never wrong. And anyway, I'm coming with you."

The two of us made our way to the other side of the cemetery, to row nineteen, plot twenty-three.

"You were right."

"Of course I was."

"Thanks."

"My pleasure." And with that, he shot off up the nearest tree.

Who would have thought squirrels could be so entrepreneurial?

The grave, although relatively new, was obviously untended; weeds had already partially covered the headstone. In order to read the inscription, I had to first clear them away. It read:

Weep not for me,
Between a rock and a hard place,
I chose a different compass,
And still it waits,
Where you stand. Where you fail.

What on earth did all that nonsense mean? As Orson had said, it did mention the word compass, but was it a clue to the whereabouts of the stone or was it simply the had no choice but to walk down each row.

"Need any assistance?"

I looked around to see who had spoken, but there was no sign of anyone.

"Are you looking for a particular grave?"

"Who's there?" Was someone hiding behind one of the headstones? "Stand up so I can see you."

"I'm up here."

"Up *where*?"

"Right here. Above your head."

I looked up to find a squirrel sitting on the branch of an old oak tree. "Did you say that?"

"I don't see anyone else around, do you? So, are you looking for a particular grave?"

"Yeah, but I'm not having much luck."

"I could help you with that."

"I don't see how."

"I have all the graves catalogued in a database."

"Of course you do."

"It's true."

"Why would you do that?"

"It's how I earn a crust. People like you come into the cemetery every day, looking for the grave of a relative or friend. For a small fee, I save them the time and bother of having to find it themselves."

"How *small* a fee?"

"Ten pounds. More than reasonable, I'm sure you'd agree."

"Let's say I was to give you the money, how do I know you won't just do a runner?"

"Look at my face. Don't I look trustworthy?"

"You do, actually." I took out my purse and handed

Chapter 15

All the memories came flooding back to me. The first time I'd visited Candlefield cemetery, many years ago, was for the funeral of my birth mother. That was just a matter of days after I'd stood by her deathbed, and she'd uttered the words that were to change my life forever: *You're a witch.*

I almost hadn't made it to the funeral that day because I'd been unable to find my way to Candlefield in the car. As a result, I'd arrived too late for the actual ceremony. It had been a grey, rainy day—befitting really.

So much had happened since then. I was now considered one of the most powerful witches in Candlefield, and I was married with a beautiful daughter. What would have happened, I wondered, if I'd decided not to attend the funeral? If I'd rejected the notion that I was a witch? Knowing Aunt Lucy as I now did, I doubt she would have given up on me.

Did I have any regrets? If I could go back to my old life—the one before I discovered I was a witch—would I? That was an easy question to answer. Emphatically no. I loved being a witch. I loved my family, both human and sup. I wouldn't change a thing.

Except perhaps for today's weather. Once again, my visit to the cemetery had coincided with the heavens opening. At least this time I had an umbrella with me, which was just as well because I'd already spent over thirty minutes trying to locate Ma Chivers' grave. One might have expected the more recent graves to be clustered together, but that clearly wasn't the case, so I

to be reminded of her every time someone addressed me. Sorry."

"It's okay. Thanks anyway." I stood up and started for the door.

"There is just one thing."

"Yes?"

"My mother left very specific instructions about her funeral arrangements. She wanted no ceremony and no guests, which was just as well because no one would have attended anyway."

"I see." I actually *didn't* see the relevance, but I figured I owed it to him to allow him to get it off his chest. "I'm surprised you agreed to oversee it."

"I didn't want to, but there wasn't anyone else. Anyway, the point is that she also left precise instructions for the wording that was to be engraved on her headstone."

"Okay?"

"It didn't make any sense to me at the time, but I didn't really care. I do remember it said something about a compass."

"A compass *stone*?"

"No, I don't think so. I just remember it including the word compass. It might be nothing."

"Do you still have a copy of the wording?"

"No. Why would I keep it?"

"In that case, can you tell me where I can find her grave?"

"Sorry, but I can't do that."

"Who are you, anyway?"

"My name is Jill Maxwell. I used to be Jill Gooder."

"Of course. I thought I recognised you. My mother hated you."

"From what I remember, your mother hated most people."

"That's true, but she hated you with a particular passion."

"Where is she, Orson? Why are you protecting her?"

"*Protecting her*?" He scoffed. "Why would I do that? It's not like she ever protected me. Do you have any idea what it's like to grow up the son of the most hated woman in Candlefield?"

"It can't have been easy."

"It was hell. Not that she cared. She only cared about one person and that was herself."

"Tell me where I can find her, please. It's really important."

"She's dead."

"What? Are you lying?"

"Why would I lie? She died two years ago."

"Oh no." I slumped into one of the chairs.

"Why do you care if she's dead? You have more reason to hate her than most."

I spent the next ten minutes telling him about Braxmore, the compass stones and the threat to Florence.

"What happened to your mother's possessions? Maybe the clue to the whereabouts of the compass stone is amongst them somewhere."

"I burnt everything. I didn't want to leave any trace of that evil woman. I changed my name so I wouldn't have

"I did try knocking but no one answered. I'm looking for Orson Wellington."

"Orson!" She shouted down the office. "There's someone here to see you."

"*Me*? Who is it?" The wizard walking towards me looked nothing like Ma Chivers.

"Don't know." The witch shrugged. "Her face is familiar though."

Orson Wellington clearly had a penchant for the check. His suit, shirt and tie were all checked. It shouldn't have worked, but somehow it did.

"Are you looking for me?"

"Orson?"

"Yeah."

"Is there somewhere we can talk in private?"

"I—err—guess so. There's the staff room. No one will be in there just now."

"Great."

The staff room had a table, four chairs, and incredibly, three microwaves.

"What's this all about?" Orson asked.

"I believe your mother is Martha Chivers?"

His face fell. "Sorry, I can't help you."

He started for the door, but I moved to block his way.

"I just want to know where I can find your mother. Tell me that, and I'll be on my way."

"I can't."

"I assume by the fact that you've changed your name you and she aren't on the best of terms."

"That's none of your business."

"Just tell me where she is, and I'll leave you be."

"Move out of my way."

you tell me where I'll find your three Orsons, please?"

"Orson Green and Orson Hall both work in the vampire section. Orson Wellington works in the admin office."

"Where's that?"

"On the first floor."

"Okay, thanks."

In the vampire section of the museum, I found two young men working on a new exhibit, the centrepiece of which was a giant set of fangs.

"Excuse me, I'm looking for Orson."

"That's me," they chorused.

"I'm Orson Green."

"And I'm Orson Hall."

"Hi. I'm Jill. I was actually looking for the son of a woman with the surname of Chivers. Is that either of you, by any chance?"

"You want Orson Wellington," Orson Hall said.

"He works upstairs in admin." His namesake pointed to the stairs.

"Right, thanks. I assume he changed his name?"

"Yes. A couple of years ago, but I wouldn't mention it. It's a rather touchy subject with him."

"Okay, thanks for the advice."

The door to the admin office had frosted glass, so I couldn't see inside. I tried knocking but there was no response, so I just walked in. The large open-plan office wasn't exactly a hive of activity. In fact, most of the desks were unoccupied.

"Can I help?" A witch, with curly blonde hair, shouted from halfway down the office. "You're not supposed to be in here."

with fingers crossed, I made my way inside.

The museum was an enormous building, divided into a number of different sections: wizards and witches, werewolves, vampires etc. I had no idea where to start, and it didn't help that I didn't even know what Orson looked like. Perhaps he'd look like his mother—poor devil.

After wandering around aimlessly, looking for any man who looked like Ma Chivers, I did what I should have done in the first place; I approached the information desk.

"Excuse me, I wonder if you can help me?"

"I'll do my best, madam." The female werewolf behind the desk sported a smart blue uniform, which made her look like a flight attendant who had lost her way.

"Do you have someone working here by the name of Orson?"

"We do, yes."

"Awesome."

"Yes, Orson."

"No, I meant—never mind. Can you tell me where I can find him?"

"Which one?"

"Which one *what*?"

"Which Orson are you looking for?"

"You have more than one?"

"Three, actually."

"Oh. I'm after Orson Chivers."

"Sorry, we don't have an Orson Chivers. We have Orson Green, Orson Hall and Orson Wel—"

"Wells?"

"Wellington."

"Okay. I suppose I could have got the name wrong. Can

"That's right."

"Forget it." He threw one of the cases onto the sofa and started to unpack.

"What's wrong?"

"What do you think is wrong? Have you forgotten cats hate water?"

"I—err—it had never occurred to me."

"I can't possibly live next to a river. I'd be terrified to go out. And how are my friends supposed to visit?"

"I—err—"

"It's no good trying to change my mind. The river is a dealbreaker."

"Oh well. If you're absolutely sure."

Yes! Yes! Yes! What a result!

Snigger!

***

What's that saying? Like father like son? I was hoping that it wouldn't be a case of like *mother* like son when it came to Ma Chivers' son, Orson. Since I'd discovered I was a witch, I'd had the misfortune to meet many undesirable characters, but there weren't many worse than that woman. For many years, she'd done her best to make my life a misery, but she'd never really got the better of me. The thought that I needed her help to locate the third compass stone filled me with dread. I couldn't imagine her helping me willingly, at least not without something in exchange.

But first I had to find her, which is why I was standing outside Candlefield Museum. I wasn't even sure if her son still worked there, but it was my one and only lead. So,

"You said you'd talk it over with Jack, and that guy is too nice for his own good, so he was never going to say no."

"If you give the dog or goldfish any grief, you'll be out of there so quickly your paws won't touch the ground."

"Understood. We just need to finalise the arrangements."

"What *arrangements*?"

"How many days I'll spend there and how many I'll spend here."

"You can't commute back and forth between the two."

"You do."

"That's different."

"How is it?"

"Because I'm—err—it just is."

"Okay, I suppose I can make that work. I'll just have to let everyone know my new address."

"Everyone? *Everyone* who?"

"Friends, business acquaintances, girlfriends."

"Hold on. I don't want to be overrun by cats."

"Don't worry. I'll make sure they don't all visit at the same time."

"You'll need to warn them about the river."

"River? What river?"

"The one that runs by the house."

"You never said anything about a river."

"You know we live at the old watermill, so of course there's a river next to the house."

"I just thought that was a name. Like Dunroamin."

"It used to be a working mill. The wheel is still there."

"Are you telling me there's a river right next to your place?"

door. "Hello!"

Nothing.

I hammered even harder on the door this time, and I was just considering magicking myself inside when the door cracked open a few inches and one of the creepy men poked his head out. "Yes?"

"There's a burning smell and it seems to be coming from your unit. Is everything okay in there?"

"Yes, it's all under control."

"What was it?"

"Err, a power tool burned out. Nothing to worry about."

And before I could press him further, he had closed the door.

"What was it?" Mrs V handed me a cup of tea.

"The guy said it was a faulty power tool, but I'm not sure I believe him."

"Did you have a power cut last night, Jill?"

"Yeah, we did. You too?"

"Yes. Right at the interesting part in Greenside Mysteries."

"The chauffeur did it."

"Oh no! You shouldn't have told me. I was going to watch it on Rewind tonight."

"Sorry, Mrs V. I still think it was the butler."

When I'd told Jack that Winky would already have his cases packed, I'd been joking. At least, I thought I had, but there they were, beside the sofa.

"Have you got plenty of salmon in?" Winky said.

"Aren't you rather jumping the gun? I haven't said you can come and live with us yet."

Maybe I could pretend to be your mother."

"I'm afraid not. The people running this scam have a reputation for extreme violence. It wouldn't be safe for you to be here, in case things go pear-shaped."

"Should you really be exposing yourself to such danger, Jill?"

"It comes with the job. It's what my clients pay me for."

"You're welcome to use this place whenever you like. Let me know when it will be, and I'll use the opportunity to take a shopping trip to London. It's ages since I was there."

"That's very kind, Caroline."

***

As soon as I stepped into the office building, I became aware of a burning smell, so I dashed up the stairs, and into the office.

"Is everything okay in here, Mrs V?"

"Do you mean that burning smell?"

"Yeah. I can't smell it in here, but it was quite strong on the stairs and landing."

"I noticed it as soon as I walked through the door."

"It must be coming from down the corridor. I'd better go and check everything is okay down there."

"Shall I put the kettle on?"

"That would be great, thanks."

As I walked down the corridor towards my mysterious new neighbours, the burning smell became stronger. The front of the unit was still boarded up with no indication of what kind of business it was to be.

"Hello! Anyone in there?" I knocked on the makeshift

"That's right."

"I'm Sears. Do come in."

The first thing I noticed was that the house was considerably warmer than on my previous visits, when the dire state of the finances had meant much of the house went unheated. The exterior wasn't the only part of the house to have benefitted from a fresh coat of paint. The hallway too was looking a hundred times better than it had the last time I'd been there.

Sears led the way to the same dining room where I'd first met Lady Tweaking, and just as on my first visit, she had Olivia, a cream-coloured Persian cat, on her lap. As soon as the cat spotted me, she jumped down and scurried out of the room.

"Sorry about Olivia, Jill. She doesn't get any less anti-social."

"Thanks for seeing me at such short notice, Caroline."

"My pleasure. I'll be forever in your debt for what you did for Tweaking Manor. You said on the phone that you needed a favour."

"That's right, and it's rather a big one, I'm afraid."

"Ask away."

Obviously, I couldn't tell Caroline the truth about Ghost Town and the Restore scam. If I had, she would have thought I'd lost my mind.

"I'm working on a case that involves huge scale art fraud. To try and snare the people behind this, I need to pose as someone with the means to spend a large sum of money on a painting they claim is a Vermeer. If I could bring them here, it will lend credibility to my claim to be minor aristocracy."

"How very exciting. Is there anything I can do to help?

"I didn't realise she had one."

"Neither did I."

"What did her son have to say?"

"I haven't caught up with him yet."

"Chop-chop, then. There's no time to lose."

"I'm doing my best. You could always lend a hand if you wanted to."

"No, thanks. I have too much on my plate as it is. Which reminds me, I need to get back to supervise the breakfasts."

"Grandma, wait."

"What is it? I'm already running late."

"Take it easy on the Peeps."

"On the *what*?"

"Joe and Flo Peep. They're the ones who have taken over the tea room. I saw you making a scene in there yesterday."

"I wasn't making a scene. I was simply pointing out that they had no blackcurrant jam."

"At the top of your voice. Look, they're a really nice couple. I'm just asking you to be nice."

"You want me to be nice to the competition? What a quaint idea."

***

The exterior of Tweaking Manor was looking much better than on my last visit. Much of the brickwork had obviously been repointed, and the woodwork repainted.

"Mrs Maxwell?" The butler who answered the door was several years younger than Mulgrave, the previous holder of that post, who had died in tragic circumstances.

widespread because Kathy's went off too."

"It simply isn't good enough. I had to step in to make sure none of my guests were inconvenienced."

"When you say you *stepped in,* do you mean you have a backup generator?"

"Don't be silly. Why would I go to such unnecessary expense?"

"Please tell me you didn't use magic."

"Of course I did, but it was quite a faff."

"You have to be careful, Grandma. What if the rogue retrievers get a whiff of it?"

"Why would they? Everyone will assume the hotel's backup generator came to the rescue."

"The one you don't have?"

"Correct. Anyway, the reason I came to see you is to ask if you've tracked down Ma Chivers yet."

"Not yet, but—"

"What's taking you so long?"

"I was about to say that I managed to speak to that young sidekick of hers."

"Alicia?"

"No, the young guy."

"Cecil?"

"It's Cyril, but yes. He's put on quite a bit of weight over the years."

"Do you think I care about his physique?"

"Probably not. Anyway, he doesn't know where Ma Chivers is, but—"

"That was a fat lot of good, then."

"If you'd just let me finish for once."

"Go on."

"He told me where I can find Ma Chivers' son."

Breakfast finished, I turned to Jack. "Okay, I'm ready for them."

"Ready for what?"

"The three excuses I can give Winky why he can't come and live with us."

"I couldn't come up with—"

"Okay, two will do."

"Any."

"What? None at all?"

"I racked my brains, but I couldn't think of a single legitimate reason other than the dog and the goldfish, and he's already said he's fine with those."

"Well, that's just great. I was relying on you to rescue us."

"I'm sorry, but if you couldn't come up with any, I don't know how you expected me to."

"That's it, then. I'm going to have to bring him home with me tonight."

"That soon?"

"If I know Winky, he'll already have his case packed."

I was on my way out to the car when someone called my name. That someone was Grandma, so I pretended I hadn't heard her and climbed in anyway. I was just about to set off when she stepped in front of the car and glared at me.

I lowered the window. "Morning, Grandma."

She came to the driver's side. "I suppose you're going to pretend you didn't hear me?"

"I didn't. I was thinking about a case."

"Hmm. What happened to the power last night?"

"I've no idea, but the problem must have been

Chapter 14

Thankfully, by the next morning, the power was back on. By the time I got downstairs, Jack and Florence were already tucking into their breakfasts—if you can call sawdust a breakfast, and for some reason Jack had a great big grin on his face.

"What are you looking so happy about at this time of the morning?" I took the box of Strawberrycandy Pops out of the cupboard and poured myself a bowl.

"I know who did it."

"Who did *what*?"

"The murder."

"You know who killed Sushi?"

"No. I'm talking about Greenside Mysteries. I looked it up online."

"Who was it? The butler?"

"No. It was the chauffeur."

"I thought he was dead too?"

"Apparently, he faked his own death."

"What a load of rubbish. I hate those convoluted mysteries which make no sense."

"I wonder if Kathy knows. You should call and tell her."

"I don't have time. I have to go to Tweaking Manor this morning."

"Are they having more problems over there?"

"No. I'm hoping Lady Tweaking will do me a favour."

My phone beeped with a text. It was another photo from Ava Todfoster who was taking an early morning swim. I quickly sent it with a brief message to her husband, and then got stuck into my breakfast (a real breakfast, I might add).

"It's dark in that basement."

"In case you hadn't noticed, it's dark everywhere at the moment. Use the flashlight app on your phone."

"I don't have it installed."

"Fine, I'll do it."

The stairs leading down to the basement were treacherous, but I managed to get down there without breaking any limbs.

"It's not the fuses," I shouted to Jack who was standing at the top of the stairs.

"I'll go and see if anyone else's lights are out."

When I joined him by the lounge window, it was clear that the whole village was in darkness.

"You should have checked this before you sent me down to the basement. I could have broken my neck on those stairs."

"I didn't send you down there. You volunteered. Do you think I should call the power people?"

"There's no point. If the whole area is out, I'm pretty sure they'll be aware there's an issue."

"Give Kathy a call."

"Why? What can she do about it?"

"I meant to find out who the murderer was."

"Good idea." I grabbed my phone and made the call. "It's me. Have you been watching Greenside Murders?"

"Yeah."

"Who was the murderer? Our power just went out."

"I've no idea. We're in darkness too."

speak to him?"

"That would be great, Jill, thanks."

***

Poor old Humpy had been relegated to the windowsill because Florence had insisted on taking her two favourite beanies (who will not be named) to bed with her. Jack and I had for once managed to agree on something we'd both like to watch on TV. It was a classic whodunit and, with only ten minutes left of the show, neither of us had a clue who the murderer was.

What do you mean that doesn't bode well for a P.I? I don't recall asking for your opinion.

"It must have been the vicar," Jack said. "He was fishing at the lake, and that's where the body was found."

"Rubbish. That was clearly a red herring. *Fishing? Red herring?* Get it?"

"That was beyond terrible. Who do you think did it, then?"

"The butler."

"Why?"

"Because the butler always does it."

"Is that the kind of logic you apply to your real-life cases?"

Before I could respond, the TV died, and all the lights went out.

"What happened?" Jack said.

"I'll take a wild guess and say the power just went out. Go and check the fuses."

"Why do I have to do it?"

"Because you're the man of the house."

"Will you and Flo be able to cope by yourselves? Ms Drinkwater used to have two or three people working for her."

"We'll definitely need to employ at least a couple of people. In fact, a lovely young woman was supposed to start today, but she phoned yesterday to say she'd changed her mind."

"I may have spoken too soon," Flo said in a hushed voice. "I think we may have our first difficult customer."

I didn't need to ask who she was talking about.

"I'd better get going. You two should be really proud of what you've done with this place."

That brought a smile back to Flo's face. "Thanks, Jill. Just wait until we get the garden open too."

"*Garden*? I didn't realise there was one."

"Come and see." She beckoned me to follow her through the kitchen, and then pointed out of the window. "I can't understand why the previous owner didn't utilise this space. There's room for at least ten tables out there. We just need to spruce it up a little: buy some tables and chairs, plant a few flowers, invest in some garden ornaments, and we'll be ready to roll."

"Garden ornaments? Like gnomes?"

"Yes, that kind of thing."

"It just so happens that a friend of mine is in the garden ornament business, and he's about to retire. I know he's trying to get rid of all his stock. I'm sure he'll have something that would be just perfect for you."

"I'm afraid we're on rather a tight budget."

"Don't worry about that. It won't cost you a penny."

"Really?"

"Yes. He just wants it all gone. Would you like me to

Jack and I eventually opted for the afternoon tea for two, which as it turned out was more than enough for the three of us.

"These sandwiches are yummy, Mummy. Why don't you make these at home?"

"I didn't know you liked salmon."

"I do." And to prove it she shoved half a sandwich into her mouth.

Flo spotted that we'd finished and came over to give us the bill.

"That was lovely," I said.

"Thanks. All the customers have been really nice so far."

The words were no sooner out of her mouth than who should walk through the door, but Grandma.

"Is there any chance of getting some service?" she demanded.

"I'll be with you in a moment," Flo said. "You can pay at the counter, Jill."

"Thanks."

Jack took Florence outside while I went to settle the bill. While I was waiting for Joe to come through from the kitchen, I heard a raised voice, and I didn't need two guesses who it was.

"No blackcurrant jam?" Grandma sighed. "How disappointing."

It was obvious that Flo was doing her best to placate her, but it was also obvious that Grandma was deliberately causing a fuss.

"Sorry to keep you waiting, Jill." Joe took my bill and credit card. "Things have been rather hectic."

completely over it now."

"Hmm."

"Mummy, can I have a strawberry milkshake like last time?"

"The tea room has new owners, so we'll have to see if they still do them."

The official opening of Peep Inside had taken place that morning, so by the time we got there, there were a number of tables free.

"Jill, I'm so pleased you could make it." Joe Peep was full of smiles. "What do you think of the place?"

"It's lovely. Very quaint. Although I did think you might have gone for a railway theme."

"To tell you the truth, I wanted to, but Flo insisted we keep the décor very simple."

"My ears are burning." Flo appeared at his side.

"I was just telling Jill that you wouldn't allow me to turn this place into a homage to the GWR."

"Much as I love Joe and the railways, I couldn't allow him to do that with this beautiful little tea room."

"I for one think it looks great," Jack said.

"Do you have strawberry milkshakes?" Florence asked.

"She's had one in here before," I explained. "But I warned her you might not still do them."

"What kind of tea room would we be if we didn't sell those?" Flo grinned. "Would you like cream on top?"

"Yes, please."

"Okay, why don't you grab a table. I'll get this young lady's milkshake while you two take a look at the menu and decide what you'd like."

The new menu had slightly more offerings than had been available under Ms Drinkwater's ownership, and world."

"I don't get it. Ghosts won't have money in the human world because, when they died, their assets would have been disposed of according to their Will. Or have I misunderstood what you're saying?"

"No, you're spot on."

"Okay, so what am I missing?"

"The customers they're targeting are ghosts that have connected to a member of their family who is still alive. From what I can make out, in order to be accepted on the program, you must have living relatives who agree to pay the exorbitant fees these crooks are demanding. Unfortunately, Jill, that seems to rule me out because I don't have any living relatives. At least, none I'm in contact with or who have that kind of money."

"That's a blow, but there still might be a way we can make this work."

"I don't see how."

"Can you leave it with me for a while, Colonel? There's someone I need to speak to."

"Of course. Give me a call."

***

Florence insisted on taking her two favourite beanies, Crystal (real name: Sunshine) and Rainbow (real name: Sprinkle), with her to the Peeps' tea room.

"What does it matter what she calls them?" Jack whispered. "They're *her* toys now."

"It doesn't. Why would you think it matters to me?"

"Because you cringe every time she uses their names."

"Because those aren't their names. Forget it. I'm

that happen?" Kathy turned to the two girls. "You two had better start putting the beanies back in the bags."

On the drive home, Florence was in seventh heaven, as she took one beanie after another out of the bag.

"I'm going to call this one Crystal."

"Its name is actually Sunshine."

"I like Crystal better. And this one will be Rainbow."

This was going to be even harder than I'd imagined.

Jack wasn't home when we got back, so I made sandwiches for Florence and me. Not that she was interested in eating. All she could think about was the beanies. When she'd finally managed to force down the sandwiches, she went up to her room, dragging the bags of beanies with her.

I had just taken a seat in the lounge when the temperature dropped, and the colonel appeared.

"Jill, I hope you don't mind me dropping in on you at home. I could see you were alone."

"It's fine. To be honest, I'm glad of the company. Would you like a drink?"

"That's very kind of you, but I can't stay. I've promised Cilla that we'll take a walk this afternoon. I just wanted to report back on those blighters at Restore."

"How did you get on? Better than my mother, I hope?"

"That remains to be seen. It appears to be rather more complicated than your mother assumed."

"How do you mean?"

"Whoever is behind this doesn't seem particularly interested in money that is held in GT."

"Now you've lost me."

"They're only interested in making money in the human

"Where would you go?"
"Can't we live in your car again?" Henry said.
"I didn't think you liked it in the glove compartment."
"We don't, but anything is better than this."
"I'm afraid that's not going to work."
"We can't stay here, Jill. This isn't what we signed up for."
"Okay, I hear you."
"What are you going to do about it?"
"I don't know. You'll have to give me a couple of days to come up with something."
"Promise you won't abandon us."
"I promise."
I was about to leave, but Henry hadn't done with me yet.
"It's not just us."
"What do you mean?"
"The two gnomes feel the same. When we told them that we were going to speak to you, they asked if you'd get them out of here too."
"How am I supposed to do that?"
"Please, Jill."
"Okay, okay. I'll do my best."
Sheesh!
I'd thought Kathy and I might have chance to catch up on each other's news, but I didn't get a look-in because it was beanie central. Eventually, I could take no more.
"Right, Florence, we'd better be making tracks."
"Already?" Kathy sounded disappointed. "You've only just got here."
"We've been here two and a half hours."
"Really?" She stared in disbelief at her watch. "How did

telling us what you were doing."

"I didn't like to bother you."

"I thought Pete was joking when he told me that you'd been caught on the CCTV."

Luckily, the two girls came running downstairs, and saved me from further interrogation.

"Look, Mummy, there's millions of them." She and Lizzie were each carrying a bag full of beanies. "Do you want to see them?"

It was obviously a rhetorical question because, without waiting for my reply, she tipped the bag's contents onto the floor. Lizzie did the same with her bag. Kathy immediately joined the two girls, and the three of them started to examine the beanies. Lizzie seemed particularly keen to show Florence the bizarre creatures that she and her mother had created in their laboratory of horror.

"While you three are doing that, I'm going to take a walk in the garden, if that's okay?"

"Are you feeling alright?" Kathy said.

"Yeah. I just thought I might get some ideas for our garden. It's looking a bit boring at the moment."

"You know what you need, don't you?"

"What's that?"

"Gnomes."

"I don't think so."

The three of them were engrossed with the beanies, so this was the perfect opportunity to check what Henry was up to. As soon as I stepped into the summerhouse, he and Henrietta were both on my case.

"You have to get us out of here," Henry said.

"We can't do anything now they've installed those." Henrietta pointed to the cameras.

"Morning."

"I assume Florence has told you about the beanies?"

"That you've decided to return the stolen property, you mean?"

"Wow! You always did know how to hold a grudge."

"How many of them are still in their original form?"

"What do you mean?"

"I mean how many haven't been ripped apart in order to create some Frankensteinesque monster?"

"Probably half."

"That's something, I guess."

"Would you like a coffee, grumpy?"

"Yes, please, but only if we can have it in the *orangery*."

"Has anyone ever told you that sarcasm doesn't become you?"

"No. Never."

The kids had gone upstairs, so while Kathy was making the coffee, I took a seat in the conservatory. I'd no sooner sat down than a sudden movement outside caught my eye. And yet, everything out there seemed to be still. Even the gnomes who normally waved to me were as still as statues—presumably worried they'd be caught on CCTV. I was just beginning to think I'd imagined it when I saw it again. Henry was waving frantically to me from the window of the summerhouse; he was clearly beckoning me to go over there.

"Where is it?" Kathy put the coffee on the table.

"Where is what?"

She pointed to my hand. "The ring that Jack bought you for your birthday?"

Oh bum! "I—err—had to take it in to get it resized."

"I still can't believe you came around here without

Chapter 13

It was Sunday morning, and we had a busy day ahead. When I say *we*, I actually mean *me* because Jack was gallivanting off to the golf course.

"I'm going to try to get back for two o'clock," he said. "I thought the three of us could check out the tea room this afternoon. I'll be interested to see what the Peeps have done with it."

"Don't you go overdoing it, Jack. I don't want you to do yourself a mischief."

"Sarcasm doesn't become you."

"Of course it does. It's my stock-in-trade."

"Is it time to go to Auntie Kathy's yet, Mummy?" So far that morning, Florence had asked me that question every five minutes since she'd climbed out of bed.

"Just about, yes."

"Yay! What will we carry all the beanies home in?"

"I'm sure Auntie Kathy will have a box or some bags."

"Daddy's going golfing now, pumpkin." Jack crouched down. "Give me a big kiss."

The quick kiss that Florence planted on his forehead was rather half-hearted because she was more interested in how quickly she could drag me out of the house.

"Look! Lizzie's there!" Florence yelled as we approached their house.

Peter's car was missing, so I parked on the driveway behind Kathy's. As soon as I'd opened the car door, Florence jumped out, and she and Lizzie went inside.

"Good morning, sis." Kathy stepped out of the house just as the kids ran inside.

baffled.

"Thanks. Is it time to go, Mummy?"

"It is, darling. Say goodbye to everyone."

As we made our way back to the old watermill, we passed a waste bin, into which Florence deposited her 'basket'.

"Why did you do that?"

"It was rubbish."

"It wasn't all that bad." It was.

"I don't want to go to basket-weaving anymore."

"I thought you liked it."

"It's no fun if I can't use magic. All that weaving in and out is boring."

No arguments from me there.

Florence? Michelle is over there."

"Okay." She went running over to the kids' table.

"And there's a spare seat next to Suzanne for you, Jill."

"Great, thanks."

When Suzanne spotted me, her face fell.

"Hello, Jill. I wasn't sure we'd see you again."

Which I'm pretty sure was code for *you're the worst basket-weaver in the world.*

"Well, here I am."

"Okay. I think maybe we should try you with something really simple today."

"That's probably best."

If proof were still needed that I wasn't cut out for basket-weaving, you had only to look at the thing lying in front of me on the table. For the last hour, I'd followed all of Suzanne's instructions to the letter. And yet, everyone else had the beginnings of a basket in front of them. I had what is known in the business as a hot mess.

"Never mind, Jill," Olga said. "I'm sure you'll get the hang of it in time. Shall we go and see how Florence has got on?"

"Sure."

I followed her to the kids' table where Michelle was telling the children it was time to call it a day.

"How did our little superstar do today, Michelle?" Olga said.

"Err, okay. Not quite as good as last time, but she'll get better, I'm sure."

Florence jumped up from the table and handed me her creation, which looked not dissimilar to mine.

"That's—err—very nice, Florence." Olga was clearly

"It doesn't sound like it. Anyway, they'll be back home tomorrow."

"Hmm."

"What's wrong?"

"Have you forgotten what Kathy and Lizzie have done to my beloved beanies? They turned them into Frankenstein monsters."

***

Florence was still buzzing about the beanies as we made our way across the village to the basket-weaving class.

"How many beanies does Lizzie have, Mummy?"

"I'm not sure. A lot. It might be better if you just brought two or three of them home."

"No! Lizzie said I can have all of them, and I've made space in my bedroom."

"Okay." I knew when I was beaten. "When we get to the basket-weaving class, there's no using magic this time."

"Aww—not fair."

"It is fair. None of the other children can use magic."

"Okay."

As soon as we entered the hall, Olga made a beeline for us.

"Hello, you two. Have you missed the basket-weaving as much as the rest of us?"

"I have," Florence said.

I realised Olga was waiting for my response.

"Absolutely. My Saturdays have been quite empty without it."

"Do you want to go and join the other children,

"Seems not, but they insist they're not going to allow themselves to become distracted this time."

"No soft furnishings, then?"

"Apparently not."

The fish and chips went down a treat, witnessed by the fact that everyone cleared their plates. I was just about to clear the table when I got a call from Kathy. Hopefully, she was going to tell me that they had to cancel our visit to their house the following day.

"Hey, Kathy."

"It's Lizzie, Auntie Jill."

"Oh? Is your mum okay?"

"Yeah. She's cleaning the gnomes."

"Right."

"Could I speak to Florence, please?"

"Sure." I held out the phone. "Florence, it's Lizzie."

"Hello?" Florence said, rather nervously. "Yeah. Yeah. Yes, please. Thank you. Bye." She turned to me and squealed. "Lizzie says I can have her beanies."

"Which ones?"

"All of them. She said she doesn't play with them anymore, so I can have them."

"That's great, pumpkin," Jack said. "You'd better go and tidy your bedroom to make room for them."

"Okay." She jumped down from the chair and went charging up the stairs.

"That was nice of Lizzie, wasn't it?" Jack said.

"Returning them to their rightful owner, you mean?"

"I can't believe you're still holding a grudge about that."

"I'm not."

"We thought about it, but we wanted this to be a brand new start. If we'd kept the old name, it wouldn't have felt like that."

"I wish you the very best of luck."

"I assume you don't still live in Smallwash? It's a long way to come for some fish and chips."

"No. We live in Middle Tweaking now. I'll make sure to tell everyone in the village that you're here."

"Thanks. That's very kind. I'll give you extra chips for that."

"Mmm, something smells nice." Jack took the fish and chips from me at the door.

"Did you get me a fish, Mummy?" Florence said.

"Of course I did, darling."

"Yummy. I love fish and chips."

"Daddy told me that Thomas was at the dance class this morning."

"Yes, he was."

"Was he naughty?"

"No. He didn't do any magic."

"That's good. Do you think he enjoyed it?"

"Don't know." She shrugged.

Jack dished out the food and we all sat around the table.

"Mmm, this fish is delicious," Jack said.

"You'll never guess who the chippy belongs to."

"Don't tell me it's your grandmother's. That woman is slowly taking over."

"No. It's Tish and Chip's."

"From Smallwash?"

"Yeah."

"I thought they were done with chippies."

Unfortunately, the owners of this new shop had let the side down by calling the shop Grange Fish & Chips. How very boring! Hopefully, their fish and chips would be better than their name.

When I stepped inside, I was in for a surprise because, behind the counter, were none other than Tish and Chip who had run the chip shop near us in Smallwash.

"Hello, you two. I thought you'd given up on the fish and chip business."

"Hi." Tish clearly recognised me from all the fish suppers I'd bought from her previous shop. "Not really, but we felt like we'd lost our way at Smallwash and needed a fresh start."

"We allowed ourselves to diversify too much," Chip said, as he poured a huge bucket full of freshly cut chips into the fryer. "I don't know if you remember, but we'd moved into soft furnishings."

"I always thought that was a bit of a strange decision."

"We did a few daft things like that. That's why we took a break, to give us time to decide what we wanted to do with our future. The weird thing is, we both came to the same conclusion: that we wanted to stay with the fish and chips."

"They're in our blood," Tish chipped in.

Chipped in—get it? Come on, that's comedy gold right there.

"We decided to start again, but this time it's strictly fish and chips only. Definitely no soft furnishings."

"That's a pity because I only called in to see if I could pick up some cushions." I laughed. "Just kidding. I'm surprised you didn't use your old name: Never Battered was brilliant."

I'd just got back to the car when Jack phoned.

"How's the Todfoster case going?"

"Okay. I've just finished. How was dancing?"

"You'll never guess who started there this morning."

"No idea. It must be someone from outside the village because all the little girls who live in Middle Tweaking are already enrolled."

"It's someone from the village."

"Who?"

"Thomas."

"No."

"Yes, I'm afraid so. Cindymindy was there to enrol him."

"Did he get up to any of his tricks?"

"No. To be fair, he was well behaved. He actually seemed to be enjoying himself."

"Let's hope it stays that way. What are we having for lunch?"

"That's one of the reasons I called. Have you seen the new chippy that's opened on the Grange Estate?"

"No, but then I haven't driven through there for a while."

"I thought you might call in there on your way home and grab some for lunch."

"Why not. I quite fancy fish and chips."

I took Jack and Florence's orders, then set off for the Grange Estate, which was a small village five miles from Middle Tweaking. I had been delighted to hear the news about the new chip shop because until then, the nearest one had been fifteen miles away.

I loved to see fish and chip shops with elaborate puns for their names; there were some absolute crackers.

Christine, but a little bird told me that Jill is actually a suspect, which is a crazy idea. Is that true?"

"Jack, I can't discuss that."

"I know. I know. But from what I can make out, the only reason Jill is in the picture is because she stepped out of the room just before Susan did, which is ridiculous. If I remember rightly, you had already left the room, and no one considers you to be a suspect."

"I really do have to go, Jack."

"Of course. Just tell me one thing, Christine, please. It might help Jill."

"What's that?"

"Were you in the loo with Susan and Jill? Did you see or hear what happened in there?"

"I wasn't in there. I only left the dining room to go outside for a cigarette." She opened the car door. "Sorry, but I really do have to go."

That was the exact opposite of the result I'd been hoping for. Either Christine Hoyle was an expert liar, or she really hadn't been the person in the occupied cubicle. Over the years I'd developed a sixth sense that told me if someone was lying, and it wasn't tingling. If it wasn't her, then who had been in the loo with us? When I (posing as Jack) had asked Christine if I was a suspect, she'd deliberately avoided the question, which confirmed what I already knew: They had made their minds up that I was the killer.

Great!

***

"Unfortunately, yes."

"The Jelly Monster is after me." Florence came giggling into the kitchen and shot off upstairs again.

"That daughter of yours can be very strange at times," I said.

***

I'd planned to use magic to gain access to West Chipping police station, in order to find Christine Hoyle's home address. As it turned out, I didn't need to do that because I'd just arrived at the police station when she came out of the side entrance and headed for the car park.

I couldn't simply walk over and start firing questions at her, so instead I cast the 'doppelganger' spell and made myself resemble someone she might be more willing to talk to.

"Jack? You made me jump." She took a step back from her car. "Where did you spring from?"

"Sorry, Christine. I was just on my way inside to see Robbie."

"Terrible business with Susan."

"I still can't believe it. Are they any closer to finding out who did it?"

"You know I can't discuss that, Jack."

"Sorry, of course. Old habits die hard."

"I didn't really get a chance to speak to you and your wife the other night. Her name is Jill, isn't it?"

"Yeah. I'm one lucky guy. They don't come any better. And she's so pretty, don't you think?"

"Err, yeah. Look, I mustn't keep you."

"I know you can't discuss the details of the case,

us?"

"For years now I've been telling him that the only reason he can't move in with us is that Florence is allergic to cat fur."

"She never has been."

"Duh! I know that, but Winky didn't until you and she turned up at the office yesterday."

"Right. And you don't think he'll buy that excuse any longer?"

"Not after she spent all that time hugging him."

"Why am I the one who has to come up with excuses?"

"Because I did it last time."

"And why do you need *three* of them?"

"Better to be safe than sorry."

"How long do I have?"

"Until I go to work on Monday."

"Run, everyone!" Florence came rushing down the stairs. "The Jelly Monster is coming!"

She went charging out the door into the garden.

"What's this Jelly Monster she keeps going on about?" Jack said.

"Beats me." I shrugged. "Hey, seeing as you're gallivanting off to play golf tomorrow, can you take Florence to dance class this morning?"

"Sure. What will you be doing?"

"I—err—have to do some work on the Todfoster case."

"Isn't that the case where you're getting paid for doing nothing?"

"Yes, but it's not quite *nothing*. I need to send Mr Todfoster my weekly report."

"Okay. What about basket-weaving? Will you be back for that?"

the details."

"Tell me what you know."

"They worked together in Shawtown, and from what I heard, they were good friends."

"And?"

"They had some kind of falling out."

"That was pretty obvious from the way they were glaring at one another at the dinner. What did they fall out about?"

"Like I said, I've only heard rumours."

"For goodness sake, Jack, just tell me what you heard."

"Okay. They were working together on a case and they had a disagreement about how to proceed."

"What case?"

"I don't know. Honestly. Anyway, Sushi prevailed, and it must have turned out she was right because, shortly afterwards, she was promoted."

"What about Hoyle?"

"From all accounts, she'd been expected to get that promotion."

"So there's bad blood between them?"

"I guess so."

"Does Christine still work in Shawtown?"

"No. The last I heard she was at West Chipping. Hang on. Does this mean you've been sticking your nose into Susan's murder?"

"No, of course not."

"You'd better not. It will only end badly."

Time to change the subject, methinks. "Jack, I need you to come up with three reasons why Winky can't come and live with us."

"Where did that come from? Why would he live with

Chapter 12

It was Saturday morning, and I was determined to find out more about the woman who had attended the dinner alone. If my suspicions were correct, she had been in the loo at the same time as Sushi and me, which meant she would have been alone with Sushi after I'd left.

Jack had just finished his muesli and was reading the newspaper.

"Don't you know it's rude to read at the table?" I said.

"That's rich coming from you."

"I never read at the table."

"You do realise that reading on your phone is still reading, don't you?"

"That's totally different. I can't even see your face behind that thing."

"Fine." He folded the paper and put it onto the table. "What would you like to talk about?"

"How are your team doing in the bowling league?"

He laughed. "Since when were you interested in my bowling?"

"I've always been interested."

"O—kay. We're in third position at the moment. If we manage to beat—"

"Who was that woman by herself at the dinner? The one who was seated opposite Sushi?"

"I thought you wanted to know about my bowling team?"

"I did. I do. Third spot is very good. So, who is she?"

"Her name is Christine Hoyle."

"What's the story with those two?"

"It all kicked off after I'd left the service, so I don't know seats. Everyone that is except Sushi who, by that point, was probably dead.

"Hmm."

At least with the computer operational again, I was able to look at the CCTV from the Red Lion. I started with the footage from the reception, but that wasn't particularly illuminating. The early part of the tape showed the staff signing in, and then later all the guests arrived.

I was much more interested in the footage taken from the dining room, which I whizzed forward to the point where everyone had just taken their seats around the table. Sushi and the woman who arrived late were glaring at one another, then Sushi's husband said something to her, which resulted in those two having heated words. The waitress and waiter appeared, and began to go around the table, taking everyone's orders. Nothing much happened for a few minutes, other than the inane chatter between Norman Whitelea and his guests.

Whether she was bored by the mundane conversation or simply desperate for a cigarette, the single woman stood up and left the room. Shortly afterwards, I too stood up and made my way out of the room, en route to the toilet.

A few minutes later, the two servers returned with the starters. It was while doing that, that the waitress spilled soup on Sushi, who stood up and began to berate the hapless woman.

A man, who I assumed to be the manager, intervened; he sent the waitress, who was clearly upset, out of the room. His efforts to try and placate Sushi had obviously fallen on deaf ears because she stormed out. Shortly afterwards, Sushi's husband stood up and left the room too. Where had he gone?

Over the next few minutes, everyone returned to their

"It's already done. In a manner of speaking."

"What does *in a manner of speaking* mean? Is it working or not?"

"It certainly is."

"What was wrong with it?"

"It's what we in the trade call NPI."

I hated people who spoke in acronyms. "What does that stand for?"

"Not. Plugged. In."

"What? Of course it was plugged in."

"Nah, it wasn't. The plug was still hanging in the socket, but just barely. I pushed it in properly and Bob's your uncle. So, the good news is there are no parts to pay for."

"Good."

"And no labour either. I can hardly charge you for pushing in a plug, can I?"

"That's very kind of you."

"It'll just be the call-out charge."

"How much is that?"

"Fifty quid."

"Fifty pounds? Just for turning up?"

"Plus VAT, of course."

As soon as the computer guy had left, Winky came out from under the sofa with a huge grin on his face.

"Don't say a word," I said.

"I wouldn't dream of it. I was just going to ask which bright spark forgot to check the plug?"

"Did you pull it out?"

"Of course I didn't. It was probably Mimi. That cat has a vindictive streak."

"Barry, it's Jill Maxwell."

"Jill. I was hoping we might hear from you before the weekend. Do you have any news for us?"

"I do and I'm pleased to report it's good news. You won't be getting any more trouble from the man at DOPA."

"Are you sure about that?"

"Positive."

"That's excellent news. How did you manage it?"

"Let's just say I 'persuaded' him not to trouble you again."

"I must say I'm very impressed. If you let us have your bill, I'll make sure it's paid immediately."

"I'll do that."

Back at the office, Mrs V pointed to my office door. "The computer man is here."

"That was quick. Has he been here long?"

"Only a couple of minutes."

"Can you send an invoice to those three gentlemen who were here earlier in the week? Charge them for one day at the usual rate."

"Will do. What shall I put down for the description?"

"Err—put *privacy protection*."

"Right you are."

The computer guy wasn't exactly breaking into a sweat. In fact, he'd made himself comfortable in my chair, with his feet on the desk, and he was staring at his phone.

"Hello, love, are you the boss?"

"Yes. Jill Maxwell. Shouldn't you be trying to repair that?"

sure if his office was in the city centre, or if he was on his way to his car.

I had my answer when he walked into the multi-storey car park. I continued to follow him in the hope that his car would be parked in a quiet spot with no one around. Instead of taking the stairs, he headed straight for the lift. When the doors opened, he stepped back to allow an elderly man to exit. As soon as Charlie stepped inside, I followed. When the doors closed, there were just the two of us in there.

"Hello, Charlie."

"Oh, hello. Aren't you—?"

I didn't have any time to waste, so I held out my phone and showed him the photo of my three clients.

"I'm sorry. I don't understand. Who are these gentlemen?"

I quickly cast the 'ignore' spell, which I'd found on my app shortly after the visit from Harry, Barry and Gordon.

"You will ignore these gentlemen from now on. Is that clear?"

"I will ignore these gentlemen."

"You have no interest in them and will not pursue them for any reason."

"I have no interest in them and will not pursue them for any reason."

"That's very good, Charlie." The lift doors opened. "This is where you get out."

"Right."

As soon as he'd stepped out, I pressed the button to take me back to ground level.

Now, that's what I call a result. Once I was outside, I made a phone call.

get it from her.

Wow! My luck was in, for a change.

As I approached the shop, I saw that Charlie was in there, talking to Rita. That called for a quick change of plan, and as you know, I'm nothing if not nimble on my feet. I hurried across the road, and pretended to look in the window of the shop directly opposite. In fact, I was simply looking at the reflection so I could see when Charlie came out.

"Has anything caught your eye?" said a strange little man who had just poked his head out of the shop.

"I—err—" It was only then that I realised I was staring at a window full of model kits. This had to be the shop that Jack had been so excited about.

"The Hawker Hurricane is one of our most popular lines." He came over and stood right next to me, which blocked my view of the shop opposite.

"Err, no. I don't think so. What about that one?" I pointed to the far side of the window in the hope that he'd move out of my line of vision.

"The Bristol Blenheim? Also, very popular. Would you like to come inside and take a closer look?"

Just then, Charlie came out of the shop opposite.

"I—err—I have to get back to work. Maybe I'll call in later."

"We close at six. Shall I put the Blenheim to one side for you?"

"Err, if you like."

"I usually ask for a ten percent deposit, Ms—?"

I was already on my way up the high street. I didn't want Charlie to spot me, so I stayed on the opposite side of the road and followed him at a distance. I wasn't even

My main doubt was the length of time since the conviction. Would he really wait so long to make a move?

The second article was more promising and related to a man recently released from prison. Carl Harper had been released on licence after serving ten years of a fifteen-year sentence for manslaughter. The Harper case had been one of the first Sushi worked on after being promoted to detective. On checking through the archives for information about the original trial, I found another article that reported he had also made death threats to Sushi. Harper was reported to be living in the Norwich area.

There were several other articles, but none which specifically mentioned threats to Sushi. One of them was about a murder case which had fallen apart in court, with the result that the accused was acquitted. Clearly bitter at the outcome, Sushi was reported as saying that they were not looking for anyone else in connection with the enquiry. Yet another article reported the death of a man in prison. He had been three years into a twenty-year sentence following his conviction for murder. His daughters were said to be inconsolable at their father's death, following what they described as a gross miscarriage of justice.

***

I decided to take a walk down the high street to On A Sixpence. I needed to find Rita's husband, Charlie, so I could 'dissuade' him from harassing my three clients: Harry, Barry and Gordon. I doubted Rita would voluntarily tell me the address of her husband's super-secret offices, but I was hoping that a little magic might

"Will do. I'd better get back or Cilla will be accusing me of chasing the ladies again."

With no computer, I couldn't check the CCTV, but there was another angle I could explore. I needed to find out who might have a motive to kill Sushi. Someone with a grudge against her.

In her job, Sushi would inevitably have made her fair share of enemies. Perhaps someone she had put behind bars had recently been released. Or maybe, a friend or relative of someone she had recently sent to prison was out for revenge.

I did a search on my phone for Detective Susan Shay. There were dozens of articles, most of which were from within the last week and covered her murder. By changing the search criteria, so that the results were in reverse date order, I came across several entries which pre-dated her death. Most of them were trivial, but a few did catch my eye. The first was dated almost four years ago and came from the Shawtown Herald. Sushi had transferred from Washbridge to Shawtown about a year before that. The article was about the conviction of Dave 'The Sword' Fisher who had been jailed for life for the murder of a man called Ricky Harrow, in what was described as a gangland killing. Sushi had been the lead detective on the case, and according to the article, Dave Fisher's brother had had to be restrained when the verdict was read out. He was reported to have shouted, "You're dead, Shay!"

It's true that many empty threats are made in courtrooms, but given the reputation of the Fisher brothers, this was something that I needed to check out.

"I'd just taken a seat at my desk when my phone pinged with a message from Ava Todfoster. It was a photo of her taken at the beautician where she appeared to be having a pedicure. As usual, I forwarded it to her husband.

Restore's rejection of my mother's application was a setback, but a great P.I. always has a backup plan.

What do you mean, that's all well and good, but what did *I* intend to do? Cheek! I'll have you know that I was voted best P.I. in Washbridge and surrounding districts. By whom? A popular magazine, but not one you would have heard of.

As I was saying, it was time to go to Plan B.

"Colonel? It's Jill."

"Hello there, young lady. It's not very often I get a call from you. Is everything okay?"

"Everything's fine. I was wondering if you might have some spare time soon for a quick chat?"

"How does right now sound?"

"It sounds great. Are you sure you aren't busy?"

"Positive. Cilla has just gone to the hairdressers, so I'm at a bit of a loose end for the next hour or so. Hang on. I'll be with you in a jiffy."

And so he was, but not before Winky had scooted off under the sofa.

"Thanks for popping over, Colonel."

"No problem at all. What is it I can do for you?"

I told him about the Restore scam and how my mother had tried to sign up but had been turned away. "I thought you would have a much better chance of being accepted."

"I'm sure I'll be able to persuade those bounders to let me sign up."

"Great. Here's the info. Let me know how you get on."

Chapter 11

I'd decided to try again with the CCTV footage from the Red Lion, but when I switched on the computer, it was as dead as a dodo.

Great! Just great!

"Mrs V, my computer isn't working."

"Oh dear. Would you like me to take a look at it for you?"

"Do you know anything about computers?"

"No, but I mended my sister's sewing machine when I was down there. How much more difficult can it be?"

"Don't we have a business card for a computer techie type guy? I seem to remember he called in on spec a few months ago."

"Let me take a look." She pulled open her drawer and took out a handful of business cards. "Michael Green – Vermin control, Sadie Newton – Office stationery, Kevin Tong – Watercoolers. I still think you should have bought one of those."

"Focus, Mrs V. Is there one for a computer guy?"

"Right. Alan Dale – Office cleaning. I really think that would—"

"Mrs V!"

"Sorry. Here it is: Warren Nerding – All things IT."

"Would you give him a call and get him to come out and look at my computer ASAP?"

"Is that the model?"

"Is *what* the model?"

"ASAP?"

"No, Mrs V. That's ASAP, as in as soon as possible."

"Of course. Silly me. I'll get right on it."

"I love goldfish. I could watch them for hours."

"I'm not sure."

"Come on. You've said all along that if it wasn't for Florence's allergy I could live with you."

"Did I? I don't remember."

"Yes, you do. Those were your exact words. You're not going to go back on it now, are you?"

"I'll have to speak with Jack."

"Call him now."

"I can't. He'll be in the cinema. I'll speak to him over the weekend and let you know what he says on Monday."

"Promise?"

"You have my word."

This scenario was all my nightmares rolled into one. The idea of Winky living with us didn't bear thinking about, but how could I get out of it?

"Didn't you ask?"

"Of course I did, but they gave me some mealy-mouthed answer about not being able to disclose that for commercial reasons."

"How can they possibly know if you can't afford it if they won't even tell you the cost?"

"I asked the same question, but they just closed down the conversation. I should have lied about my finances. Maybe then, I'd have been accepted."

"Never mind. Thanks for trying, anyway."

"What will you do now?"

"Don't worry. I'll think of something."

When I ended the call I realised that Winky was still staring at me, tapping his paw impatiently. "I'm still waiting."

"For what?"

"An explanation as to how your daughter, who is supposedly allergic to cat fur, just spent five minutes hugging me without so much as a sniffle or a sneeze."

"What can I tell you? It's clearly a miracle. The doctor did say that she might grow out of it one day, and it looks like she has."

"Hmm." He could not have looked any less convinced. "You know what this means, don't you?"

Only too well. "No. What?"

"It means I can come and live with you at the old watermill."

"If only it was that simple."

"Why isn't it?"

"Because we now have a dog living in the house."

"So what? I can get along with dogs when I have to."

"And two goldfish."

Donna and Wendy there."

"We're going to see The Elephant's Jewel, Mummy." Florence was still stroking Winky who was lapping it up.

"That sounds great. I wish I could come with you."

"Can't you skive off work for a few hours?" Jack said.

"I can't. I'm snowed under at the moment."

"Come on, Florence." Jack took her hand. "Or we'll miss the start of the film."

"Bye, you two. Enjoy your film."

"See you tonight." Jack gave me a peck on the cheek. "And don't go doing anything stupid."

"What a lovely little girl," Winky said after they'd left.

"Isn't she just?"

"Don't you find it rather strange, though?"

"Find *what* rather strange?"

"How she could hug me like that without bringing on an allergic reaction. What with her being allergic to cat fur and all."

Oh bum!

Luckily, my phone rang and rescued me from Winky's ire. If only temporarily.

"Jill, it's your mother."

"Hi. How did you get on with Restore?"

"I didn't."

"Why not? You promised you'd contact them."

"And I did, but they don't want to know me."

"How come?"

"They asked a lot of questions, including about my finances. They didn't say as much, but I got the distinct impression I'm not wealthy enough for them."

"How much does it cost?"

"I don't actually know."

There was no point in worrying about The Bugle article, so I took out the DVD that Surefoot had given me and put it into the computer. I was just about to start watching it when the door to my office opened and in walked Jack and Florence. If Jack had seen that I was looking at CCTV footage from the Red Lion, he would have gone crazy, so in a panic, I switched off the computer.

"Surprise, Mummy!" Florence came running over and gave me a big hug.

"How come you aren't in school?"

"It's insect day, silly."

"She means *inset*, and I did tell you about it," Jack said.

"Oh yeah. Sorry, I forgot. This is a lovely surprise."

"What a cute cat!" Florence squealed and ran over to give Winky a big hug.

"I called to warn you about the article in The Bugle," Jack glanced at the newspaper on my desk. "But I can see you've already read it."

"It's outrageous. I've a good mind to go around to their offices and kick a few butts."

"That would only make things worse. If you ignore it, it'll all be forgotten within a few days."

"Someone must have fed them this information, and we know who that is, don't we?"

"Don't go jumping to any conclusions, Jill."

"I'd bet good money that this is the work of Leo Riley or Big Mac."

"You can't know that for sure."

"You didn't come into town just to tell me about the newspaper article, did you?"

"No. I'm taking Florence to the cinema. We're meeting

Back at the office, Winky was seated on the windowsill.

"How goes it, wuss?" I said.

"I wasn't really scared of those mice."

"You could have fooled me."

"It was just an act. I wanted Mimi to think she'd got one over on me."

"From where I was standing, she got *two* over on you. First, you try to embarrass her by planting mice at her apartment, but she comes out of it smelling of roses. Then she gets the pleasure of seeing you wuss out."

"At least I'm not the one looking at serious jail time."

"What are you talking about?"

"I take it you haven't seen this morning's paper?"

"No. Why?"

He jumped down from the windowsill, disappeared under the sofa, and came back out clutching a copy of The Bugle. "Police home in on suspect in detective murder case."

"Let me see that." I snatched the paper from his paws. "I don't believe this!"

The headline he'd just read was accompanied by a photo of me. I had to sit down while I read the full article.

"I should sue them."

"Good luck with that." Winky grinned. "They don't actually say you're the suspect."

"No, but it's my photo next to the article."

"But the caption reads: *Jill Maxwell was one of the guests at the dinner that night*. The way they've done it is quite clever if you think about it."

"I'm glad you're impressed. Meanwhile, this article makes me look as guilty as hell."

then we should be out of your hair for good."

"Okay. What do you need?"

"Copies of the CCTV footage from the night of the incident."

"I don't understand. I gave a copy to your colleagues who were here before."

"Unfortunately, those copies have become corrupted. I take it you still have the original?"

"Of course, but as I explained to your colleagues, it doesn't cover the corridor where the toilets are. We only have CCTV from the main dining room and the reception area."

"That's fine."

"It may take me a few minutes to make copies. I could get someone to drop it by the police station later to save you having to wait."

"I'd prefer to take it with me."

"As you wish."

He turned to the receptionist. "Veronica, would you make a drink for the police officer, please. And bring through a selection of our cakes."

"That's very kind of you," I said.

One cup of tea, a slice of angel cake and a chocolate éclair later, Surefoot returned with the discs. "Is there anything else you need?"

"No, just these. Oh wait, there is one more thing. I wouldn't want the tech people who caused the previous disk to corrupt, to get into trouble, so I'd appreciate it if you didn't mention this to the boss if she comes around."

"No problem. I wouldn't want to get anyone the sack."

***

"Aarghh!" Winky screamed. "Get those horrible creatures out of here!"

What an absolute wuss that cat of mine was. He refused point blank to get off the sofa until I'd caught and removed all the mice.

***

According to Jack, the police had released the scene of Sushi's murder. When he'd mentioned it, I'd pretended to be uninterested because I didn't want to alert him to what I had planned. He definitely would not have approved.

Although I say it myself, I do look good in a uniform.

I'd parked my car just down the road from the Red Lion restaurant, and after making sure no one was around, I'd magicked myself into the uniform of a police constable.

"Good morning, officer," said the woman on reception.

"Good morning. Would you tell the manager I'd like a word with him, please?"

"Certainly." She picked up the phone. "Mr Surefoot, I have a police officer in reception. She'd like to speak to you." The receptionist replaced the receiver and turned to me. "He'll be through in a minute."

Ironically, Mr Surefoot almost tripped over his own feet as he walked into reception.

"Good morning. I'm Terry Surefoot." He offered his hand. "I thought your people had everything they needed."

"Indeed we have, Mr Surefoot."

"Please call me Terry."

"I'm just here to clear up a few loose ends, Terry, and

"Is one of you going to tell me what happened or do I have to throw you both out onto the street?"

"I'll tell you, Jill," Mimi said. "And I apologise for the disturbance, but I'm sure you'll understand when I explain."

"I'm listening."

"This pathetic excuse for a feline released a box full of mice in the apartment where I live."

"All lies," Winky said. "Don't listen to her."

"Carry on, Mimi."

"Can you imagine what that could have done to my reputation as a mouser, Jill? The two-leggeds might have lost all confidence in me."

"What do you mean, *might have*?" Winky laughed. "I bet they're looking for your replacement as we speak."

"And that's where you're wrong because, as always, Winky, you underestimated me."

"What do you mean?"

"The two-leggeds did see the mice, but they also saw me catch them in double-quick time, with the result that instead of being trashed, my reputation has been enhanced."

"You're lying." Winky looked totally deflated.

"You know that I'm not."

"I think you should apologise to Mimi," I said.

"Never!"

"It's alright, Jill. I don't need his apology. In fact, to show there's no ill feeling, I've even brought him a little present." She jumped down behind my desk, then reappeared with a small box. "These are for you, Winky." She opened the box and three little mice dashed out. "Bye, Jill." And with that, she disappeared out of the window.

them attempted to make eye contact with me.

But my motto has always been if at first you don't succeed, try, try again. "You seem to be struggling with that thing. Can I give you a hand?"

"No!" The shorter man snapped. "Stay back!"

Charming! Something told me these were not going to be good neighbours.

Five minutes later, the two men had finally got the box to the top of the stairs and started down the corridor.

"What is it you guys do?" I shouted after them.

They did not respond.

"Good morning, Mrs V. You were right about our new neighbours."

"They are undertakers?"

"No. At least, I don't think so. I meant about them being rude. I tried to engage them in conversation, but they blanked me. I even offered to help them carry their box upstairs, but they weren't interested. Why can't we have some nice normal neighbours for a change?"

Before Mrs V could respond, there was the horrific sound of two cats going at it in my office.

"Whatever is going on in there?" Mrs V said.

"Stay here. I'll sort it out."

Winky was standing on the sofa; Mimi was sitting on my desk. Their gazes were locked together as they threw a stream of insults at one another.

"That's enough!" I had to yell in order to get their attention. "What on earth is going on in here?"

"Why don't you ask him?" Mimi said.

"Winky?"

"She just can't take a joke."

"How can you call that a joke?"

"When I came over the other day, I reckon it must have slipped off my finger."

"Why didn't you say something?"

"I didn't realise I'd lost it at the time."

"I mean when you came over last night, why didn't you knock on the door and tell us what you were doing?"

"I didn't like to disturb you."

"Did you find it?"

"Yes, thanks. It's safely back on my finger."

"It looked to me like you were talking to the gnomes and elves."

"What?" I laughed. "Of course I wasn't. That would be crazy. What's that, Jack? Okay, I'm coming. Sorry, Kathy, I have to go. See you on Sunday."

While I'd been talking to Kathy, Jack had been sitting at the kitchen table, desperately trying not to laugh. As soon as I ended the call, he let it all out. "Priceless! She must think you're a total nutjob."

"As if she didn't already."

***

When I arrived at my office building, I found two men struggling to carry a large wooden box up the stairs. Judging by their attire (very undertaker chic), they must have been the same men Mrs V had encountered the other day. She'd told me that they had blanked her, but then she didn't really have my winning personality.

"Good morning, gentlemen. My name is Jill Maxwell. It seems we are to be neighbours."

The taller of the two made some kind of grunt, which was more than his colleague could manage. Neither of

Chapter 10

The next morning, I left my phone on the kitchen table while I nipped upstairs to check what Florence was up to.

"Are you alright under there, darling?" I had to get down on all fours to see under the bed.

"Me and humpy are hiding from the monster."

"Which monster?"

"The Jelly Monster. It's big and green and full of jelly." She giggled. "Be careful it doesn't get you."

"O—kay."

"You can get under here with us if you like, Mummy."

"I can't because I have to go to work. Try not to bump your head when you come out."

When I got downstairs, Jack was on *my* phone. "No, I have no idea. Yes, it does sound a little strange. She's here now. I'm sure she'll be able to explain. I'll pass you to her." He handed me the phone and mouthed, "Kathy."

"Hi."

"What were you up to last night, Jill?"

"Nothing much. Just watching TV."

"I mean what were you up to in our back garden?"

Oh bum, and quadruple bum! How had she seen me?

"I—err."

"We checked the CCTV this morning, and imagine our shock when we saw you on it."

"You've had it installed already?"

"Yes, a couple of days ago. So? What were you up to?"

"I—err—I was looking for my ring. The one Jack gave me for my last birthday. You remember it."

"No, I don't, but never mind that. Why would it be in our garden?"

had expected Henry and Henrietta to be in the summerhouse, but they were standing next to one another in front of it.

"Hi, you two. I just wanted to warn you that my sister is having CCTV installed soon, so no more night-time shenanigans."

Neither of them responded. It was almost as though they'd lost the ability to speak, but I didn't have time to worry about that because Kathy or Peter might appear in the conservatory at any moment. It was time for me to skedaddle.

Don't you just love that word? I should definitely skedaddle more often.

goodness only knows what it might catch Henry and Henrietta getting up to." I stood up and made for the door. "I shouldn't be long."

"Don't worry. I'll tell you what happens."

I'd parked a couple of streets away from Kathy's house, so they wouldn't spot my car. I had considered using the 'invisible' spell, but then the gnomes and elves wouldn't have been able to see me, and I didn't want to make them jump in case they did something that would get them noticed. The darkness should give me enough cover to get into the back garden, long enough to deliver my warning, and get out again. The only potential problem was if Kathy, Peter or the kids were in the conservatory.

The light was on in the lounge and the curtains were drawn, so hopefully Kathy and Peter were in there. The kids would most likely be in their bedrooms, which were also on the front of the house. So far, so good. After sneaking down the side of the house, I peered around the back to check the conservatory; it was in darkness. Result!

The two gnomes were standing side by side under the tree.

"Hey, guys, it's me. Jill."

No response.

"Listen, I wanted to warn you that my sister is having CCTV installed soon, so you're going to have to curtail your night-time activities."

Still nothing.

"Did you hear me?"

They still didn't respond. I wasn't sure what I'd done to upset them, and I didn't have time to worry about it. I'd delivered the message and that was all that mattered. I

me.

"If you come any closer, I'll do it again."

"Ricky, come on." Cindymindy took hold of his arm. "Let's go."

They'd no sooner left than Jack came out of the kitchen. "That was hilarious."

"You heard all of that, I take it?"

"I was peeping through the gap in the door. Do you think it will do any good?"

"We can only live in hope."

***

I found it hard to take movies about the paranormal serious these days. The depiction of witches, vampires, werewolves and the like were ridiculous. It occurred to me that I should offer my services as a consultant on such films, but it might be difficult to explain how I was qualified to provide such a service. I mention this only because we were watching a new series which, inexplicably, Jack had fallen in love with.

"Why are we watching this nonsense?" I sighed.

"It's good. The king of the vampires is about to lose his throne."

"Why do you care? Why would *anyone* care?"

"Shush! Isn't there something else you can be doing?"

"No, there—oh bum!"

"What?"

"I've just remembered I need to go over to Kathy's to warn the gnomes and elves that she's having CCTV installed. Otherwise, they're likely to be caught on camera, moving around and talking to one another. And

"Please, Jack."

"Okay, but don't make things even worse."

Cindymindy was standing at the door with a small cardboard box in her hand.

"Have you bought me a present?" I said. "You really shouldn't have."

"Change him back!"

"I'm sorry? Change who back to what?"

"You know very well what I mean." She pulled open one of the box's flaps, and the rat poked his nose out.

"What a lovely rat. What do you call him?"

"You've had your fun. Now change Ricky back."

"Not a chance."

"But you can't leave him like this forever."

"I think you'll find I can." I began to close the door.

"Wait. Please, Jill, you have to change him back."

"I'll do it, but only if you give me your word that you and Ricky will start to take your parenting responsibilities seriously. Specifically, that you'll stop Thomas using magic at school."

"But it isn't that easy. Thomas doesn't always listen to us."

"You're going to have to find a way to make him listen. Stop his pocket money. Confiscate his game console. Do whatever it takes to make him take notice."

"Okay, we'll try. I promise."

"You'd better step inside and put the box down. I wouldn't want to scare any of our neighbours."

Once she'd placed the box on the floor, I reversed my spell, and Ricky reappeared; he was only marginally better looking than the rat.

"How dare you do that to me?" He took a step towards

then Ricky said, "There's nothing to be done. Boys will be boys. A bit of fun never hurt anyone."

"That's where you're wrong." After a quick check to make sure there was no one else around, I cast the spell.

"What did you do?" Cindymindy yelled. "You've turned Ricky into a rat!"

"You'd better grab him before he runs away."

"But I hate rats."

"Please yourself."

"You think you're so clever, don't you, but I'll just turn him back."

"Good luck with that." As I walked away, Cindymindy was trying desperately to reverse my spell, but she simply wasn't powerful enough. "If you'd like to talk about the Thomas situation, you know where to find me."

***

We'd finished dinner and Florence had gone upstairs to play in her 'den'. This new game involved her sliding under our bed and squeezing in amongst the various boxes that were under there.

"I wish you'd tell me what happened with Cindymindy," Jack said as he started to load the dishwasher.

"You'll find out soon enough, I'm sure."

"I hope you haven't done something I'll regret."

Before I could reply there was a knock at the door. "I wonder who that could be?" I grinned. Jack made to follow me into the hallway, but I put up my hand. "Wait here."

"But I—"

"What happened?"

"They cleared the classroom and then sent texts to all the parents, asking them to come and pick their child up early. Miss Hope said they were calling in a plumber."

"This can't go on."

"I don't see what we can do about it."

"Just watch me." I started for the door.

"Where are you going?"

"Where do you think? To see Cindymindy."

"Don't do anything rash."

I didn't bother using the ridiculous broom-shaped knocker. Instead, I hammered on the door as hard as I could with my fist.

Cindymindy was wearing a weird green facemask and looked as though she was feeling seasick.

"I wondered how long it would be before you turned up," she said through a mouthful of gum.

"This has to stop, and it has to stop now!"

Ricky appeared at her side, dressed as usual in his string vest and shorts. "What's up?"

"Miss nosey-parker is here again, lover." Cindymindy planted a kiss on his lips.

It was truly nauseating.

"My daughter and the rest of the class were sent home early today thanks to that son of yours."

"No need to thank us," Cindymindy said. "I bet the kids were made up to get out early. I would have been when I was at school."

"I don't doubt that for one minute. What do you intend to do about this situation?"

The two of them looked at one another, grinned and

moment, so I'll call it a day and see you shortly."

"Skiving off again?" Winky said, as I tidied away the papers on my desk.

"I'm the boss. I can leave whenever I like." I went through to the outer office. "I'm going home, Mrs V. Something has cropped up at school."

"Is Florence okay?"

"Yeah, she's fine. There's been some trouble with one of the little boys. I'm sure it's nothing. I'll see you in the morning."

***

"He did what?" I said much louder than I'd intended.

"Shush!" Jack put his finger to his lips. "I don't think we should let Florence hear us discussing this."

"Where is she?"

"In her bedroom with Wendy. The last time I looked, they were playing with the dolls' house. Let's go through to the lounge."

"Hey, you!" Wanda shouted. "I have a complaint."

"It'll have to wait. I have more important fish to fry."

"What a terrible thing to say to a fish."

"Sorry, I didn't mean—it's just a saying. I have something urgent to attend to at the moment."

"Charming." The fish turned her back on me.

"What's up with Wanda?" Jack asked.

"Never mind her. Let me get this straight; are you telling me that Thomas made it rain in the classroom?"

"Yes. According to Florence, he used the 'rain' spell."

"Did Florence get wet?"

"No. Apparently, he only made it rain on the teacher."

he simply watched the ball bounce down the slope.

Fifty minutes later, we made our way back to Aunt Lucy's house. I was exhausted after having walked up and down the park a dozen times.

"That was fun, wasn't it, Jill?" Barry said.

"It was great, but it might have been even better if you'd fetched the ball occasionally."

"When can we do it again?"

"I'll have to see. I'm really busy at the moment."

Aunt Lucy was standing in the front garden waiting for us. "Did you enjoy that, Barry?"

"It was great. Jill is really good at throwing the ball."

"I've put your dinner out, boy."

"Yummy!" As soon as I unclipped his lead, he dashed past Aunt Lucy into the house.

"You could have warned me that he doesn't have a clue what to do."

"I could have, but that wouldn't have been as funny."

***

I spent the next couple of hours back at the office, catching up on paperwork. Yawn and double yawn.

Jack called, and I was expecting that to provide a welcome distraction, but I was wrong.

"Jill, there's been some trouble at the school. I thought I'd better let you know."

"What kind of trouble? Is Florence alright?"

"She's fine. It's that Thomas boy again."

"What has he done now?"

"It might be best if I tell you when you get back."

"Okay, there's nothing much happening here at the

"Steady on, boy!"

"Lucy told me that you have another dog."

"That's right. His name is Buddy."

"Is he like me?"

"No, he's nothing like you, Barry."

"Is he big or small?"

"He's tiny, but he has a lot to say for himself."

"Will you bring him to see me one day?"

"Maybe. We'll have to see."

Once we were in the park, I let Barry off the lead, and held up the ball. "Are you ready?"

"I'm ready. I'm ready." He was spinning around in anticipation.

I threw it as hard as I could. "Fetch it, boy!"

Barry didn't move. He simply turned and watched the ball bounce away, then said, "This is fun, isn't it, Jill?"

"Err, isn't this the bit where you go and fetch it?"

"*Fetch it*?"

"The ball."

"Okay." He didn't move.

Just then, my phone beeped with a text from Aunt Lucy which read:

Forgot to mention. Barry hasn't figured out he's supposed to fetch it.

The message ended with a smiley emoji.

"Do it again, Jill," Barry said.

"Err, okay." I walked down the park with Barry at my side, and collected the ball. "This time when I throw it, you have to run after it, pick it up and bring it back to me. Okay?"

"Yeah! Throw it."

I did, but still Barry didn't move from the spot. Instead,

there.

While I was in Candlefield I thought I may as well pay Aunt Lucy a visit. And, yes, I was hoping for a cup of tea. I would have had one in Cuppy C, but there was a long queue and no free tables.

"Jill, how lovely to see you. Cuppa?" Aunt Lucy gave me a hug.

"That would be nice."

I'd barely got through the door before Barry came charging down the stairs and pinned me to the wall.

"Jill! I haven't seen you for ages and ages."

"It hasn't been all that long."

"Have you come to take me for a walk?"

"I hadn't, but after I've had a cup of tea, I will."

"Yay!" He was so excited that he ran up and then back downstairs.

"You'll have to calm down first."

"I am calm." He ran back upstairs. "Promise." Then back down again.

By the time Aunt Lucy and I had finished our tea and cake, Barry was a little calmer (not much, but a little).

"Come on then, boy, let's go to the park." I fastened the lead to his collar.

"Wait, Jill," Aunt Lucy called after us. "You'd better take his ball."

"I didn't realise he had one."

"It's his favourite thing at the moment."

"I love my ball." Barry tried to grab it from my hand.

"Not yet. You can have it when we get to the park."

As always, Barry practically pulled me there. It took all my strength just to keep a hold of the lead.

This man was much more self-assured than the young man who'd been a permanent feature at Ma Chivers' side.

"You're right. I didn't. I'm trying to track down Ma Chivers, but no one seems to have any idea about where she is. I thought—"

"That I would know? Well, I don't. I've not seen her for more than three years."

"And you've had no contact since then?"

"None. One day she was here, the next *puff*! Gone!"

"Do you think something could have happened to her?"

"Don't know." He shrugged. "Do you ever see Alicia?"

"No. Not for years."

"I miss her." He sighed. "If you do happen to see her, will you tell her I asked after her?"

"Of course." I stood up. "Thanks anyway."

"Jill."

"Yes?"

"Did you know Ma Chivers has a son?"

"I didn't realise she had any children."

"His name is Orson."

"You don't happen to know where he lives, do you?"

"No, but the last I heard, he was working at Candlefield Museum. You could try there."

"I will. Thanks, Cyril."

***

Closed?

For reasons known only to them, the museum was only open six days a week. And wouldn't you know it, it was closed on Thursdays. Still, at least Cyril had been able to give me a lead. Hopefully, Ma Chivers' son still worked

Chapter 9

I was still fuming about the visit from Dawn Brakes (seriously, what kind of stupid name is that?) when my phone rang.

"Jill, it's Amber."

"Why are you whispering?"

"He's here."

"Who's where?"

"Cyril. He's in the tea room."

"Okay, thanks. I'll be straight over."

Cuppy C was much busier than usual, which I suspected was down to Bobby. I saw several people clutching signed photographs of the cute little dragon.

"He's over there!" Pearl gestured.

When the twins had told me that Cyril had put on a few pounds, they hadn't been exaggerating. If I'd seen him on the street, I'm not sure I would have recognised him. I had no idea what kind of reception I was going to get because we'd hardly been bosom buddies in the past.

"Cyril?"

He looked up from his cup of hot chocolate. "Yes?"

"You probably don't remember me, but I'm—"

"Of course I remember you. Who could forget the great Jill Maxwell?" His tone was more sarcastic than aggressive, which gave me a glimmer of hope.

"Do you mind if I join you?"

"It's a free country."

I took the seat opposite him. "How have you been keeping, Cyril?"

"I'm sure you didn't come over here to ask about my health or to make small talk."

"Why else would the door be closed?"

Ignoring my question, she stood up. "Thank you for your time, Jill. I really do appreciate it."

"My pleasure."

She started for the door, but then hesitated. "Just one more thing. I've been told by Leo Riley and others that you have a habit of—how shall I say this—inserting yourself into live police investigations. I must ask you not to do that this time."

If she was expecting a response, she was to be disappointed.

"I don't think she's a fan," Winky said, after she'd left.

"The feeling is mutual."

"So, did you?"

"Did I what?"

"Murder the Sushi-meister?"

present at the dinner, I've been brought in to oversee the investigation. I'm normally based in Lancashire."

"Okay."

"Cards on the table, Jill, it's been brought to my attention that you have not had the best of relationships with several of the people present at last night's meal, including Susan Shay."

"Was that a question?"

"Would you say that's a fair comment?"

"Yes."

"I understand your husband is ex-force too?"

"That's right. He's the only reason I was at the dinner."

"Of course. I believe that you went to the toilet a few minutes before Susan Shay."

"That's correct."

"What happened when she came into the loo?"

"She was angry because the waitress had spilled soup on her."

"Apart from that, did she say anything to you?"

"She expressed surprise that Jack and I were still together, and then she told me that I'd wrecked his career."

"That must have annoyed you."

"Not enough to kill her, if that's what you're insinuating."

"That's not what I meant."

"Susan Shay was fine when I walked out of the loo. You should be trying to find out who was in the other stall."

"Did you actually hear anyone in there?"

"No, I didn't."

"If you didn't see anyone, and didn't hear anyone, you can't be certain there was someone in there, can you?"

"That's for me to know and you to wonder."

My phone beeped; it was a photo of Ava taken in Washbridge library. After sending a quick acknowledgement to her, I tapped out a brief email to Richard and sent it with the photo attached. The Todfoster case was proving to be some of the easiest money I'd ever made.

***

Mrs V came through to the office and closed the door behind her.

"There's a Detective Brakes out there."

"What does he want?"

"It's a woman. She said she'd like to ask you a few questions about the incident at the Red Lion."

"You'd better send her in, I suppose."

Detective Brakes walked straight up to my desk and extended her hand. "Dawn Brakes. I'm very pleased to make your acquaintance, Mrs Maxwell."

Dawn Breaks? Seriously? Surely, she had to be taking the mickey.

"It's Jill. Have a seat."

"Thank you for seeing me. I know you must be busy."

This woman was being much too nice for my liking. If she thought her smarmy manner would get me to drop my defences, she had another think coming.

"Needless to say, I'd like to ask you a few questions about what happened at the Red Lion restaurant last night."

"What would you like to know?"

"First of all, I should explain that because of the people

"Young? Old?"

"In their fifties, I would say. Both very weird looking."

"Weird *how*?"

"They were dressed like undertakers. To tell you the truth, Jill, they gave me the creeps."

"That doesn't sound very promising."

"How was your dinner last night."

"Apart from the woman who was murdered in the loo? Okay, I guess."

"I assume you're joking?"

"I'm afraid not. Do you remember Sushi?"

"The lady detective?"

"Yeah. She was there with her husband. Someone bashed her over the head."

"How dreadful."

"That's not all. Muggins here is the prime suspect."

"Surely not. No one could believe you would do something like that."

"And yet, they do. It doesn't help that I was the last person to see her alive."

"What's going to happen?"

"I'm going to find out who the real murderer is."

"Is that wise?"

"Probably not, but I'm going to do it anyway."

"You're in deep trouble," I said to Winky who was sitting on the windowsill.

"What did I do this time?"

"Not with me. Mimi was in here yesterday and she was not a happy kitty."

He laughed. "Serves her right."

"What did you do?"

Town. Some scam artists have set up a company that supposedly offers to bring ghosts back to life."

"Surely no one would fall for that," Daze said.

"You wouldn't think so, but apparently several people have already handed over a small fortune."

"There's one born every minute."

"That reminds me of The Count," Blaze said. "Do you remember him, Daze?"

"Oh yeah. I'd forgotten about him."

"Who's The Count?" I said.

"A wizard who claimed he could bring the dead back to life. The guy was a complete headcase."

"What happened to him?"

"The last I heard, they'd committed him to an asylum somewhere near the Dark Forest."

"Can we get two flat whites, please?" said one of the two hipster types who had appeared behind me.

That was my cue to leave, so I said my goodbyes and headed off. It was only when I reached the office building that I realised I hadn't paid for the coffee.

Whoops!

Mrs V was practising her Morris dancing; this time, thankfully, minus the bells.

"Good morning, Jill. Tea?"

"No, thanks. I've just had a coffee from the van in the car park."

"Did you see the two men from down the corridor?"

"No. There wasn't anyone there just now."

"They arrived at the same time as I did. I tried to engage them in conversation, but they ignored me. Very rude if you ask me."

groaned. "Daze just stands there taking the orders."

"Are you going to make that coffee for Jill or not?" Daze snapped. "She has to get to the office."

"Coming right up." He pulled a face behind her back. A brave move considering Daze rarely missed anything.

"I take it this isn't a permanent career change for you two?"

"It isn't, although I could definitely get used to it. It's quite undemanding."

"For some," Blaze sniped.

"Ignore him, Jill. As you may have already guessed, we're working undercover on one of our more unusual assignments."

"We're after Big Foot." Blaze handed me my coffee. "There have been a number of reported sightings of him around these parts."

"Big Foot? Do you mean a yeti?"

"No, Jill, there are no such things as yetis. He's a werewolf, and they call him that because one of his feet is bigger than the other."

"Right. What's he wanted for?"

"He isn't a criminal. He's a missing person."

"How does someone that size go missing?"

"That's a very good question."

"How come you two are involved in a missing person case?"

"The official reason is that we know Washbridge better than the other rogue retrievers, but the real reason is that Big Foot is a cousin of our boss."

"Talking of weird jobs, I've landed a doozy."

"Weirder than Big Foot?" Blaze said.

"Yeah, I'd say so. I'm working for the police in Ghost

DVD, and then call the number at the end of the presentation."

"What shall I say?"

"That you're interested in their service and that you'd like to visit their offices to find out more."

"Then what?"

"Once you have an appointment, I'll fix you up with a mini-camera and mic so you can record what goes on in there."

"Like a spy?"

"Something like that." I stood up and put my empty plate in the sink. "I have to get back now. I'll wait to hear from you."

Like a spy? I was already beginning to have grave misgivings about this.

***

For the first time ever, there was a coffee van in the car park where I always left my car during the week. It would have been remiss of me not to take advantage.

As I approached the serving hatch, I recognised the person behind the counter.

"Daze?"

"Morning, Jill. I believe yours is a caramel latte, isn't it?"

"That's right. Thanks."

"Blaze, Jill would like a caramel latte."

"I'm not deaf. I heard her." He stepped forward to stand next to Daze. "Morning, Jill."

"Good morning, Blaze. I had no idea you two had trained as baristas."

"I'm the only one who had to do the training." He

"Yes, but that beauty spot is miles from anywhere, so by the time we'd found a pub and eaten our meal, it was time to come home. Anyway, enough of my woes, what did you want me for?"

"It might be easier for me to pop over and explain. Where are you at the moment? At the shop?"

"No, it's my day for a late start. I was just about to have breakfast. Have you eaten yet?"

"Not yet, no."

"If you come over now, I'll make you something."

"Okay."

Twenty minutes later, I was tucking into a fry-up.

"This is delicious. These sausages are fantastic."

"Alberto reckons he only married me for my fry-ups. What was it you wanted to talk to me about?"

I told her about 'Restore' and their claims to be able to bring ghosts back to life.

"How much does it cost? I'd definitely be up for that. Being a ghost isn't all it's cracked up to be."

"You're missing the point, Mum. It's a big con."

"How can you be so sure? What if some really clever person has come up with a way to do it?"

"Trust me, it's definitely a scam. Now, are you up for helping me put these crooks out of business?"

"Of course. What do you need me to do?"

I took out the promotional DVD and handed it to her. "Take a look at this."

"I don't have a DVD player."

"Don't you know anyone who does?"

"I think Blodwyn might have one."

"Okay, ask her if you can borrow it, take a look at the

Mummy." Before she stole them.

"Auntie Kathy showed me photos of them. They're really funny. They're a bit of one animal and a bit of another one."

"Hmm."

"She said I can go to their house and see them."

"Did she?"

"When can I go, Mummy?"

"I don't know. We'll have to see."

"Can we go on Saturday?"

"You've got dancing and basket-weaving on Saturday."

"Sunday."

"I'm not sure. We might all be doing something on Sunday."

"I'm golfing on Sunday," Jack said. "You two will have plenty of time to go to Kathy's."

"Thanks, Jack."

"Yay!" Florence did a happy jig.

Me? I wasn't in a jigging mood.

My phone rang; it was my mother.

"Blodwyn told me you called yesterday. You should have rung me on this number."

"It wasn't urgent, and I didn't want to spoil your day out with Alberto."

"Don't mention that man's name to me."

"I take it the day out wasn't a roaring success."

"We were supposed to be having a picnic, but when we got to the beauty spot, he realised he'd left the hamper on the kitchen table."

"Oh dear." Somehow, I managed not to laugh. "What did you do? Go to the pub?"

Chapter 8

The next morning, Jack and I were back on speaking terms after making up overnight. And, no, I'm not going into the details of how we made up. Sheesh, can't a woman have any privacy?

Unfortunately, the peaceful accord didn't last for long because, over breakfast, I had made the mistake of telling him that I intended to find out who'd killed Sushi.

"That's a terrible idea, Jill."

"Why is it? As things stand, I'm the prime suspect, so if *I* don't find out who the real murderer is, I'll probably be behind bars this time next year."

"You're being ridiculous again."

"How am I? You can't honestly expect those clowns, Leo and Big Mac, to find out who did it."

"They won't be the ones working on the case because they were present when the murder took place. They'll more than likely bring in—"

"Another set of clowns?"

"I was going to say detectives from another force. You don't have much faith in the police to sort this out, do you?"

"That's not true. I don't have *any* faith that they will."

"You do realise that if you go sticking your nose in where it's not wanted, there's a good chance you could make things even worse."

"How could it be worse than being the prime suspect in a murder case?"

Florence came running into the kitchen. "Mummy, Auntie Kathy has loads of Beanie Babies."

"Yes, I know, darling. Most of them used to belong to

"Why? Not over something silly, I hope?"

"Of course not. It's just that my darling husband has accused me of being a murderer."

"She wasn't my biggest fan."

"You two have a history, then?"

"I work as a private investigator. Our paths have crossed a number of times."

"You didn't like her, I take it?"

"We didn't particularly like one another."

"Was she okay when you left the loo?"

"She was fine."

"What did they ask you?" Jack said in the taxi on the drive home.

"If I'd seen Sushi in the loo. I said I had and that we'd had words."

"Was that wise?"

"I told the truth. Are you suggesting I should have lied?"

"Of course not."

"It's not like I have anything to hide."

"I know, but—" He hesitated.

"Hang on. You think I did it, don't you?"

"Don't be ridiculous. Of course I don't."

"Then why are you worried about what I may or may not have said?"

"Forget it."

The rest of the journey passed in silence.

"I wasn't expecting you two back yet," Kathy said when we marched into the lounge. "Did you have a nice time?"

"I'm going to get a beer," Jack said, heading towards the kitchen.

"Have you two fallen out?"

"Looks that way."

"No, although I think there might have been someone in one of the cubicles."

Big Mac came back into the room and banged his hand on the table. "Everyone, can I have your attention? You've no doubt heard the tragic news. Most of you here know the drill. This is now a crime scene, and no one should try to leave until the police have spoken to you. I called the station; they should have someone over here in about fifteen minutes. Until then, I suggest we all stay in this room and remain seated."

Susan's husband was being consoled by Leo's wife. Everyone else was talking in hushed voices.

"They all think I did it," I whispered to Jack.

"Don't be ridiculous."

"Why do they keep looking at me, then?"

"They aren't."

They definitely were.

The police commandeered the restaurant manager's office and used it to interview all the guests individually. I was one of the last to be called. After asking me a few routine questions, the police officer said, "A number of people have mentioned that you were out of the dining room when the deceased went to the toilet."

"That's right. I was in the loo. Susan came in while I was still there."

"Did you speak to her?"

"Briefly."

"About what?"

"She expressed surprise that my husband and I were still together."

"Why would she say something like that?"

"Turning her into a cockroach?"

"Of course not. She's already one of those."

I took a sip of my soup. "This is tepid."

"It wasn't when they served it." Jack tutted. "Everyone else has finished theirs."

Duly admonished, I slurped down the cold soup without another word of complaint.

The waiters had just started to serve the main course when Sushi's husband, Donald, spoke up. "Excuse me, everyone. Susan has been gone for an awfully long time and I'm beginning to worry. Would one of you ladies mind checking the loo to see that she's okay?"

Leo's wife got to her feet. "I'll go and see."

I was just about to take a bite of roast pork when there was a blood-curdling scream from outside the room. Donald, Leo, Big Mac and Jack all shot out of the room to see what was going on. I considered following them, but I wasn't sure my presence would be appreciated.

A few minutes later, Jack, and Leo and his wife returned, and it was obvious from their expressions that something was seriously wrong. Leo's wife was in tears.

"What's going on?" I asked Jack as he returned to his seat next to me.

"It's Susan."

"What's wrong with her?"

"She's dead."

"What? How?"

"It looks like someone hit her over the head. You didn't—"

"Didn't *what*? Kill her? Is that what you think?"

"Of course not. I was going to say you didn't see anyone else in there, did you?"

for a few minutes. Jack owed me big time for dragging me there.

The sign on the door to the ladies' loo read 'Powder Room'. Seriously? Give me strength!

Once inside, I stood by the sinks and played around on my phone. I planned to stay there for as long as I thought I could get away with before Jack sent out a search party to look for me. I was just about to make my way back to the dining room when the door opened and in walked Sushi, who was clearly raging about something.

"Hello, Susan."

"Look what that stupid woman did." She pointed to what appeared to be soup on her jacket.

"Oh dear. That's unfortunate. Do you need a hand?"

"Not from you. I have to say I'm surprised that you and Jack are still together."

"Why wouldn't we be?"

She shrugged. "No reason. I thought he might have started to resent you for curtailing his promising career."

"What did you just say? I did not *curtail* his career. He chose to leave the force to do something else."

"I suppose it makes it easier to tell yourself that."

I would have loved to grab her by the hair, force her face-first into the toilet bowl, and flush it, but there was someone in one of the other cubicles, so I thought I'd better not. Instead, I said, "Nice speaking to you, Susan."

"I thought you'd run off," Jack said when I got back.

"No. Just shooting the breeze with my pal, Sushi."

"The waitress spilled soup on her."

"I know." I grinned.

"You didn't do anything stupid, did you?"

"Like what?"

her husband and Big Mac and his wife. Leo, Sushi and Big Mac seemed to be competing with one another to offer me the coldest greeting.

"They're all talking about me," I whispered to Jack.

"Of course they aren't. You're just being paranoid."

"It isn't paranoia if it's true. Look at Leo. If looks could kill, I'd be dead by now."

A couple of minutes later, a woman arrived by herself, and took the only remaining spare seat, which was directly opposite Sushi. As soon as she was seated, she began to glare at Sushi. Almost as if she could feel the woman's eyes burning into her, Sushi looked up and their gazes met. No words were exchanged between the two of them, but Sushi was now returning the woman's gaze with interest.

"What's going on with those two?" I whispered to Jack.

"Nothing."

"Something clearly is. They look like they want to kill one another."

"I'll tell you later."

Sushi's husband said something in her ear that resulted in the two of them exchanging heated words. Their argument didn't last long because a waitress and a waiter came over to the table and began to take our orders.

The conversation was mindbogglingly boring, as most of the people around the table did their best to outdo the others with their tales of Norm.

The woman who had been glaring at Sushi must have found the conversation as tedious as I did because she got up from her chair and left the room.

"I need the loo." I stood up.

I didn't, but I did need to get away from that crowd just

both have a drink—something told me I was going to need one.

The taxi arrived outside the old watermill bang on time.

"It's Jill, isn't it?" the driver said.

"Err, yeah?" The man's face was familiar, but I couldn't put a name to it.

"Jim. Jim Keeper. Long time no see."

"Hi, Jim. How are you?"

"Fine, thanks."

"How long have you been driving a taxi?"

"It's four years now. The dating agency didn't work out, so I started on the taxis, just as a stopgap until I could find something else. But I found I really enjoy it, and I've been doing it ever since. Red Lion, isn't it?"

"Yes, please."

"They do some great grub in there. Me and my missus went there for our wedding anniversary."

"Who was that?" Jack asked when we'd been dropped off outside the restaurant.

"He used to be a grim reaper."

"He certainly has the name for it. Jim Keeper the grim reaper." He laughed.

"Thanks for pointing that out. I never would have noticed."

"Come on. Let's go and say hello to everyone."

"If we must."

All my worst nightmares had been realised. After Jack had spoken to the host and his wife, we joined the others in the dining room that had been booked for our party. Around the table were Leo Riley and his wife, Sushi and the last half-hour, putting on one suit, and then another.

"What do you think about this one, Jill?"

"I think the same thing about it as I did twenty-minutes ago, the first time you put it on."

"I'm not sure." He took another look in the wardrobe mirror. "Maybe it's too dark."

"It's fine, Jack."

His phone rang, and as soon as he answered it, I could tell something was amiss. With a bit of luck, the dinner had been cancelled.

"That was Sarah's mother." He sighed. "Sarah has a tummy bug, so she can't sit for us."

"Oh dear." It took all my self-control not to fist pump the air. "Never mind. You'll just have to go by yourself."

"Don't be silly. I'll call Kathy. She's always saying she'd sit for us if we needed her to."

"Kathy is—err—"

"What?"

"She said she had a thing tonight."

Ignoring me, he gave her a call. "Kathy? It's Jack. I don't suppose you could babysit Florence tonight, could you? I know it's short notice, but our usual sitter has taken ill. You can? Great! Jill thought you might have something arranged. Thanks. See you shortly." He finished the call and shot me a look.

"What? I must have got the nights mixed up."

***

My last-ditch efforts to escape the dreadful night out had failed, so we were waiting for a taxi to take us to the Red Lion. We'd decided to take a cab so that we could it, but it was locked. From inside, came the sound of more banging. Clearly whoever had taken the unit was having lots of work done.

"Any idea who is moving in down the corridor, Mrs V?"

"No dear, but I hope they aren't going to keep up that racket for much longer. It's giving me a headache."

The smell of bacon still lingered, and I was just about to call Jack, to tell him we should have a fry-up for dinner, when I remembered it was that awful meal at the Red Lion tonight. I couldn't imagine they'd have bacon cobs on the menu.

There was a cat on my desk, but it wasn't Winky.

"Where is he?" Mimi hissed.

"Winky? I've no idea."

"Are you hiding him, Jill?"

"No. He was here when I left earlier. You look a little upset."

"*Upset*? I'm way beyond upset."

"What has he done?"

"I don't want to talk about it. Just tell him that when I catch up with him, he'll wish he'd never been born."

Winky never did show up that afternoon, and judging by the look on Mimi's face, that was probably a wise decision.

***

Florence had finished her dinner; Jack and I had just eaten a few crackers because we didn't want to spoil our appetite for the meal that evening. It took me no time at all to pick my outfit, but Jack had been faffing about for

Chapter 7

Back in Washbridge, I made my way down the high street, with the intention of dropping in on Rita at On A Sixpence. I needed an audience with her husband, Charles. He was DOPA's representative in the area, and he was causing my clients: Barry, Harry and Gordon a certain amount of consternation.

I was plain out of luck because the shop was closed. According to the opening times printed on the window, it closed on Sundays and Wednesdays. Drat! I considered going across the road to Coffee Animal, but even I couldn't justify that, having just visited Cuppy C.

As I walked back to the office, I gave my mother a call at Cakey C.

"Cakey C, Blodwyn speaking, how can I help you today?"

"Blodwyn, it's Jill. Is my mother there?"

"It's her day off. She and Alberto have gone for a run out into the countryside. You could try her mobile."

"It's alright. It'll wait until tomorrow."

"Okay. I'll have to go, Jill, I've got a queue."

"No problem."

Was I the only person working today? It was certainly beginning to feel that way.

As I made my way up the stairs, I could hear some banging coming from down the corridor. Had someone moved in already? I decided to investigate, but it didn't do me any good. Sheets of hardboard covered what had until recently been Bubbles. The only access now was via a temporary door set in the middle of the boarding. I tried

"No. Cyril."

"I remember him. Skinny guy."

"He's not skinny anymore. He's plonked on the pounds over the last few years."

"Little wonder," Pearl said. "He's the only person I know who eats more muffins than you do, Jill."

"I'm surprised you allow him in here."

"The first time he came in, we didn't realise who he was until we'd already served him. He's never caused any problem, though, has he, Amber?"

"No. He just sits in the corner, minding his own business, and he never speaks to anyone."

"When was the last time he was in here?"

They both shrugged, then Pearl said, "It must be at least a month."

"I don't suppose you know where he lives, do you?"

"No idea. What's this about, Jill?" Amber said.

"I could tell you, but then I'd have to kill you. Do me a favour, would you? The next time he comes in here, give me a call."

No, I had no idea dragons could write either. Live and learn.

"Jill!" He spotted me and beckoned me over.

"You're very popular."

"It's like this every day."

"Don't let the twins overwork you."

"This isn't work. I love it. Everyone is so friendly."

"Are you sure you wouldn't like to take a look at the Dragon Rescue centre? You might like it."

"Maybe one day, but not now. I'm really happy here."

"Excuse me, are you going to be much longer?" asked the impatient vampire standing behind me.

"I'd better leave you to your fans, Bobby."

"It was nice to see you again, Jill. Would you remind the twins that it'll be time for my cake in ten minutes?"

"Sure."

"Bobby said to remind you to take his cake upstairs in ten minutes, Pearl."

"Don't worry. We're on it."

"I don't suppose either of you have seen Ma Chivers recently, have you?"

"No, thank goodness," Amber said. "And I hope we never see her again."

"Why are you asking about that awful woman?" Pearl said.

"No reason. It just seems strange that she's disappeared without a trace."

"That woman was always going to meet a sticky end."

"That sidekick of hers does come in here occasionally, though," Amber said.

"Alicia?"

It was a very long time since I'd seen both the twins looking so happy.

"Hi, Jill." Amber beamed. "Your usual?"

"Yes, please."

"Isn't it a beautiful day?" Pearl said.

"What's got into you two?"

"What do you mean?" Amber gave me a puzzled look.

"Why are you so happy? Did you win the lottery and forget to tell me?"

"One word," Pearl said. "Bobby."

"He's still upstairs, I take it?"

"He certainly is, and he's welcome to stay there for as long as he wishes."

"I assume he's bringing in the punters?"

"They can't get enough of him, but that's not the only reason we're so happy. It's just having Bobby around. He's such a lovely person. It lifts the spirit just being in his company. You must have noticed that, Jill?"

"To be honest, I didn't get the chance to spend much time with him."

"You should go upstairs and say hi."

"I will." I picked up my coffee and muffin and started for the stairs.

"Hey, you haven't paid the entrance fee," Pearl called after me.

"Oh, right. How much is it?"

"Just kidding. It's free for family."

Wow! The twins really were in a good mood.

Bobby was at the far side of the room, posing for a selfie with a woman and her young son. After that, he signed a couple of photos for two teenage witches.

"I don't know who he is, but we'd like you to put a stop to it."

"As it happens, I've met the gentleman in question, and I found him very susceptible to magic, so I don't think I'll have any problem throwing him off the scent."

"Excellent, it seems that Raymond's friend was right about you. What will this cost us, Jill?"

"My rates are on here." I took out one of my standard contracts and handed it to him.

"That seems most acceptable." He stood up and shook my hand. "You'll let us know when you've dealt with the matter?"

"Of course, but before you go, would you mind if I took a photo of the three of you?"

"Why do you need that?"

"I'll use this as part of the spell I cast on the man from DOPA, to make sure he doesn't trouble you again."

"Okay." The three of them stood together while I snapped a photo on my phone.

Even after they'd left, I still had no idea what kind of sups they were. Not that it mattered. I would just need a few minutes with Rita's husband, Charlie, and I was confident that I could disrupt his search for proof that sups were living in the human world.

More easy money.

***

This week was just getting better and better, so I decided a trip to Cuppy C was in order. What better way to celebrate this sudden uptick in my fortune than a rendezvous with a coffee and a blueberry muffin?

"They get a terrible press, but most of them are stand-up individuals. Anyway, I digress. When we put out the word that we needed a private investigator who was also a sup, it was Raymond's friend who came up with your name."

It was now clear that these three gentlemen were sups, but I had no idea what kind, and I didn't like to ask for fear of looking naive.

"How can I help the three of you?"

"Harry, Gordon and I all live and work here in the human world, and although I say so myself, we have fitted in very well. This is our fifth year and—"

"Sixth," Gordon interrupted.

Barry hesitated while he thought about it. "You're right. This is now our *sixth* year and, until recently, everything was going rather well."

"I take it something has changed."

"Unfortunately, yes. We no longer feel safe here in the human world."

"What happened to change things?"

"We fear that our cover is about to be blown and we'll be forced to go back to the sup world."

"All sups have to be careful not to do anything to draw attention to themselves."

"This is different. It has recently come to our attention that a human has made it his business to expose us."

"DOPA," I said.

"Really! There's no need for insults."

"No, you misheard. I didn't say dope. I said DOPA. It stands for Department Of Paranormal Activity. One of their people has been posted to Washbridge. That must be who you're talking about."

I was still trying to figure out what Winky was up to when Mrs V came through to my office and closed the door behind her. Whenever she did that, you could be sure that whoever was in the outer office came under the heading of weird.

"There are three weird gentlemen out there, Jill."

What did I tell you? Am I psychic or what?

"Weird how?"

"It's hard to describe, but they're most definitely weird. Shall I tell them that you've had to go out?"

"Not if they're potential clients. I can't afford to turn anyone away, weird or otherwise. Why don't you show them through?"

What the three men lacked in stature they made up for with flamboyance. All three were dressed in checked double-breasted suits. They looked as though they might be brothers with their thick, curly hair, thick sideburns and beards.

One of them stepped forward. "Thank you for seeing us, young lady. I'm Barry."

"I'm Harry," said the man to his left.

"And I'm G—"

"Let me guess. Gary?"

"It's Gordon, actually."

"My name is Jill. Won't you take a seat?" Barry took the chair opposite me; the other two sat on the sofa. "What is it I can do for you gentlemen?"

"We got your name from a friend of a fiend."

"You mean a friend of a *friend*."

"No, actually. One of our neighbours, Raymond, is a fiend. Have you had many dealings with fiends, Jill?"

"None."

had a sneaking suspicion I knew what it was.

"Morning, Mrs V."

Chewing desperately, she managed to say something that sounded a bit like, "Good morning, Jill." She swallowed. "Sorry about that. I was just finishing my cereal bar."

"Really?" I sniffed the air. "Was it bacon flavoured?"

"I simply couldn't resist." She opened the drawer and took out the half-eaten bacon cob. "A new takeaway has opened around the corner. As I walked by, the smell of bacon drew me inside."

"It's just as well you've taken up the Morris dancing."

"We have a practice session every night this week and next week, so I should burn off a few of these calories. Will you be going out on surveillance today, Jill?"

"No, that's all finished now."

"Already? Shall I prepare the bill?"

"Not yet. I'll let you know when."

Winky was sniggering to himself, which was never a good sign.

"What are you up to?"

"Me? Nothing."

"Don't give me that. What are you sniggering at?"

"Let's just say revenge is a dish best served cold."

"O—kay. Who are you planning revenge against? Not me, I hope?"

"Relax, you have nothing to worry about."

"Not Mrs V?"

"No, I don't have time to waste on the old bag lady."

"Just make sure whatever you're plotting doesn't come back on me."

let Florence come into the lounge while I'm watching it."

"Okay."

The presentation was slick with a capital 'S'. The man fronting it was as smooth as they come, and he oozed false sincerity. He exhorted the benefits of returning to life just as easily as if he had been selling life insurance or a timeshare. I couldn't help but admire the conviction he managed to convey despite the fact that the whole enterprise was clearly nonsensical. He concluded the presentation with the following lines:

"For those of you for whom haunting is no longer enough, we offer an alternative solution. As you'd expect, a premium service like this isn't cheap, but I'm convinced you'll agree it's worth every penny. To learn more, call us now on Restore-999-999."

I'd been hoping for more details on how the so-called service worked, but there were none. To find out more, I would need to get inside their operation, but that presented a problem. Although I could fall back on magic for many things, I wasn't capable of presenting myself as a ghost. I needed an actual ghost to help me, and I knew just the person.

***

As I walked up the stairs to the office, I caught a whiff of bacon. Just the smell of it made my tummy rumble. I glanced down the corridor to see if the smell was coming from the empty unit, but there was no sign of any activity down there.

As I stepped into the outer office, Mrs V shoved something in her drawer and slammed it closed. And I

know that the Stock sisters have got a trophy on display in the shop?"

"Yeah, I saw it when I called in there last night."

"What did you and your grandmother do with your cup? Does she have it at the hotel?"

"There is no cup. The only reason the Stock sisters have one is because they bought it from a shop in Washbridge."

"Wow! That's pretty vain of them. I'm surprised you haven't done that too."

"I am *not* vain. I prefer to keep my light under one of those whatchamacallits."

"Bushels."

"Yeah, those things. Whatever they are."

"Are you back on surveillance duty today?"

"No, thank goodness. There's no more surveillance for me."

"Have you wrapped up that case already? That was jolly quick."

"No, it's still on-going." I told Jack all about the arrangement I'd come to with Ava Todfoster.

"So, effectively, you're getting paid for doing nothing?"

"Not quite nothing. I have to send a brief report and a photo to her husband every now and then."

"And you're going to get a nice bonus when it's all done?"

"Yep."

"Nice work if you can get it."

"I doubt the other case I'm working on will prove to be so simple."

"Is that the 'Restore' scam thing?"

"Yeah. In fact, that reminds me, I need to take a look at their promotional DVD. Do me a favour, will you? Don't

Chapter 6

The next morning, Jack was being unbearably jolly. "I can't wait for tonight. I just took a quick look at the Red Lion's menu, and it looks fantastic."

"Are you sure you wouldn't rather go by yourself? I could call the babysitter and cancel."

Before Jack could respond, Florence had her two-penn'orth, "I am not a *baby*!"

"I know you aren't, darling." I gave her a kiss on the top of her head.

"Why do I have a babysitter, then?"

"It's just what people call someone who looks after little children."

"I'm *not* little!"

"No, right. Sarah is more like your older friend, isn't she?"

"Why do you give her money to be my friend?"

"Err, I—" I looked across at Jack who was barely containing a laugh. "Feel free to jump in here."

"But you're doing so well without me."

"We don't pay Sarah to be your friend," I said. "We pay her for her time."

Florence considered this for a while before saying, "Why don't you pay *me* for *my* time?"

"We do. That's why we give you pocket money each week."

"Okay. I'm going to practise my spells."

"Be careful. Don't choose any dangerous ones."

"I won't."

Jack started to load the dishwasher. "Hey, Jill, did you

"Absolutely. I've never been able to get on with those new-fangled calculators."

"Right. I couldn't help but notice you have a cup on display."

"Quite a few people have commented on it."

"Did you receive it in the post? I didn't realise they were issuing them."

"No. We got it from Washbridge."

"Got it from *where* in Washbridge?"

"Wash Trophies. It's in the marketplace. Their prices are very reasonable."

"Hold on. Do you mean you bought it yourselves?"

"That's right. We felt we needed something to commemorate our success."

"O—kay. I just popped in to see if you've had a delivery of Chococandy Pops."

"Not yet, I'm afraid, but we still have plenty of Strawberrycandy Pops."

"That's okay. I still have half a box of those. I'll just take some custard creams."

"We're all out of those too. We sold the last three packets this afternoon."

"Three packets? That's just greedy. You should really think about rationing them."

"It was your husband who bought them. He popped in with that darling little girl of yours."

"Oh, well, that's okay, then. Thanks, Marjorie."

"Would you like me to give you the phone number for Wash Trophies?"

"No, it's okay, thanks."

windows had been blacked out. I was about to walk away when the door opened and out stepped Joe and Flo Peep.

"It's Jill, isn't it?" Flo said.

"That's right. I see your perseverance paid off."

"Indeed," Joe said. "We thought we'd lost our opportunity, but here we are."

"And you open on Sunday?"

"That's right. I hope you'll join us then."

"I'll do my best. Can I get a quick preview?"

"I'm afraid not. That would spoil the surprise."

"Fair enough. Good luck with your new venture."

"Thanks, Jill."

As I stepped into the village store, I almost walked straight into the plinth that had been placed close to the door. On top of the plinth was a glass case, inside which was a silver cup. I had to put my nose close to the glass in order to see the inscription:

Cross-swords crossword tournament.
Awarded to Cynthia and Marjorie Stock.

Hang on. How come they got a cup when Grandma and I had finished two places higher than them, and we had received nothing?

Marjorie was behind the counter pushing beads back and forth on an abacus.

"Hi, Marjorie."

"Just a second," she said without looking up. After moving the beads back and forth a few more times, she picked up a pencil and wrote a number on her notepad. "I do hate doing accounts, don't you, Jill?"

"You use this for your accounts?"

it?"

"I don't think that's necessary. I can get someone to take a photo of me and I'll forward it to you. Then you can send your report complete with photo to Richard."

"I'm not sure about all this."

"Please, Jill, you'd be doing me a massive favour. Once Richard is convinced that I'm not cheating and asks you to end the surveillance, I'll pay you a bonus of five-hundred pounds."

"Won't he notice if that amount of money disappears from your account?"

"No. We have a joint account, but we also have our own individual accounts. What do you say?"

I hesitated, but only for a few seconds. Essentially, she was offering me the chance to get paid just to send a photo and a brief report to Richard, without the hassle of having to do the surveillance. And on top of that, she was going to give me a hefty bonus at the end. Hmm, difficult decision.

"Sure. I'm in."

***

I parked outside the old watermill and then made my way to the village store. Before I got there, though, I noticed that the tea room had a new sign:

Peep Inside

Intrigued, I went over to take a closer look. A handwritten notice stuck to the window announced that the tea room, which was now under new ownership, would open on Sunday. I tried to look inside to see what changes, if any, the new owners had made, but the

"Right."

"If I magic myself back and forth between here and the sup world while Richard is around, he's bound to notice sooner or later. I suppose I could use the 'forget' spell on him, but it doesn't seem right to put him through that so often."

"Is your mother expected to make a full recovery?"

"Fortunately, yes, but it's going to take a couple of weeks at least. What are you going to tell Richard?"

"I'm not sure. I can hardly tell him that you're a witch, can I?"

"I have a suggestion if you're amenable to the idea."

"Go on. I'm listening."

"I love Richard. I've never cheated on him, and I never will."

"Okay?"

"Why don't you pretend to continue with the case? You can report back to him, confirming everything I've told him is the truth."

"Lie to him in other words?"

"Yes, but it would be in a good cause."

"I'd be taking his money under false pretences."

"We can afford it. We're loaded."

"It might not be sufficient for me to simply tell him everything is hunky-dory. He may want proof."

"Hmm, I hadn't thought of that." She took a sip of coffee. "How about this? From now on, whenever I make an excuse to leave the house, I'll go and see my mother, but then I'll spend some time doing whatever it is I told Richard I was going to do. That way I won't actually be lying."

"And you'll let me know, so I can be there to witness

"What did my husband say when he hired you?"

"That you're the most wonderful woman in the world and that he loves you very much, but he's worried you might be seeing someone else."

"I would never cheat on him. I love him more than life itself."

"He doesn't understand why you've started going out on your own so often. He said you'd told him you were going to the opticians today."

"I never was any good at lying."

"Why *are* you lying to him?"

"It's my mother. She was taken ill a few weeks ago, and she has asked me to go around to her place to help with the cleaning, shopping, that kind of thing."

"I'm sorry to hear that. Does your mother live in Candlefield?"

"Yes."

"Then I don't really understand the problem. Why not just nip outside, and magic yourself over there? When you get back, time won't have moved on here in the human world, so Richard would be none the wiser."

"If only it was that easy." She managed the weakest of smiles. "Have you heard of Donovan's Delay Syndrome?"

"I can't say that I have. What is it?"

"It's named after the first sup who is known to have contracted it. It's very rare, but those who suffer from it experience a delay of anything up to two minutes when they magic themselves between the sup world and this one. Fortunately, mine isn't that bad, but there's still up to a minute's delay."

"I assume you just nipped to Candlefield?"

"Yes. I was doing some shopping for my mum."

around. I started back up the alley and was almost back at the road when I heard a sound behind me: it was Ava.

"Oh?" She took a step back. The look of surprise on her face must have matched my own. "Thank goodness you're a sup. I thought for a minute I'd blown my cover."

Discovering she was a witch had put me in a very difficult position, and I wasn't entirely sure how to proceed.

"It's Ava, isn't it?"

"Yes. How did you know? Do I know you from somewhere?"

"Do you think we could go and get a drink and have a chat?"

"I guess so."

We found a quiet coffee shop and took a table where we wouldn't be overheard.

"My name is Jill Maxwell."

"I thought your face was familiar. I saw you in the Levels Competition some years ago. I still don't understand how you know my name, though."

"I work as a private investigator here in the human world."

"Really? How very—just a minute, does that mean you were following me?"

"Yes, I was."

"Richard?"

"Yes."

"Oh no. I feared something like this might happen. How long have you been tailing me?"

"Only since yesterday. I was supposed to follow you on your morning jog, but I—err—let's just say something came up."

Mrs V. Incidentally, have you seen Ma Chivers lately?"

"Not for years. Why do you ask?"

"No reason. Someone mentioned her name the other day and it occurred to me I hadn't seen her for ages."

"She was always a bad egg. Maybe she crossed the wrong person."

"Yeah, maybe."

***

Back on the Todfoster case, I'd parked a hundred yards up the street from their house and was waiting for Ava to appear.

I didn't have long to wait because, just after one-thirty, she left the house, climbed into the car, and headed into Washbridge. I followed at a discreet distance. She parked in the same car park that I used every day, and it was only when I followed her on foot that I sensed she was a witch. Ava made her way down the high street and then took a left past Kathy's shop. Three doors down from there was an optician, so it was beginning to look like she'd been telling her husband the truth. Perhaps her new glasses were causing her problems and she was going to get them adjusted.

But then, she walked straight past the opticians and stepped into the alleyway at the side of the shop. When I followed her, the alley appeared to be deserted. I walked the full-length of it just in case she'd hidden behind one of the industrial bins, but there was no sign of her. Could she have spotted me? I didn't see how, but it was possible. Whatever the reason, she had obviously magicked herself somewhere else, so there was no point in my hanging

"I haven't seen Lester in ages. Is he okay?"

"I don't see very much of him myself. He leaves at the crack of dawn and doesn't get back until late."

"I didn't realise being a fishmonger required such long hours."

"I keep telling him he should set on an assistant, but he won't entertain the idea. Still, he's happier than I've ever seen him, and that's all that matters. Have you been to Cuppy C this week?"

"Not yet. There's nothing wrong, is there?"

"Quite the opposite. That dragon is proving very popular."

"Surely not more popular than the cork museum." I grinned.

"Apparently so, but why people would prefer to see a dragon than a cork collection is beyond my understanding."

"He's not just any dragon. Bobby is pink with green spots."

"That explains it, then." She rolled her eyes. "And what kind of name is Bobby for a dragon?"

"It suits him. I have to admit he is rather cute."

"Florence hasn't magicked up any more creatures, has she?"

"No, thank goodness. I take it Barry isn't here."

"He's with Dot. He was asking me when he can go to the groomers again."

"Hmm, that might be a problem. Bubbles has moved out of my building."

"That was rather sudden, wasn't it?"

"Yeah. The owner, Farah, has found more suitable premises. I'll have to see if she left her new address with

Chapter 5

Aunt Lucy had kindly invited me over for lunch. Well, technically speaking, I'd invited myself, but I could tell that she was really pleased to see me. She'd made one of her delicious shepherd's pies, which was much better than the sandwich I would have had if I'd stayed in Washbridge. Much cheaper too.

"You wolfed that down, Jill. Didn't you have any breakfast?"

"Only a little fruit. I had to go out early on a case I'm working on."

"Anything exciting?"

"Not really, but I have just landed a new case that is really unusual."

"Oh? What's that?"

"Some scam artist in Ghost Town is supposedly offering to bring the residents there back to life."

Yes, yes, I know I'd promised Constance that I wouldn't discuss the case with anyone else, but family doesn't count. Obviously.

"Some people will fall for anything." Aunt Lucy shook her head.

"I dropped in at Cakey C while I was in GT."

"How is Darlene?"

"She's fine. She gave me a bit of a hard time because I hadn't been over there for a while."

"You really should make the effort to spend more time with your mother."

"I know. Maybe if she made meals like yours, I would."

"Don't let her hear you saying that, or you'll be in trouble."

walk."

"Not to worry. Ava has just called me to say she's going to the opticians this afternoon at two o'clock."

"That doesn't sound particularly suspicious."

"She only had new glasses a month ago."

"I see. Okay, I'm on it."

By the time I'd finished on the call, Winky was out from under the sofa, and he was looking very pleased with himself.

"What are you looking so happy about?"

"Voila!" He held out a glass bottle, inside which was a galleon. "What do you think of it?"

"You didn't do this."

"Of course I did. What do you think I was doing just now?"

"It's—err—"

"*Brilliant* is the word you're looking for."

"It's certainly better than those monstrosities that Mrs K made."

"You can have it."

"Thanks."

"For twenty-pounds."

"I'm not paying for it."

"It's worth double that."

"I don't care. I don't want it that badly."

"Please yourself. I'll sell it easily online." He took back the bottle. "And what was that rubbish about a cow?"

"You shouldn't have been listening to my call."

"You are without doubt the world's worst liar."

"I don't remember asking for your opinion."

address and key before then."

"Great. Thanks, Kathy."

***

"Mr Todfoster phoned while you were out, Jill," Mrs V said. "He asked if you'd give him a call back."

"Okay, will do."

I went through to my office and was pleasantly surprised to find that all Winky's Feline Fortune boxes had disappeared. He was under the sofa, doing something, but I couldn't make out what he was up to because he had his back to me.

"What are you up to under there?"

"You'll see in a minute."

I made a call to Richard Todfoster.

"Richard? You called me earlier, I believe."

"Yes, I'm very keen to know what happened this morning."

"I—err—unfortunately, I had to cut short the surveillance."

"Why?"

"I was following your wife as agreed, but then I encountered a—err—cow in the road."

"A *cow*? In Under Wash?"

"Yes, it must have got out of the farmer's field, so I had to hang onto it until its owner turned up."

"That's strange."

"You're telling me."

"I meant it's strange because there are no farms around Under Wash."

"How weird. Perhaps the man was just taking it for a

tomorrow."

After our meeting had concluded, Mad and I walked out together.

"Are you and Brad really going away or did you just say that to get out of this crazy case?"

"We really are going away, but I'm not sorry to miss out on this one. The whole thing sounds nuts."

"Where are you going?"

"Spain."

"Very nice. We're off to Filey soon. At least we will be if my sister lets us stay at her new holiday house, which reminds me, I was supposed to call her."

"I'll leave you to it, Jill. Good luck with the case."

"Thanks. Enjoy Spain." Once Mad had left, I called Kathy. "It's me."

"Jill? Where are you? It's a terrible line."

"I—err—" I should have waited until I was back in the human world before making the phone call. "I'm in a layby. The signal here isn't very strong. Can you hear me?"

"Just about."

"You said we could use your holiday house in Filey."

"Yeah, but I didn't think you sounded very enthusiastic."

"Of course I am. And Florence and Jack definitely are. When could we go there?"

"Pretty much anytime you like at the moment."

"How about in a couple of weeks' time?"

"That's fine. How long do you want it for?"

"Just a week, if that's okay."

"That's fine. I'll pencil you in. I'll let you have the

of money for the service."

I was beginning to feel exasperated at having to listen to this nonsense. "How are they managing to convince anyone to hand over good money for this scam?"

"That's what I'm hoping you can find out."

"Far be it from me to turn away work, but wouldn't this be better investigated by your own people?"

"There's a limit to what we can do because the scam spans the ghost and human worlds. That's why I thought of you and Mad."

"There's a slight problem from my end," Mad said. "Brad and I are going away for a week the day after tomorrow. Sorry."

"What about the shop?" I said.

"Brad's brother is coming down to run it for us. He used to work in the Glasgow shop."

"What about you, Jill?" Constance turned to me. "Have you got capacity to take this on?"

I hesitated, conscious that the Todfoster case would take up a lot of my time, but then I remembered the upcoming rent increase. "Sure, I can do it."

"Great." She opened her drawer, took out a DVD, and handed it to me. "We managed to get hold of a copy of Restore's promotional material. It should act as a starting point for your investigation."

"What exactly do you want me to do? Shut down their operation?"

"Ultimately, yes, but first I want you to find out exactly what they're doing. Specifically, how are they convincing otherwise-sensible people to hand over good money to them?"

"Okay. I'll take a look at this tonight and make a start

"That's right. Florence is five now."

"Cripes. Has it really been that long? How do you manage to juggle everything?"

"Jack works from home, so that makes things easier."

"Thanks for agreeing to come over at such short notice."

"No problem. I hope I can help."

"Me too. First things first, though. I have to ask both of you to give me your word that what I tell you today won't go beyond these four walls."

"Sure." Mad nodded.

"Yeah, no problem." I was becoming more and more intrigued.

"Okay. Over the last few months, we've become aware of an outfit who go under the name of Restore. These guys are offering to 'restore' their clients to life."

Mad and I exchanged the same puzzled look, but she got in with her question first. "Restore them to life? Are you talking about a zombie? I can't see there'll be much demand for that."

"No," Constance said. "Not like a zombie."

I chimed in at this point. "I think I must be misunderstanding you, Constance. You surely can't be saying that they're offering to bring people back to life?"

"That's exactly what I'm saying. Or to be more precise, it's what they're claiming."

"But that's impossible," Mad said. "Isn't it?"

"Of course it is." Constance sat back in her chair.

"I might be missing something here," I said. "But why are we even discussing this nonsense? You surely can't be taking it seriously?"

"We have to, for the simple reason that people are signing up for it, and of course, handing over huge sums

"What does she want to talk to you about?"
"I have no idea."
"How's little Florence?"
"She's great, but she's a bit of a handful."
"All kids are at that age."
"Yes, but most kids in the human world can't do magic. She seems to learn a new spell every day."
"The last I heard, you were going to wait until she was older before you let her loose on too much magic."
"That was the original plan, but Grandma persuaded me to have a rethink."
"I might have known. You should have told her to keep her nose out."
"Easier said than done. I hear Dad has taken up fishing?"
"Yeah." She laughed. "Anything to get away from Blodwyn."
"Shush, she'll hear you."
"I'm only joking."
"How are you and Blodwyn getting along these days?"
"Fine. She's much easier to work with than that nightmare, Yvonne. How's your business doing?"
"Things are a bit quiet at the moment, but they'll pick up. They always do."

I met Mad outside the police station and the two of us were escorted to a small conference room where Constance joined us a few minutes later.
"Hello, Jill. It's nice to see you again."
"Likewise."
"I understand from Mad that you've had an addition to the family since we last spoke."

"Is there any chance of a drink?"

"What is it you drink again? It's been so long."

"I can always find another café."

"Grab a seat. I'll bring it over. I suppose you'll be wanting a muffin?"

"Is it on the house?"

"Of course."

"Okay, then."

I'd no sooner taken a seat than Blodwyn, my father's partner, came over. "Hey, Jill, long time no see."

"Don't you start. My mother has already given me a hard time for not visiting in a while."

"Sorry, I didn't mean it like that. It just feels like ages since we saw you."

"How's my father doing? Is he here?"

"No. He's gone fishing. He's always fishing these days."

"I didn't realise he was a fisherman."

"He only took it up a couple of months ago, but he virtually lives at the lake nowadays."

"How do you feel about that?"

"I'm okay with it." She smiled. "To tell you the truth, I like the me-time it gives me."

"One latte and a blueberry muffin." My mother placed them on the table and then pulled up a seat. Blodwyn said goodbye and went back behind the counter.

"Thanks, I need this." I inhaled the blueberry muffinness.

"So, what brings you to GT? And don't say you came to see me because I know that's not true."

"I've got a meeting with Constance Bowler."

"The policewoman?"

"Yeah."

time I'd walked from where I'd parked the car to their street, she was coming out of the house. Ava was wearing what was clearly a brand new tracksuit and trainers. She set off at a brisk pace down the street, and then cut across the fields.

Oh bum! It had never occurred to me that she might take to the fields. The muddy ground was still sodden from the previous night's rain, and I certainly wasn't dressed for a cross country run.

Epic fail, Jill.

I made my way back to the car, and made a call to Mad.

"Jill? I thought you were going to be tied up on surveillance?"

"Slight change of plan. Are you two free now?"

"Let me check with Constance. I'll get straight back to you."

"Okay."

Sure enough, Mad came back to me within a matter of minutes and said that Constance would be free in an hour's time, so we arranged to meet at her office.

***

If I'd paid a visit to Ghost Town but failed to drop in on my mother at Cakey C, I would never have heard the end of it, so as I had an hour to kill, I magicked myself over to her tea shop.

"Don't I know you?" said my mother. "Your name is on the tip of my tongue."

"You're hilarious. There's nothing to stop you visiting me, you know."

"I have this place to run. I never get a day off."

"Where is it?"

"In Chipping Green. It's only a small restaurant."

"No chance of me sneaking out, then?"

"None. Are you going to ask Kathy about Filey?"

"Yeah, I'll give her a call later today."

I'd just finished the last spoonful of cereal when my phone rang; it was Mad.

"Jill, I wasn't sure if you'd be up yet."

"What's wrong?"

"Constance Bowler called me a few minutes ago. She asked me to check with you to see if the three of us can get together sometime. Today if possible."

"What's it about?"

"She wouldn't go into detail on the phone. She said she'd prefer to do it when you were there. The fact that she called at this hour of the day suggests it must be important."

"It might be difficult. I'm just about to start surveillance on a case I'm working on, and I have no idea how long I'm going to be tied up. I could call you once I'm free, if that's okay."

"Sure. I'll let Constance know."

"Okay. I'd better be making tracks. Speak again later, probably."

***

In his text, Todfoster had said that he expected his wife to leave the house between seven and seven-thirty, so to be on the safe side, I arrived in Under Wash a little before six-forty-five. It's just as well that I did because, by the

Chapter 4

The next morning, I was up at the crack of dawn because, the previous evening, Richard Todfoster had sent me a text in which he'd said his wife would be going for an early morning jog. According to his message, she'd only recently taken up this early morning activity, and he was suspicious she might be meeting someone.

It took all my strength just to keep my eyes open while I was eating my Strawberrycandy Pops.

"Good morning." Jack yawned; he was still in his dressing gown.

"Is it? I'll tell you when I'm awake."

"I don't know how you can eat those." He pulled a face. "I can taste the sugar from here."

"I need something to fortify me for the morning ahead."

"There's a bowl full of *real* fruit over there."

"I don't need you giving me a hard time, thanks."

"What's your plan this morning?"

"There isn't really a plan. I'll just follow the target and see what she gets up to. I'm pretty sure this is all a complete waste of time, but the client pays the bill."

"I don't remember you taking on many of this kind of case."

"That's because I try to avoid them like the plague, but needs must at the moment."

He filled the kettle. "I'm really looking forward to that dinner tomorrow night."

"That makes one of us."

"You'll enjoy it when you get there. I've heard very good things about the Red Lion. The chef is supposed to be excellent."

"Don't be daft. She said we could use it, didn't she?"

"Yeah. It just makes me feel like the poor relation."

"You can't let your pride stand in the way of Florence's holiday."

"You're right. I'll have a word with her tomorrow."

"I've fed Buddy, Mummy." Florence came bouncing in. "When are we going on holiday?"

"I'm going to talk to your Auntie Kathy tomorrow, to see if we can stay at her house in Filey."

"Is that the seaside?"

"Yes, it is."

"Do they have donkeys?"

I hoped not. "I'm sure they do."

"Yay!"

"I saw the vicar on the way in. The village hall is back in business, so you'll be able to go to dance class and basket-weaving on Saturday."

"Double yay!"

"Great." There went my Saturday.

"Mummy, Wendy is going on holiday soon," Florence said, before I'd even got through the door.

"That's nice for her."

"When are *we* going on holiday?"

"I don't know."

"I want to go to the seaside, so I can go on the donkeys again. It was fun last time, wasn't it?"

"Hmm." Fun wasn't the word I would have used to describe it. "Let me get inside."

"Can we, Mummy?"

"We'll see. Have you fed Buddy since you got home from school?"

"Yes."

Jack came out of the kitchen, shook his head, and mouthed, "She hasn't."

"Florence." I crouched down so I was at her eye-level. "Tell Mummy the truth. Have you fed Buddy?"

"I forgot."

"Off you go and feed him, then. He'll be really hungry by now."

"Alright." She huffed, and off she trotted.

"She's been banging on about that holiday ever since I picked her up from school," Jack said.

"What did you tell her?"

"That we'd have to see."

"Where's Wendy going?"

"Donna said they were having a week in Margate."

"Everywhere is so expensive."

"Not if we go to Kathy's place in Filey."

"I hate the idea of having to ask her."

band."

"I *am* a one-woman band."

"Some people won't want to do business with such a small outfit. My version made it sound like you were a bigger organisation."

"It doesn't matter, anyway. I doubt anyone is ever going to see the ad. It took me all my time to track down a copy of the magazine."

"Didn't I tell you? You should have spent that money on Feline Fortune."

***

By the time I got back to Middle Tweaking, I was feeling a little more positive. Granted, it was only one case, and certainly not one I would have chosen, but at least it meant I would be bringing some money in. Before Richard Todfoster had walked into my office, I was beginning to think I might have to take Kathy up on her job offer. Can you imagine what a disaster that would have been?

"Yes, madam, that pink monstrosity really suits you."

I'd just stepped out of the car when someone called my name; hurrying down the road was the vicar.

"I'm glad I caught you, Jill. I believe your daughter attends the dance classes at the village hall."

"When it's open, yeah."

"That's what I wanted to tell you. Good news, the village hall is once again open for business. Am I right in thinking you both attend the basket-weaving too?"

"That's right." Unfortunately.

"In that case, it's double good news for you. Olga has confirmed the classes will restart too."

"That's no problem."

"In that case, if you sign at the bottom of the page, I'll get started straight away."

"Excellent."

"Sleazy work that, isn't it?" Winky said after Todfoster had left.

"Beggars can't be choosers, particularly now the rent is going up."

"You should work from home, then you wouldn't need to pay for office space."

"That would never work. Jack and I would kill each other within a week. And besides, where would that leave you?"

"I'd come and live with you."

"We've been over this a thousand times. Florence is allergic to—"

"Yes, yes, I know. She's allergic to cat fur."

Infidelity cases were my least favourite kind of case, which I tried to avoid if at all possible, but needs must at the moment.

"How's your nose?"

"Still sore. I hope you're going to get that window sorted out."

"Don't worry, I will. Oh yes, and I have a bone to pick with you."

"What am I supposed to have done now?"

"You sent an updated version of my ad to P.I. Monthly."

"You should thank me."

"There was nothing wrong with the one I wrote."

"Your copy made it sound like you were a one-woman

"So many different places. Since we got married, she's joined a Pilates club, joined a book club, taken up cycling, and there are others. Just this week, she told me she was thinking of joining the local W.I."

"I see. Do you also have shared interests?"

"Oh yes. We do lots of things together too. We're members of the sailing club, play badminton and go to the theatre."

"It sounds like you both have a very active social life."

"We certainly do."

"Have the two of you been arguing a lot recently?"

"Not at all. We're perfectly happy. Be honest with me, Jill, do you think I'm being stupid?"

"Are you sure you want me to be honest?"

"Absolutely."

"You probably are. What you've just described sounds like a healthy, happy relationship."

"You're probably right. I certainly hope so. Even so, I'd feel much better if you could put my mind at ease once and for all."

"Are you absolutely sure you want to do this? I realise that I'm in danger of talking myself out of a job, but it seems to me that this could backfire on you."

"What do you mean?"

"By asking me to do this, you're essentially saying you don't trust your wife."

"You're right." He pondered on the matter for a minute. "But I know that until I'm sure nothing is going on, I'll never rest. If you're willing to take the case, I'd like you to start as soon as possible."

"Okay." I took out my standard contract from the drawer. "These are my hourly rates."

"Mrs Maxwell." He offered his hand. "It's very good of you to see me at such short notice like this."

"No problem, and please call me Jill."

"Jill it is, and you must call me Richard."

"*Richard*? Sorry, my PA told me your name was Todd."

"It's Richard Todfoster."

"I see. What can I do for you, Richard?"

"It's a matter of the utmost delicacy, so I trust I can rely on your total discretion."

"Of course. Anything you tell me is subject to investigator/client privilege."

"Excellent. Three months ago, I married the most wonderful, beautiful woman in the world."

"Congratulations."

"Thank you. Ava is my everything, which is why I feel so bad about being here today."

"I'm not sure I follow."

"I assume you investigate possible infidelity?"

"Err, yes, of course, but you said you had only recently married."

"Quite, and I'm sure it's nothing more than my overactive imagination, but I shan't rest until you've put my mind at ease."

"It might be best if you tell me the reasons for your suspicions. Have you seen her with someone? Seen messages on her phone?"

"No, nothing like that. This is probably going to make me sound a little silly."

"You're unlikely to say anything I haven't heard before."

"It's just that Ava goes out such a lot."

"Goes out? Goes out *where*?"

close the window without having to get up from my desk.

Just brilliant!

I cast the spell and the window slammed closed. Unfortunately, I did it just as Winky was about to jump inside. He hit the glass face-first and slid slowly down the pane.

I used the same spell to open the window and then rushed over to check on him.

"Are you okay?"

"Where am I?"

I lifted him up and placed him on the sofa. "Winky, look at me. Are you alright?"

"I think so." He gave his head a shake. "What happened?"

"The window closed."

"How?"

"The catch must be faulty." I shrugged. "I'll take a look at it." I walked over to the window and fiddled around with the 'faulty' catch. "All sorted. It won't happen again."

What? If I'd told him what had really happened, he would have made my life a misery.

***

Ahead of my visitor's arrival, I'd made Winky stack all his boxes in the corner. I figured that seeing an office full of cat products wouldn't have given Mr Foster the professional impression I was shooting for.

The man virtually oozed money; the cost of his suit would have covered the rent on my office for the next five years.

clearly wondering how I'd returned to my office without her seeing me.

"You'll be pleased to know the fire escape is in good working order, Mrs V."

"Sorry?"

"I thought it was about time I checked it out."

"Doesn't the landlord usually do that?"

"Of course, but one can never be too careful, can one?"

"I suppose not." She walked over to one of the open boxes. "That's an awful lot of cat litter."

"I—err—believe in buying in bulk."

"I've never actually seen that horrible cat of yours use his tray."

"He doesn't very often. Still, best to have too much stock than get caught short. Don't worry, I'll be moving this all out of here tonight."

"Right. You had a call while you were out."

"A new client?" I asked with more hope than expectation.

"Yes, Mr Todd Foster. He asked if he could come and see you this afternoon at two o'clock. I said that was okay. I hope that's alright."

"That's fine. In fact, it's absolutely great."

Maybe things were starting to turn around at last.

While browsing the spells on my newly installed app, I came across one called the 'window open/close' spell. Having to leave the window almost permanently open to accommodate Winky's comings and goings caused an awful draught, but I couldn't be bothered to keep getting up to open and close it. This spell would be like having my own remote control and would mean I could open and

"Before you go, we've been invited to a dinner on Wednesday night."

"Invited by who?"

"It's for Norman Whitelea. I worked with him at Washbridge nick. He's taking early retirement."

"You said *we'd* been invited."

"Yeah."

"Why would he invite me? I don't know the guy."

"I assume it's a couples thing."

"You don't want me there."

"Of course I do. It'll look pretty weird if I'm the only one whose partner isn't with them."

"I'll feel like a spare part."

"Please, Jill. I don't ask you to do many things."

Jack knew exactly how to guilt-trip me. "Okay, I'll go. They've not given us much notice though."

"It sounds like the invitations went out some time ago, but it took Norman a while to track me down."

"You'd better make sure the babysitter is free. If she isn't, you'll have to go alone."

"Already done. Sarah has confirmed she's available."

"Great. Anyway, I'd better get back."

"Okay. See you later." He stood up and gave me a quick peck on the cheek.

Back at the office, I cast the 'password' spell, and I'd just started to scroll through the spells on the app when the door opened, and Mrs V walked in.

"Jill?" She did a double take.

I'd been so keen to get back to the office to try the app that I'd totally forgotten I'd been on the high street before I'd magicked myself to the old watermill. Mrs V was

Chapter 3

Bumping into Hilary had been a real spot of luck. If I hadn't, I may never have found out that the spell book was available on app. After she'd left me, I brought up the app store on my phone, and searched for Worm Counter. Needless to say, there was only one. Eager to check it out, I downloaded the app and clicked on the icon, which was a cute little worm.

Enter password:

Oh bum! I'd forgotten I needed that. I could have waited until the evening when I was back home, but it wasn't like I had anything else to do, so I found a deserted alleyway and magicked myself to the old watermill.

"Jill?" Jack looked up from his computer. "Where did you come from?"

"I need to check something in the spell book."

"What was so urgent that you had to use magic to get back here?"

"I need the 'password' spell to get into an app."

"Which app?"

"The spell book."

"Yes, I know that's why you came back, but what's the app for?"

"The app is the spell book in digital form."

"O—kay?"

"I bumped into Hilary from Love Spell. She was the one who told me about it."

"Let me get this straight. You magicked yourself home to check the spell book, so you can access the spell book?"

"Why don't you go back to your work. I'll be gone in two ticks."

"Don't you have the app?"

"*App*?"

"Yeah. The spell book is available on app, didn't you know?"

"I had no idea. How is that even possible when there's no internet in Candlefield?"

"One of the members of WOW is a bit of a computer geek. She created the app and made it available here in the human world."

"Isn't that dangerous? What if a human sees it and downloads it?"

"It's not called spell book or anything like that. It's in the app store under Worm Counter."

"Who would want to count worms?"

"No one. That's just the point. No human will give the app a second glance. And even if they did download it, they'd need to use the 'password' spell to gain access to it."

"The '*password*' spell?"

"It's in the spell book."

"Of course. Thanks, Hilary, I'll give the app a try."

"Hey, Jill, are you by yourself?" It was Hilary from Love Spell.

"Yeah. Come and join me."

"Thanks. Are you okay? You looked a little glum. I wasn't sure if I should bother you or not."

"I'm fine. The business is just going through a bit of a rough patch at the moment."

"I'm sorry to hear that. I'm sure things will pick up for you soon."

"I hope so."

"How's that little witch of yours?"

"Florence is great. She's learning more spells every week."

"That must be quite challenging for you."

"It is, that's why I've taken to studying the spell book."

"You?" She laughed. "Why would you need to do that? Everyone knows there isn't a more powerful witch in Candlefield."

"That may be true, but I'm familiar with only a fraction of the spells in that book. I want to make sure I know what Florence is up to. It's going to take me ages, though, because the book is crammed full of spells, a good number of which are useless. I found one yesterday to make toast, if you can believe that."

"I use that one all the time."

"You do?"

"Yes. My toaster packed up a few months ago and I figured why go to the expense of buying a new one when I could just use magic?"

"I guess. I just wish the spell book wasn't so heavy. I'd like to bring it to work with me to study when things are quiet, like they are at the moment."

section it should go in." He looked up and down the shelves of magazines. "Ah yes, I remember. I put it next to The Emergency Services Gazette. Here it is." He handed me a copy.

"Thanks. How much is it?"

"Nine-pounds, ninety-five pence."

"*How much*?"

"These niche publications always have a high price tag, I'm afraid. Shall I put it back?"

"No, I'll take it."

Once I was outside, I quickly flicked through the magazine, which didn't take long because there weren't many pages. My advert was on the second to last page under an article entitled Covert Surveillance And The Call Of Nature. The ad read:

Jill and Winky, ace investigators. No case too big or too small.

That wasn't the copy I'd submitted to them. Winky must have sent in that version behind my back; that cat was in so much trouble. I didn't think the lack of response was due to the ad copy, though. Based on the difficulty I'd had tracking it down, it was much more likely that no one had actually seen the magazine. So much for Patsy Puggins and her promises.

***

Feeling somewhat deflated, I decided to try to cheer myself up with coffee and a muffin at Coffee Animal. Fortunately, it was no-animal day, so I didn't have to listen to some annoying creature beseeching me to feed them.

"Yes. Do you have it?"

"I don't think so. I'll check the computer." He went behind the desk and tapped away on the keyboard. "It's listed here."

"Do you have it?"

"No, we haven't ordered any copies."

"Can you tell if it's been published yet?"

"Yeah, it came out on the twenty-second."

"Any idea where I might get a copy?"

"It's a bit niche. I doubt any of the smaller newsagents will stock it. You could try Browns. They have everything."

"Right, thanks."

Browns was one of the biggest and oldest stores in Washbridge. They sold pretty much everything, and they had one floor dedicated to stationery, books, newspapers and magazines. On my way over there, I called in at a couple of other small newsagents, but neither of them had heard of P.I. Monthly.

"Yes, we do have it, madam." The smartly dressed man standing behind the counter at Browns sounded very confident. "You'll find it in between Soufflé World and Stew Weekly."

"I think you must have misheard. I didn't say Pie Monthly. I said P.I. Monthly."

"That's new, isn't it?"

"Yes, the first issue should have come out a few days ago, but I think it might have been delayed."

"I don't think it was. I remember seeing it now. Where did I put it?" He led the way over to the racks of magazines. "Hmm, I remember trying to work out which much more important. "What's it called?"

"P.I. Monthly. Do you know if you have it?"

"Yeah. We do." Back to her tapping.

It took all my self-control not to snatch the phone from her hand, and crush it under my foot.

"Do you think you could possibly get it for me because I couldn't see it?"

"Okay." More sighs. She came out from behind the counter, walked over to the rack of magazines, and returned with one in her hand. "There you go."

"This is *Pie* Monthly."

"That's what you said."

"No, I didn't. I said P.I. Monthly."

"What's that?"

"It stands for private investigator."

That seemed to catch her attention at last. "So, are you a P.I., then?"

"Yeah."

"Cool."

"So, do you have it?"

"What?"

"The magazine."

"No. Never heard of it."

"It's new. The first issue should have just come out."

"Hey, Gazza!" She shouted to a spotty young man who was wearing a badge that declared him to be the assistant manager. "This lady wants to know if we have P.I. Monthly."

"Yeah, they're next to Pie and Mash Quarterly."

"Not Pie Monthly. P.I. Monthly," the young woman said. "It's for private investigators."

"How cool." He turned to me. "Are you one?"

"What date is the magazine published?"

"The twenty-second."

"That was last Friday."

"No, it wasn't. It's—oh bum, you're right."

"And yet, phone calls there have been none." He smirked.

"There was probably a delay in publishing. I'm sure that kind of thing happens all the time when launching a new title."

"Sure. You keep telling yourself that. Instead of squandering money on that advert you'd have been better off buying a Feline Fortune starter pack."

"Rubbish. I'm going out. Just make sure you get Steve the Storage to get this lot out of here tonight."

"It's Stu."

"Whatever. Just get it out of here." I hurried out of the office. "I'm going out for a while, Mrs V."

"Is everything alright, dear?"

"Everything is fine."

Was the magazine really out already? If so, why hadn't I had any enquiries? The nearest newsagent was three streets away. The young woman behind the counter was tapping away on her phone, and didn't even look up until I coughed.

"Yeah?"

"I'm looking for a magazine."

"They're over there." She gestured to the racks on the opposite wall, and then went back to tapping on her phone.

"I've already had a quick look, but I couldn't see it."

She sighed. I was clearly keeping her from something

"We're in temporary accommodation in GT, but we're hoping to find somewhere more suitable over here."

"That rental place is awful," Priscilla said. "The shower drips and the oven is useless. I've told Briggsy that if he doesn't find somewhere for us soon, I'm moving out."

"That's actually the reason we're here today," the colonel said. "We'd both prefer to be based somewhere in the Washbridge area, and I wondered if you could suggest anywhere suitable."

"Not really, sorry."

"No problem. We'll just have to keep looking. I'm sorry to have interrupted you, Jill. I know how busy you are."

"Keep me posted on your house-hunting."

"We will. Bye, Jill."

"Bye, Colonel. Bye, Priscilla."

Hopefully, the colonel would be able to find somewhere suitable soon because Priscilla clearly wasn't happy in GT, and she obviously hadn't forgiven the colonel for the mixed sauna incident.

"It's time we made this a no-ghost zone," Winky came out from under the sofa. "Those things give me the creeps."

"Don't call them *things*."

He walked over to one of the piles of boxes. "Those two have made me lose track of where I was."

"You might as well throw all that lot in the skip because you'll never sell it."

"We'll see. I still think you should sign up for Feline Fortune too. It's not like you've got anything better to do at the moment."

"That'll change when my advert comes out. The phone will be ringing off the hook."

and I want it gone by tomorrow."

"Don't panic. Stu the Storage has said I can keep it at his gaff. He's coming over later to help me move it."

"Good. Make sure he does."

Winky suddenly stopped checking his boxes and shot under the sofa. At the same time, the temperature in the office dropped several degrees, and the colonel and Priscilla appeared.

"Hello, you two. I thought you were sailing the seven seas."

"We were indeed." The colonel tweaked his moustache. "And a jolly good time we had too, but all good things must come to an end."

"Hmm." Priscilla snorted. "Why don't you tell Jill the real reason we came back?"

"Jill doesn't need to hear about that little misunderstanding."

It was obvious from the look on Priscilla's face that she wasn't done with this subject yet. "*Little misunderstanding*? I wouldn't call Trixie Beechdale a *little* misunderstanding. That woman must be a 36DD."

"Please, Cilla, I've told you a hundred times, I had no idea it was a mixed sauna."

"Hey, guys, I'm not sure you should be having this conversation in front of me."

"Sorry, Jill," Priscilla said. "You're right. I apologise for mentioning that awful woman."

"That's okay. Am I to take it you're back for good?"

"We most certainly are." The colonel was visibly relieved to change the subject.

"Where are you living?"

our groups are taking part. You're welcome to come and watch."

"I don't think so. From what you've just said, it sounds like it could turn into a bloodbath."

"Please, Jill. I could really do with the support."

"I'll see, but I'm not promising anything."

I'd just started towards my office when Mrs V said, "All the stuff you ordered is in there."

"The stuff I ordered?"

"Yes. It took the man five trips to bring it all upstairs."

The office floor was covered in boxes, one of which Winky was in the process of tearing open.

"What's this lot and why is it cluttering up my office?"

"This is my path to wealth beyond my wildest dreams."

"It's that Feline Fortune rubbish, isn't it?"

"*Rubbish*? I'll have you know that Feline Fortune sell only the highest quality products." He lifted a small sack out of the box. "Voila!"

"That's cat litter."

"Not just any cat litter, though. This is the highest quality, scented cat litter. Any cat would be proud to use this."

"Would you use it?"

"I don't need to. I prefer to do my business au naturel. But if I did have occasion to use it, then this would be my cat litter of choice."

"You can't keep this lot in here. My clients won't be able to get through the door."

"What clients? The last I heard you were all out of cases."

"That's only a temporary situation. I want this lot gone

Chapter 2

"Morning, Mrs V."

"Good morning, Jill, did you have a good weekend?"

"Very quiet. We didn't get up to much. What about you?"

"Don't ask."

"What happened?"

"Armi and I went Morris dancing for the first time."

"Did you manage to agree on which group you'd both join?"

"We did not. We went our separate ways."

"Oh well, just as long as you both enjoyed it."

"I did. Very much. I left there feeling on top of the world, but that soon changed when I got back home. Armi asked me to show him the dance I'd learned, and then he proceeded to pick faults with it."

"But he's a beginner himself, isn't he?"

"Yes, and that's what I told him, but it didn't stop him criticising."

"Did he do a dance for you?"

"He did, and so I returned the compliment, by critiquing him."

"That's sounds only fair."

"Not according to Armi. He insisted his routine was perfect."

"I take it you have fallen out over this?"

"We haven't spoken since yesterday afternoon, and if he thinks I'm going to back down first, he has another think coming."

"Oh dear."

"There's a competition a week on Saturday and both of

biscuits, so I flicked to the B section. Nothing! What kind of spell book included a spell for toast but not one for biscuits?

"Jill!" Jack shouted. "Hilltop Green is starting in a couple of minutes."

"Coming." The spell book would just have to wait for another day because I didn't want to miss my favourite soap.

What? I never said I thought *all* soap-operas were rubbish. Just those that Jack likes.

"Not really. Not when you take into account how many hours of pleasure they give you." He grabbed the newspaper. "Look, they've taken a half page ad in The Bugle."

"Fascinating." Double yawn.

"Look at all these. They've got the Lancaster, the Spitfire, the Blenheim, the—"

I didn't hear the rest because I'd fallen into a boredom-induced coma.

***

When Florence was in bed, and while Jack was watching some awful soap opera, I grabbed the spell book and went through to the kitchen. I'd made a promise to myself to spend more time studying it, in order to expand my repertoire of spells. If I didn't do that, there was a real possibility that my young daughter would be running rings around me.

Where to start? That was the question. In the end, I decided to open the book at a random page and see what I got.

The 'toast' spell? Seriously? Just how lazy did you have to be to use magic to make a slice of toast when you could just as easily use a toaster? The 'dummy finder' spell? I wish I'd known about that when Florence was a baby. I'd lost track of the number of hours Jack and I had spent searching for dummies around the house.

I suddenly had a brainwave: could there be a spell to magic up custard creams? I quickly flicked to the alphabetical index at the back of the book, but there was nothing under C. Maybe there was an all-purpose spell for

"That's true."

"I'll have to nip around there after dark one night this week."

"What for?"

"She thinks someone has been moving their garden gnomes around during the night, so they're going to get CCTV installed."

"Why does that mean you need to go over there?"

"Because the gnomes aren't being moved around. They're moving around of their own accord. I need to warn them about the CCTV."

Florence came bounding into the kitchen. "When's dinner?"

"About half-an-hour," Jack said.

"Okay. I'm going upstairs to play with Humpy." And off she trotted.

"Hey, Jill." Jack suddenly became quite animated. "Have you seen what's opened up on the high street?"

"Not another wig shop, I hope. Grandma will do her nut."

"It's what Washbridge has needed for years. I'm really excited."

"Don't keep me in suspense. What is it?"

"Models."

"Why are you so excited about a model agency? Oh, hang on. Were you thinking we might sign Florence up with them? She is beautiful, just like her mother."

"Not that kind of model. I'm talking about model kits."

"That's what's got you so excited?" Yawn.

"I've always loved models, ever since I was a kid. It's ages since I made one."

"Aren't they ridiculously expensive?"

"Work for *you*? Doing what?"

"You'd have to learn the ropes first, but there's no reason why you couldn't end up managing one of my shops."

"I don't think so." I wasn't sure what horrified me the most: the thought of having to feign interest in the wedding plans of every bride-to-be that walked through the door, or having Kathy as my boss. Actually, that's not true. Having Kathy as my boss would be way worse.

"The offer is always there if you change your mind."

"Thanks."

***

"How's Kathy?" Jack asked.

"They've bought a holiday cottage in Filey."

"Nice."

"It's not exactly the Costa del Sol, is it?"

"I like Filey."

"They said we can use it free of charge whenever they aren't there."

"Great. That'll save us some money."

"You'll never guess what Kathy did."

"Does it have anything to do with gnomes?"

"Not this time. She offered me a job."

"How come? Doing what?"

"I told her I had no work on at the moment, so she offered to train me up to be one of her shop managers."

"What did you say?"

"What do you think I said? Can you imagine how it would play out if she was my boss? It doesn't bear thinking about."

"I wouldn't let Buddy hear you call him that; he'll tear you limb from limb."

"Anyway, I have some really exciting news." Kathy began to grin like the proverbial Cheshire cat.

"Have you won the Best Garden Gnomes in Washbridge competition?"

"We've put a deposit down on our holiday home."

"You don't let the grass grow, do you. Where is it?"

"Filey."

"*Filey*? I thought you said you were going to buy one in the south of France?"

"It was too expensive, and besides it's lovely in Filey."

"It may be, but it's not exactly known for its year-round heatwaves."

"You, Jack and Florence will be able to use it whenever we're not staying there."

"How much will that cost us?"

"Nothing. You're family."

"Thanks, that's very kind."

"No problem. How's business at the moment, Jill?"

"Deader than a dodo, but I do have an advert coming out in a few days."

"In The Bugle?"

"No chance. I would never advertise in that rag. No, this is a brand new magazine called P.I. Monthly."

"Hmm."

"What's that look for?"

"Isn't there a danger that the only people who will read that magazine will be other private investigators?"

"Err, no, I don't think so."

"If things ever get really bad, you could always come and work for me."

"They haven't been playing jazz at all hours again, have they?"

"No, thank goodness, but we think they might be messing around with our garden ornaments."

"How do you mean?"

"Several mornings this week, the gnomes and elves have been in the wrong place."

"Maybe Peter moved them?"

"He didn't. I checked."

"What about the kids?"

"They never go in the garden, and they certainly never get up before us. I'm convinced it's those new neighbours."

"Why would they do something like that?"

"Who knows? There are some very strange people about."

"That's true."

"Anyway, if it is them, we'll soon know."

"You're surely not planning to stay up all night to keep watch for them?"

"No need. We're getting CCTV cameras installed, so if it is them, we'll have the evidence we need."

Oh bum!

"Won't that be rather expensive?"

"Not these days. It's cheap as chips."

"Don't you think it's a bit over the top, though?"

"Not at all. If someone is marauding around our garden in the dark, I want to know about it. You should get it installed at your place."

"There's no need. We've got Buddy to scare away any intruders."

"That little rat?" She scoffed.

wanted her to rein in that son of hers.

Every time I saw Kathy, she was wearing a new outfit.

"Do you like it?" She did a little twirl.

"It's very nice, but at this rate you'll need to build a house extension to accommodate all your wardrobes."

"I have to project the right image at work." She looked me up and down.

"What?"

"Nothing. What's that on your trouser leg?"

"Milk probably. Florence has a habit of flicking her muesli all over the kitchen. Am I going to get a cup of tea or not?"

"Go and sit in the orang—"

"Conservatory?"

"I'll bring it through."

While Kathy was making the tea, I tried to rub the milk stain off my trousers.

"Hi, Jill," Henry called from the garden.

At his side, Henrietta gave me a little wave.

"Hi, you two."

"You're talking to those gnomes again, aren't you?" Kathy put the cup of tea on the table. "You'll get locked up if you carry on like that."

"Where are the custard creams?"

"Have some patience." She disappeared into the kitchen and returned a couple of minutes later with a new packet. "I left them in the packaging, so you can see they're the real McCoy."

"Thanks."

"By the way, I may have spoken too soon about our new neighbours."

ridiculous offerings. "Okay. We'll take one of those."

"Excellent." He handed one to Florence. "Be careful not to prick yourself with the pin, young lady. That'll be six pounds, please."

"*Six pounds*? For that tiny little badge?"

"As I said, all proceeds go to a worthy cause."

"Give him six pounds, Jack." I grabbed Florence's hand and took her inside.

When Ivers had left, Jack joined me in the kitchen. "How come I had to pay for the badge?"

"Because, apparently, you're the one with a soft spot for little green men."

"What does this society of his do?"

"Look for non-existent leprechauns. You should consider joining them if you're such a fan."

***

Kathy had invited me to pop over for a coffee. I'd agreed, but only after I'd established that she had plenty of custard creams, and they weren't the cheap ones she usually tried to foist on me.

As I left the house, I spotted Cindymindy on the other side of the road. It was the first time I'd seen her since I'd tried to reason with her and her waste-of-space husband. Since then, Florence hadn't mentioned any more 'Thomas' incidents, so maybe they'd had words with their son after all.

She glanced over, and I was about to wave to her, purely in the spirit of reconciliation, you understand, but she spotted me and made a show of turning away. She could please herself. I didn't need her to be my BFF; I just of WLSA."

"What's that?"

"Washbridge Leprechaun Seekers Association."

"Is this a wind-up? Did Jack put you up to this?"

"I can assure you that WLSA is not a wind-up."

"I have to go out in a couple of minutes. What exactly did you want?"

"I'm on a fundraising mission." He bent down and opened the green case at his feet. "We have leprechaun figurines, leprechaun badges, leprechaun mouse mats, leprechaun—"

"Hang on. What is WSAL?"

"It's *WLSA*, and as its name suggests, its aim is to seek out leprechauns, and prove to the world that they exist."

"But they don't."

"That, Jill, is a perfect example of what we're up against. Doubters. Unbelievers."

Just then, Jack and Florence joined me at the door.

"Why is that man dressed in green, Mummy?" Florence said.

"I'm dressed like a leprechaun, young lady." Mr Ivers took a bow.

"What's a lepper corn?"

"I'll explain later, darling. Mummy has to go out soon."

Always ready with a helpful comment, Jack said, "I've always had a soft spot for leprechauns."

"Are you sure you wouldn't like to buy anything?" Mr Ivers gestured to the open case. "What about the leprechaun bottle opener?"

"Can I have one of those badges, Mummy, please?"

I would have preferred to tell Ivers to sling his hook, but I figured the badge was likely to be the cheapest of his

"What do you think?"

"I'm sorry about that." I took out a pouch of dog food and poured the slop into his bowl. "I'll have a word with that little madam when she gets home."

"A fat lot of good that'll do."

The last time I'd seen Ma Chivers was when her team had competed in the synchronised broom flying competition, but that was years ago. How had a woman who'd had such a high profile for so long just disappeared? Grandma had made it perfectly clear that it was up to me to find out.

Jack and Florence were back from the park, and I was just about to put the kettle on when there was a knock at the door.

"Good day, Jill." Mr Ivers was wearing a green suit with matching hat and shoes.

"Hello, Mr Ivers. I was just about to go out," I lied.

"I won't keep you for more than a few minutes. I know what a busy woman you are."

"The movie newsletter can't be out yet. It's only a week since I had the last issue."

"An exceptional issue it was too, I'm sure you'll agree."

"Absolutely."

"I'm not here as editor/publisher of the newsletter; I'm here on behalf of the little green men."

"Sorry? Which *little green men*?"

"Leprechauns, of course." He gave me a little twirl.

"I'm sorry, Mr Ivers, but I really have no idea what you're talking about. Why are you dressed like a leprechaun?"

"Because it is my honour to have been elected chairman

Chapter 1

It was Sunday morning, and Jack had taken Florence to the park, so that Grandma and I could have some privacy.

"How can you not know, Grandma? You're always telling me that you know everything."

"Well, I don't know where Chivers is. As far as I'm aware, no one has seen hide nor hair of her for years."

"We have to find her; she has the clue to the whereabouts of the south compass stone."

"I'm well aware of that, Jill."

"What are we going to do?"

"I would have thought that was obvious. You'll have to find her."

"How?"

"Remind me again what it is you do for a living because I had this crazy idea that you were a private investigator."

"Sarcasm does not become you."

"Isn't finding missing people one of the things you do?"

"Yes, but—"

"Good, that's all sorted, then. Let me know when you've tracked her down and have the clue."

"But, I—"

It was too late, she'd already vanished.

I was so angry that I grabbed the nearest thing and threw it across the room.

"Hey, do you mind?" Buddy glared at me. "That salt pot almost hit me."

"Sorry."

"Is there any chance of getting any food around here? A dog could die of starvation."

"Didn't Florence feed you before she went out?"